PRA
THE SE
MYSTERIES

"A charming cozy debut with characters as sweet as the titular tea, a mystery with numerous attractive byways, and a budding romance waiting to be explored."
—*Kirkus Reviews* for *Live and Let Chai*

"Fun and intriguing. *Live and Let Chai* is filled to the brim with Southern charm."
—Kirsten Weiss, author of A Pie Town Mystery series

"Bree Baker's seaside town of Charm has everything readers could want: an intrepid and lovable heroine who owns an adorable iced tea cafe, a swoon-worthy hero—and murder. Fast-paced, smartly plotted, and full of surprises, it's as refreshing as a day at the beach!"
—Kylie Logan, bestselling author of
French Fried for *Live and Let Chai*

"A smart and likable protagonist, a vividly rendered setting, a suitably twisty plot, and some colorful supporting characters are the ingredients for a concoction as appealing as any of Everly Swan's specialty sweet teas. I can't wait to try out some of her recipes and to visit this delightful series again."
—Livia J. Washburn, national bestselling author of
the Fresh-Baked Mysteries for *Live and Let Chai*

ALSO BY BREE BAKER

SEASIDE CAFÉ MYSTERIES

Live and Let Chai

No Good Tea Goes Unpunished

Tide and Punishment

A Call for Kelp

A CALL FOR KELP

SEASIDE CAFÉ MYSTERIES, BOOK 4

BREE BAKER

Poisoned Pen
PRESS

Published by Poisoned Pen Press, an imprint of Sourcebooks
P.O. Box 4410, Naperville, Illinois 60567-4410
(630) 961-3900
sourcebooks.com

Library of Congress Cataloging-in-Publication Data

Names: Baker, Bree, author.
Title: A call for kelp / by Bree Baker.
Description: Naperville, IL : Poisoned Pen Press, [2020] | Series: Seaside
    Café Mysteries ; book 4
Identifiers: LCCN 2019050887 | (paperback)
Subjects: GSAFD: Mystery fiction.
Classification: LCC PS3602.A5847 C35 2020 | DDC 813/.6--dc23

LC record available at https://lccn.loc.gov/2019050887

Printed and bound in the United States of America.
POD

CHAPTER
ONE

Hey, y'all!" I greeted the selfie mode on the cell phone poised in my outstretched arm. "This is Everly Swan, your trusty seaside iced tea shop owner and baking addict, signing on to try something new for you this morning."

Recording short instructional videos for my café's website had become a weekly occurrence for me, and I was hoping to make things more exciting for my followers by getting out of the kitchen.

"In case you haven't heard, we've got something big going on in Charm today, and I thought you might enjoy an insider's look at the hubbub." I quickened my steps across Bay Street to the nature center, where most of my town and seemingly half the world population had gathered for a look at Mitzi Calgon, the pirate movie equivalent of Princess Leia.

A warm ocean breeze tickled my neck and cheeks as I approached the crowd, and I hoped with enough editing the video would turn out okay. I'd never recorded anything beyond the walls of my historic Victorian, but it seemed like a good day to start. Considering that this was the first time in a long time that I'd done more than put my hair in a ponytail and dressed in anything fancier than cutoffs and flip-flops, it was worth a try.

My beekeeping great-aunts had secured Mitzi Calgon's support in a documentary to save the American honeybee, and she was in town today for a celebration luncheon. In other words, the perfect time to finally give viewers a look at the postcard-perfect world outside my front door.

I nearly skipped up the front steps to the squat, brown brick building on the bay side of our little island, panning the crowd as I went. "All this buzz for the American honeybee has me dreaming of honey-laced recipes. Maybe after this we can make some good old-fashioned honey butter, muffins, or taffy." I paused the video and tucked the phone into my bag for safety as I opened the front door.

"Oops. Pardon me," I said, sucking in my gut and shimmying sideways through the crush of bodies inside the nature center.

I'd never seen so many people in one place out-side of Times Square at New Year's Eve, and I'd only seen that on television. People had traveled far and wide for a chance to meet the guest of honor. I didn't blame them. Mitzi was best known for her iconic role in the film franchise, *Blackbeard's Wife*, in which she had played the lead role some forty-plus years ago. She was a superstar by all rights, but I was interested for another reason. I'd recently learned that she'd known my grandma, who I missed so much it hurt, and I had about ten million questions about her for Mitzi.

"Eep!" I yipped as someone stepped backward onto my peep-toe sandal in what felt like cleats.

Only a little farther, I told myself, winding past a clutch of coeds wearing eye patches and plastic hooks for hands. The large double doors at the end of the hall were closer than ever, and my chances of reaching them without becoming permanently pressed between Mitzi's fans like a flower caught in an old book, were increasing with each tenacious step.

Gold and white satin banners hung from the ceiling above the doors, and a honeycomb arrangement of black octagons had been taped to the white marble floor around the entry. Honeybee advocacy and statistics posters lined the wall in both directions, and locally farmed honey was available for sample or purchase at a desk draped in black linens.

Thanks to my family's centuries-old obsession with beekeeping and my great-aunts' continued love for the practice, a production crew had arrived in Charm this week. Tomorrow the crew would film a documentary based on my aunts' lives as beekeepers, and Mitzi Calgon would do the voice work from a luxe studio in Los Angeles. Today, however, Mitzi was here to help create an early buzz.

My heart hammered as I broke free from the crowd and ducked under the velvet rope holding everyone at bay. "Hey," I said, wiggling my fingers at the straight-faced, black-suited men guarding the room. "May I?" I flashed my official pass for good measure, though I'd already spoken to both men the night before. While I'd been helping to transform the large nature center display room into a beautiful honeybee-themed luncheon area, they'd kept an eye on Mitzi and the production team.

The men parted, stoically, prying the double doors open for me to pass.

Inside, the fruits of my labor were shown abundantly. Nature center flora and fauna displays had been replaced with round tables covered in alternating white or gold tablecloths. Jars of honey from my aunts' hives had been clustered together as centerpieces, tied with thick, black satin ribbon and seated upon octagonal mirrored trays. Enormous paper pom-poms in coordinating colors hung at various heights from the ceiling, and classical music drifted softly from hidden speakers throughout the room. I liberated my phone once more and took a few still shots of the enchanting results.

A stage had been erected at the front, complete with podium and floor-to-ceiling velvet curtains. Signs along the stage and affixed to the podium carried the name of the company, Bee Loved, and the name of the film to be made, *Bee the Change*, as well as the name of the woman everyone had come to see, Mitzi Calgon.

I stood dumbstruck for a moment, second-guessing

my yellow and white sundress. I was more of a cutoff shorts and T-shirt kind of gal, and I always chose flip-flops over heels, but this was a special occasion so I'd dressed up. I reached nervously to tug the tip of my ponytail and found a neatly pinned chignon instead— one more indication that I was as much in costume as any of the folks wearing pirate gear and honeybee wings. My heart raced as I considered turning tail and running.

Then the women I'd come to see took notice of me and smiled. My great-aunts Clara and Fran waved from Mitzi's side. "Everly!"

I put my phone away and reminded myself to breathe, then fussed with the hem of my suddenly-too-tight dress and paced my steps upon approach. My aunts had dressed up too. Aunt Clara wore a long golden gown and Aunt Fran a black pantsuit. Their unintentional yin and yang wardrobes paired perfectly with their contrasting skin, hair, and eye colors, not to mention personalities. I'd gotten a lot of Aunt Clara's sweet-as-honey disposition, but I looked more like Aunt Fran with brown eyes and dark hair, though her hair was more salt than pepper these days. "Hi," I said as normally as I could manage, given the bundle of nerves tightening inside me.

My aunts took turns kissing my cheeks and squeez-ing me before Mitzi took my hands in hers as if we'd known one another for years. Her face lit up as she took me in. She was stunning in a head-to-toe white gown that emphasized her slender figure and perfect porcelain skin. Her silver hair was bobbed and tucked behind her ears with diamond-studded bobby pins whose sparkle couldn't compete with her smile.

A look of pride crinkled the skin at the corners of her striking blue eyes. "Your grandma was the most beautiful woman in Hollywood, and you look just like her, you know?"

Grandma was never "in Hollywood" the way Mitzi was. Grandma had only visited before my mother was born, but emotion clogged my throat anyway as I pulled Mitzi into a hug. A wave of grief and loss tangled up with hope and gratitude. As long as Mitzi was in Charm, I would have a piece of Grandma back. "It's so nice to meet you," I said. "It means the world to us that you're here."

"I think this is how Hazel would want it," she said. And she was right. Grandma would have loved having her here.

My aunts had only recently filled me in on my grandma's youthful escape from Charm, our little barrier island on the outskirts of North Carolina, to Los Angeles when she was barely twenty. She'd had big dreams but soon returned without explanation beyond the fact she was pregnant. I'd left home to chase a cowboy several years back, but I'd only returned with twenty-five extra pounds and a broken heart.

"Her smile lit up a room," Mitzi continued. "I took one look at her and I hated her. That's when I knew we had to be friends." She laughed. "She could've stolen every role I auditioned for with that wicked grin of hers, but she was happy to work on sets instead of onstage. America's loss, I think. But oh, how she loved her life here. Your family and this town were the main content of every letter she wrote to me. I only wish I'd made good on my promise to visit sooner. We always think we have more time."

"She wrote you letters?" I asked.

"Right up until she passed. I read about her death two days before her final letter arrived." Mitzi's eyes twinkled with emotion, maybe even a little mischief. "I kept every one of her letters. More than two hundred, accumulated over forty years, and I've brought them all with me." Her petal pink lips twisted into a perfect cat-that-ate-the-canary smile. "I brought them for you."

My jaw sank open. "What?"

"They're all yours," she said brightly. "A few photographs too." Her phone rang, and she pulled it from her beaded bag, then gave it a sour look.

Aunt Clara wrapped an arm around me, looking as pleased with the news of Grandma's letters as I felt. "Everything okay?" she asked Mitzi when her smile didn't return.

Mitzi pursed her lips and rolled her eyes before tucking her phone back into her clutch. "Yes. Sorry. Small annoyances."

"Mitzi," called a tall blond woman in a designer pantsuit and four-inch heels as she wound her way through the room of decked-out tables. "Lunchtime."

"You're not eating with us?" I asked. It was a luncheon, after all.

"I never eat in front of a camera," Mitzi said. "Too many chances to be caught with food in my teeth, on my face, or falling into my lap. Save me a seat, and as soon as I finish at the podium, I'll be down to sit with you and your lovely great-aunts. Maybe we can do something after this is over. I want to tell you everything I can remember about Hazel's life in California and you have to tell me everything she left out of her letters."

"Deal," I said, my heart expanding painfully in my chest.

Mitzi turned to leave, then backed up suddenly. "Oh my."

A pair of workers in matching nature center polos pushed a giant plexiglass box on a cart in our direction. Standing six feet high and as many feet wide and deep, the box was very familiar to me. It was my personal nightmare. Honeybees swarmed inside, occasionally bumping against the breathable mesh top. One of my aunts' educational hives sat on a clear acrylic table at the front.

I gave the box a wide berth, slipping between tables to put more space between myself and the bees I'd feared irrationally my entire life. I gasped when I bumped into someone. Mitzi was a step behind me, moving away from the bee box as well. "Sorry," I said, sighing a soft giggle of relief as the box was pushed up a ramp onto the stage and behind the velvet curtain.

"I hate bees," Mitzi said, one hand pressed to her chest. "I'm allergic. I haven't been stung since I was a child, but I'm deathly afraid now. I keep an EpiPen with me everywhere I go. Just in case."

I puzzled at the bizarre truth. "And you agreed to be the voice of this project?"

"For your grandmother." She winked. "Besides, that was as close as I'll ever get to the bees. Tomorrow I'll be back in LA, sitting comfy in a sound booth."

"But you'll stay tonight," I clarified, needing to hear again that we would talk about Grandma soon.

"Absolutely, and don't let me forget to tell you about the night she met your grandfather." Mitzi covered her mouth to stifle a bark of laughter. "He was lost for her the moment he laid eyes on her."

"You knew my grandfather?" I asked, flipping my gaze to meet Aunt Clara's and Aunt Fran's wide eyes.

"Mm hmm." Mitzi waved her beaded clutch in goodbye and followed the blond down a hallway toward the nature center's staff offices.

My grandpa's identity had always been a mystery to us. My aunts believed he was a famous actor who'd died suddenly on set a few months after Grandma's return to Charm. She'd never confirmed their theory, but according to my aunts, Grandma had grieved deeply until the birth of my mother, who promptly became her world.

According to Aunt Clara and Aunt Fran, Swan women were cursed in two ways and blessed in every other. First, we were allegedly bound to the island town our ancestors had founded after fleeing the witch trials in Salem. Second, we were cursed in love. I didn't believe in magic or curses, despite the consistency with which Swan husbands seemed to meet untimely deaths. Maybe that was naïve of me, or maybe denial was my superpower. I hadn't decided.

Aunt Clara rubbed my back. "We should have dinner at our place tonight. Offer Mitzi a room there instead of wherever she's staying."

Aunt Fran nodded sharply. "Agreed. I'll make midnight pancakes."

Midnight pancakes were a late-night tradition of my people. Anytime a Swan's heart was broken, we were stressed out, or we just couldn't sleep, Aunt Fran made pancakes. The buttery delights always helped me sleep. I used to believe the recipe, batter, or homemade syrup were magical, but now I knew it was more likely a carb coma that knocked me out afterward. Regardless, I loved midnight pancakes.

A set of figures soon appeared in the hallway where Mitzi had vanished. My best friend, Amelia Butters; her father; and Wyatt, the cowboy who'd once broken my heart, strode purposefully in my direction.

Amelia looked amazing, as usual, in a fitted blue sundress with small white buttons, a matching handbag, and heels.

Her dad, on the other hand, looked like a lunatic. It might've been the eye patch and full-blown pirate costume. "Argh!" he said with a grin. "I've come in search of me bride. The wench who has claimed me icy heart and warmed it to the point of hellfire for her service."

Aunt Clara clapped silently at his strangely accented monologue, a set of lines from Mitzi's movies, I presumed. "Bravo!"

Aunt Fran hugged Amelia, then looked at Mr. Butters with appraising eyes. "You just missed Mitzi, but she'll be back."

"Aye," he said, "and I shall be waiting."

Amelia hugged me next. "You look beautiful."

"Thanks." I blushed, per my usual, never sure what to do with a compliment. Normally, I would change the subject. "Your dad looks happy. I never knew he was such a fan."

She shook her head in disbelief. "It was as if someone uncorked fifty years of pent-up pining the minute he heard Mitzi Calgon was coming to Charm. He's binged all those old *Blackbeard's Wife* movies a half dozen times this week alone, and he reconnected with her fan club, which is online now but was originally a newsletter sent through the mail."

I wrinkled my nose and mouthed, "Wow."

"Yeah." Amelia's blue eyes were tight with humility. She and her dad were close, but he still embarrassed her on occasion. When he went out in public dressed as Blackbeard, for example.

"Mitzi went to eat lunch before the show starts," I said. "You must've just missed her."

Mr. Butters turned for a look down the hallway he'd just exited, the long plastic sword on his belt slapping against chair legs as he moved, like playing cards in the spokes of a bicycle wheel. The multitude of buckles on his knee-high pirate boots jingled with every step. "Bummer."

Wyatt frowned. "I gave up my office when her assistant said Mitzi needed a dressing room for the day. We poked our head in there after I snuck these two through the back door, but she wasn't there."

Amelia sighed. "The whole building and most of the parking lot is full of folks trying to get a look at Mitzi, so Wyatt figured the back door was our best chance of getting in without half the crowd screaming over the injustice."

"Smart," I said. "We're going to invite Mitzi to Aunt Fran and Aunt Clara's tonight for dinner. You should come." I slid my gaze to each of the three faces, extending the offer to Wyatt if he was interested.

Mr. Butters's jaw dropped.

Amelia smiled. "We'd love to."

A sudden bout of feedback screeched through the speakers and a pleasant female voice temporarily replaced my classical playlist. "Testing," drawled a woman I recognized as Rose, the documentary's producer. She gave the microphone's padded cover a few sound whacks with her finger.

Thump! Thump! Thump!

Several stagehands offered her a thumbs-up.

"Ten minutes until the doors open," she said. "This is it. Everyone in your places. Does anyone need a pep talk? Any last-minute questions?"

A handful of volunteers in Bee Loved T-shirts gathered at the front of the stage, beaming at their leader.

Rose shaded her eyes against the spotlight with one hand and squinted into the sparse audience. "Where are Mitzi and Odette?"

"Who?" Amelia asked.

Aunt Clara leaned in. "I think Odette is Mitzi's assistant's name."

"I'll get them," I volunteered, throwing one hand up and nearly shouting the words. "Be right back!" I turned and scurried away, thrilled for an excuse to talk to Mitzi again so soon.

To my great dismay, Wyatt's office was still empty. A salad sat, untouched, in its clear plastic take-out container on his desk. No signs of Mitzi or the blond. I turned in a small circle, considering the possibilities, then darted back into the hall. I headed for the staff's restroom next. "Mitzi?" I asked, pushing the door wide.

Every stall was open and the sinks were all dry. No signs anyone had been there recently.

I raised my shoulders and palms as I entered the luncheon room, all eyes on me. "I didn't see them."

Rose groaned into the microphone, then whipped a finger in large overhead circles. "Twelve o'clock."

Wyatt, now positioned at the back of the room, pulled the double doors open. The guards standing sentinel outside began accepting tickets from those lucky enough to have gotten their hands on them.

"Are you taping this for the blog?" Amelia asked.

I rubbed sweat-slicked palms over the material of my dress before taking a seat. "I think so," I said. Assuming I could keep my anxious hands from shaking.

Tables filled quickly, and the lights dimmed. I crossed my fingers under the table, hoping Mitzi was in place behind the curtain, awaiting her introduction.

A spotlight followed Rose across the stage to the podium, her trendy blouse and thick dark hair fluttering with each brisk step. "Flight of the Bumblebee" rose through the speakers, eliciting laughter from the crowd.

"Hello," Rose began in the slow, easy drawl of someone clearly from the South. "Thank y'all for coming out tonight. My name is Rose Long. I'm a member of the Bee Loved board of directors and producer of our upcoming *Bee the Change* documentary." She paused and smiled through a small amount of clapping. "I appreciate that," she said as the room quickly quieted once more. "I know who you're really here to see, and that's okay by me."

The crowd erupted.

"Mitzi Calgon is one of the kindest, most selfless, most generous people I know, and we're honored to have her here with us. Her incredible passion for the future of the American honeybee is absolutely priceless." Rose waited through a much longer round of applause before speaking again. She scanned the room slowly and carefully. Looking for someone? Something? Mitzi? She gripped the microphone in one hand and gave the curtain behind her a hopeful look. "Without further ado, Ms. Mitzi Calgon."

Rose stepped aside and the heavy velvet curtains were drawn apart with a flourish.

The spotlight hit the *X* taped to the floor, but no one was there.

Then, searching, the beam landed on the large plexiglass box situated along the far left of the stage.

A horrendous scream ripped from my throat, joining multiple others, as Mitzi's red and swollen face came into view, pressed firmly against the plexiglass from inside the bee box. Her unseeing eyes stared blankly back at the sea of horror-struck fans.

CHAPTER

ഔ

TWO

Two hours later, I sat against the wall of a room crawling with men and women in uniforms. EMTs had treated numerous audience members for shock. The coroner had examined Mitzi before loading her onto a backboard, then wheeling her away on a gurney. My heart was in a vise.

Members of the crime scene team photographed the area and searched for clues as to how a woman allergic to bees had wound up inside a giant box filled with them. Everyone already knew the answer. Murder.

Amelia leaned against her dad as they awaited their turn to speak with Detective Grady Hays, Charm's newest and only homicide detective. Grady had single-handedly interviewed every guest in the room, beginning with those farthest from the stage, dismissing them quickly until only those seated at my table remained.

"Amelia," Grady said. "Mr. Butters." He shook their hands, looking completely exhausted.

I wished I knew why, but Grady had put a substantial distance between us after kissing me under
some mistletoe at Christmas. It was rude behavior by
any standard, and I often fell asleep at night stewing
over all the ways I'd tell him about it. Strangely, the
sunrise routinely made a coward of me, so I'd kept
my thoughts on the matter to myself so far. Now that
spring had sprung, I was fairly certain any perceived
injustice I'd felt during the winter had passed its stat-
ute of limitations.

I gave Amelia an encouraging smile, then turned
to watch my aunts, now dressed in their beekeeping
attire, deal with the bees still inside the box. They'd
been given booties for their feet and instructed to
touch as little as necessary while righting the obser-
vational beehive. The fear I'd harbored for the bees
before was nothing compared to what I felt now. Still,
my aunts carried on, righting the toppled hive and
tending to the tiny killers' needs.

Grady's voice drew my attention away from the
scene onstage. "You too, huh?" he asked Mr. Butters,
examining his costume.

Mr. Butters had taken off the faux black beard
and big hat with the plume, but his ruffled white
shirt, stretchy black trousers, and tall buckled boots
remained. "Mitzi Calgon was pure talent. She was my
hero when I was a drama major."

Amelia patted her father's arm. "Mine too, Dad."

Amelia had followed in her father's footsteps,
studying art and theater, music, and literature, though

in the end she'd chosen a business degree and used it to open a bookstore on Main Street, Charming Reads.

Grady gripped his deeply creased forehead. "Any idea who'd want to hurt her?"

"No," Mr. Butters answered flatly. "It's nonsense. Mitzi was a legend. An American icon. A treasured part of cinematic history."

"Detective." One of the local cops strolled in our direction, a series of evidence bags gripped in one hand, a painting on canvas in the other. "We found these in the victim's dressing area."

Amelia's tanned cheeks went pink. Mr. Butters closed his eyes.

I made my way to their sides, unclear about the reason they both looked so uncomfortable but ready to support them however I could.

Grady flipped through the evidence bags, squinting briefly at the contents in each. The first few contained photos of Mitzi taken in Charm. She didn't seem to be aware of the photographer's presence. Next, Grady stopped at a bagged sheet of parchment paper, intentionally ragged at the edges and discolored for an aged look. "You are moonlight on the ocean," he read. "A siren song in my heart. Love me the way I love you and we shall never be apart. Deny me this gift and sorry you'll be, when your beautiful soul is swallowed by the sea. Forever your beloved." Grady grimaced. He returned the awful poem and stalker photos to the cop before taking a closer look at the painting.

I recognized the familiar strokes and style

immediately, then understood the source of Amelia and her father's discomfort.

"Is this your signature?" Grady asked, turning the painting of a youthful Mitzi to face Mr. Butters. Anyone who'd spent time in Amelia's bookstore would recognize the bulbous letter *B* and series of jagged scratches. It was a match to every fairy-tale rendition he'd made to mark her aisles. Grady's son, Denver, probably had at least one work with a matching signature on his bedroom wall.

"Yes," Mr. Butters whispered, "but it's not what you think."

Grady gave the painting another long appraisal. "It looks like a nudie version of Mitzi Calgon in her twenties."

Amelia's face went red. "It's a swimsuit!" she gasped. "This is a scene from the first movie." She covered her horrified expression with both hands and turned to me, wide eyes peeking over the tops of her fingertips.

I stared at the ethereal image of Mitzi submerged in water. A muted gray scale gave way to hints of lavender and teal along the canvas's edges, where lost air bubbles drifted away from her. Long raven hair curled over her shoulders and hovered around her iridescent skin like an apparition in the dark water. The string bikini hung low on her narrow hips, leaving little to the imagination.

Mr. Butters's work was both moving and powerful, but given the day's events and the uncanny way this image went along with the creepy parchment poem, an argument could be made that this was a work of foreshadowing. An image of Mitzi's soul returned to the sea.

Grady passed the canvas back to the waiting cop, who marched it away. "What about the letter and the photos?"

"I've never seen those before," Mr. Butters said.

"Anything at all you can think of that might be useful in some way to me right now?" Grady asked. "Maybe as a fan you've heard rumors about a stalker? Someone who was bothering her?"

Mr. Butters's grave expression fell further. "No."

Grady gave them each a business card. "Don't leave the island. Don't talk to anyone about any of this. Call me if you see, hear, or think of anything I should know." He shook their hands. Then the three of them looked at me.

"What?" I asked. My croaking voice startled us all.

Amelia smiled sadly. "If you want us to wait, we can walk home with you."

"No. I'm okay," I promised. "I'm not on your way, and I'm going to wait for my aunts."

"Okay," Amelia said.

"Detective?" A woman in a Charm PD windbreaker arrived with Odette at her side. Amelia and her dad hung back, listening covertly, I suspected, while I stared openly at the leggy blond last seen with Mitzi. "I found this one in the dressing room with the victim's lunch in her hands," the officer reported. "She says she's Ms. Calgon's personal assistant."

Grady cocked a hip. "You got a name?"

"Odette Minoa."

He nodded. "What were you doing in the victim's dressing room?"

Odette shifted her weight, looking simultaneously heartbroken and ashamed. "I went to collect her meal and clean up, but she hadn't eaten, so I was going to put the whole thing in a refrigerator if I could find one."

Her story sounded wildly suspect to me. "Where have you been?" I asked, anger burning more loudly in the words than I'd intended. "I looked for you and Mitzi, but you were nowhere. Not in Wyatt's office. Not the restroom. And now she's dead." A tidal wave of emotion crashed into my chest, stealing my breath. How had this happened? How could Mitzi Calgon be gone? We'd just met. We were going to have midnight pancakes. My knees went weak, and I collapsed onto the nearest chair.

Odette crossed her arms. "I went outside to make a phone call. I came in when I heard the sirens."

"What about Ms. Calgon?" Grady asked.

"She went to eat. I figured she'd call if she needed anything, but she rarely does. She should've been busy with her speech and the luncheon for another hour at least. If she stayed to sign autographs, she might've been here all afternoon. So I took my time."

My aunts appeared in my periphery, moving slowly in our direction, each with her protective hat and veil tucked under one arm. Their eyes were red and puffy and their faces splotchy—not from the bees, but from tears shed as they'd worked. They enveloped me in a group hug when they reached my chair, and my tears flowed freely.

Aunt Fran was the first to pull away and straighten her spine. "We never should have invited her here."

"No," I said. "Don't say that. This isn't our fault."

"Not your fault," she said, "It was Clara and I who recalled her friendship with Hazel and tried to capitalize on it. We're the ones who asked her to come. She was retired, and we dragged her out here so she could be murdered."

Odette shrieked. "Murdered! You said she'd been stung!"

Grady cleared his throat, clear gray eyes scanning Odette's face. "Ms. Calgon was in the demonstration box with the bees and educational hive when the curtain was pulled back. She was stung multiple times, but the cause of death is still being determined."

Odette swung her attention to the plexiglass box on stage. "Where is she now?" she demanded. "I want to see her."

Grady gave a stiff dip of his chin. "I have a few more questions if you wouldn't mind coming with me." He lifted a hand to the nearest cop and received an answering nod in return. Grady moved his gaze to my aunts, then to me. "You ladies going to be all right?"

Aunt Clara wiped her eyes with a small eyelet handkerchief and sniffled. "Yes. Wyatt's taking us home as soon as he finishes locking up."

Locking up? I turned for a look at the now-empty room and through the double doors, standing open and unguarded. The lobby was empty. The building quiet. Guests had been evacuated. Witnesses questioned and released. The nature center was a crime scene.

Wyatt moved into view, cutting through the doors as if on cue. He shook Grady's hand, then wrapped one strong arm around each of my aunts' narrow waists. "Everyone ready?"

I lifted an index finger to the numerous bruises lining his forearms. "Wyatt?"

"It's nothing," he said, catching my eye with a wink. "I'm good. You okay to get home? There's plenty of room in my truck. Extended cab."

"No. Thank you. I think I need the fresh air and exercise." I forced a tight smile and followed Wyatt and my aunts to the lobby and waited to be released by the officer manning the door. Grady and Odette brought up the rear.

I thanked the officer at the door for setting me free, then stopped to take in the presence of Grady's former mother-in-law on the sidewalk.

She straightened when she saw us and immediately locked her gaze onto Grady.

The officer she'd been waving her hands and barking at nearly ran when she flipped her palm to dismiss him.

I raised an exhausted hand in greeting. "Senator Denver."

"Everly." Her gaze flicked briefly to me before returning to Grady. His son had been named after the senator, his late wife's mother, and Senator Denver had recently purchased the largest manor on our island for a part-time home. She claimed to want to be near her grandson and maybe run for mayor of Charm instead of continuing her career in DC, but so far, she'd shown no sign of giving up her previous life. In fact, I suspected her underlying motivation for the move and property purchase was to persuade Grady to help her with a project. She'd said as much last winter, but since Grady had withdrawn from my life, I couldn't be sure.

Senator Denver had spent time in the military before making a move to politics, and it was evident in her disposition, posture, and stare. That was probably why her slightly unsettled expression struck me as something to worry about. If I wasn't emotionally drained already, I probably would have worried.

Instead, I turned to study the wordless exchange passing between her and Grady. A nearly imperceptible shake of his head dragged her shoulders down by two inches.

Whatever that was about, I didn't want to know. I wanted to go home, relieve my helper, and serve twenty flavors of delicious iced teas until Mitzi's swollen face was no longer in the forefront of my mind.

"See y'all later," I said quietly, stepping into the crowd corralled in the parking lot.

Apparently, escorting folks from the building

hadn't guaranteed they'd leave the premises. The crowd had easily doubled since my morning arrival, and the number of people in pirate costumes had quadrupled. Just two hours since Mitzi's death and the fans were in a frenzy. One Blackbeard impersonator was selling black armbands from a big cardboard treasure chest for five bucks a piece and calling them "remembrance bands." Other loiterers and lookie-loos carried poster boards on sticks and handmade banners proclaiming their devastation at the loss of a national treasure. Everywhere I looked there were images of Mitzi with angel wings, ascending into the clouds or sailing off on a pirate ship under captions like "The maiden's final voyage." I bit my lip against the argument that Blackbeard's wife wasn't exactly a maiden and the sign made no sense. Mitzi's death made no sense.

"Everly!" a woman called as I broke free from the thick of the crowd. I recognized her face from the local news. "Tell me," she said, hurrying in my direction as a man with a camera on one shoulder trailed after her, "Do you think Mitzi Calgon's fatal bee stings were an accident or is something foul abuzz here?"

I guffawed. Seriously? News anchor puns at a time like this?

"You're making a name for yourself as this town's unofficial gumshoe," she said. "Will you be looking into Mitzi Calgon's death as well?"

"No comment," I said weakly, my scrambled brain trying and failing to make sense of her statement. I was making a name for myself? As a gumshoe? And the local news lady had heard about it? My ears began to ring as I turned for the street and hurried away.

"Will you at least promise to keep us posted?" she called after me. "I hear Mitzi Calgon was a friend of your family. Is that true?"

My steps faltered, but I pushed on.

Her voice grew smaller with each additional word. "Did you know her well? Are you the reason she agreed to join the Bee Loved campaign?"

Grief gripped my chest and twisted my gut as my footfalls quickened, putting space between us as rapidly as possible. *Would I be looking into this? Should I be?*

Mitzi Calgon was someone my grandma had kept in touch with for more than forty years. For that alone, I owed her my very best efforts at finding justice. Didn't I?

CHAPTER

~

THREE

I hurried up the front steps of my beachfront Victorian and across the wide wraparound porch to my door. A large, hand-painted *C'mon in, y'all* sign welcomed guests from the window. The seashell wind chimes that tinkled with each opening of the door let me know when someone new had arrived.

"Welcome to Sun, Sand, and Tea," my new part-time barkeep, Denise, called from the café across the foyer.

"It's just me," I answered, hurrying over wide, white-washed floorboards and beneath a newly added sea glass chandelier.

A dozen lively voices lifted against a backdrop of Beach Boys tunes, and guests filled every seat in the room. Granted, there were only fifteen seats so far, a mix of barstools, bistro sets, and traditional tables, but the place was standing room only. I smiled as I took it in, humbled and awestruck as always. People liked my iced tea shop. Whether they came for the warm beachfront atmosphere, delicious food, or easy vibes, I couldn't be sure, but I hoped it was a combination of the three.

Business had boomed since I'd opened the café's doors last year, and it was already time for me to expand. Luckily, the home's former ballroom was situated just off the café and separated only by an ornately carved arch. I had plenty of space. What I didn't have was time.

Denise tapped an iced tea dispenser, then slid a lidless canning jar of my grandma's old-fashioned sweet tea in my direction. "I heard what happened," she said grimly as I arrived behind the counter. "How are you doing?"

"Not great." I took a long swig of the tea, letting its sweetness and familiarity soak into my bones.

Denise was Grady's son's au pair, and she was fast becoming a friend of mine. I'd originally mistaken her for his inappropriately young wife, but I quickly learned he was a widow. The senator, his deceased wife's mother, had handpicked Denise to care for her grandson while Grady pulled himself together after the funeral. According to Grady, Denise had been a lifesaver and she'd agreed to stay on, even through their move from Arlington to our little town.

She was young, blond, and beautiful—a quiet, genuine, and unassuming woman, at least on the surface. She'd surprised me last winter by reaching out and offering to help at the iced tea shop while Denver was in school. She said it would be a great way for her to acclimate to the island and meet more folks. I couldn't disagree, especially since I needed the help, so here we were. I suspected, though, that what folks saw on the surface was only the tip of the iceberg with Denise.

"Better?" she asked.

I nodded. The tea definitely soothed. "It just doesn't seem real," I muttered, my ice sloshing in the half-empty jar.

Denise checked her watch. "Maybe you should go upstairs and rest. I can ask the senator to pick Denver up from school for me."

"No." I forced a smile. "I'll be okay, but thank you."

"Don't mention it." She scanned the tables, probably making sure no one needed anything. "Okay. Then I guess I'd better get going."

"I'll walk you out." I stopped at the front door just as a big black SUV rolled into view. The back window rolled down and the senator circled one wrist outside the vehicle before powering the tinted barrier back up.

Denise pursed her lips. "I guess that's my ride. Are you sure you don't want me to stay so you can relax, maybe shower or nap? You've been through a lot this morning."

I smiled at the woman, at least five years my junior, worrying about me. Being an au pair suited her well. "I'm good," I assured her. "You should go. Hug Denver for me."

She gave the world around us a long, careful look,

then squared her shoulders and marched purposefully toward the SUV.

For the hundredth time, a deep, niggling instinct suggested to me that Denise was far more than she appeared.

I waved to the departing vehicle and hurried back inside to tend to my guests.

The space that was now my café stretched through the entire south side of the first floor, utilizing only about half of my overall square footage on this level. The previous owner had knocked out several non-load-bearing walls, creating a magnificent showcase of space. Now, the newly renovated kitchen flowed seamlessly into the former dining room and gathering area. I'd taken advantage of the wide planked floors and rear wall of windows, making the space home to my new iced tea shop. A little shiplap and wainscoting and it was the perfect seaside escape. I'd worked with a natural palette for décor. Soft shades of cream and tan for shells and sand. Brilliant blues for the sky and sea, with punches of orange and yellow for the jaw-dropping sunrises I observed every morning from my deck.

An enclosed staircase from the foyer provided passage to my private living quarters upstairs, complete with a locking door. The second and third floors were just as big and full of potential. I could probably thank the home's history as a boardinghouse for my substantial second-floor kitchen. All in all, the home was a treasured piece of the island's history, and I wished the walls could talk. Maybe they could advise me on which renovation project to take on first, café expansion aside.

I cleared tables, took orders, and kept moving for hours, thankful for every chore that kept my mind off the morning's atrocities. Still, the busyness hadn't stopped me from wrestling with Odette's claim to have been conveniently outside at the time of Mitzi's murder. Hopefully, Grady would check her cell phone records to confirm, *not that she couldn't have made a call, then left someone on hold while she went to hurt Mitzi,* I realized. I hoped Grady would look into that possibility too.

I started as Amelia and Mr. Butters appeared. I hadn't heard anyone come in.

"Two iced chai lattes, please," Amelia said, dragging herself onto a stool at the counter.

"And rum cake," her dad added. "Make mine a thick slice."

I obliged, then set the offerings before them on the counter. Mr. Butters had changed into his usual cargo shorts and untucked short-sleeve button-down, but I'd never seen him so sad. "On the house," I whispered.

"How are you holding up?" Amelia asked.

I shrugged. "It was busy when I got here. That helped for a while."

Amelia pressed the tines of her fork into her rum cake but made no move to raise the bite to her lips. "Now, it's dinnertime."

"Yeah." The menu at Sun, Sand, and Tea was

limited. Great for lunches and snacks, refreshing drinks and desserts, but folks normally headed into town for a proper meal this time of evening. "Can I make you guys some food?"

"No." They answered in unison, clearly satisfied with my most popular dessert.

I'd taken the old rum cake recipe from a handwritten cookbook in my aunts' archives and featured it on my blog for Valentine's Day, not knowing the cake would be an immediate hit. Apparently, the baking tutorial I'd created had been too complicated for the masses, so folks just started placing orders. Locals stopped by or called. Blog followers left orders in the Comments section. I'd already shipped four rum cakes out of state and a dozen throughout North Carolina. I was actively considering which of my other recipes would hold up for shipping until I realized I'd have to clone myself if I wanted to bake any more than I already did.

"What do you think we should do?" Amelia asked, dragging me back to the moment. "Those pictures and that note were creepy. They were probably from the same person, and Detective Hays thought Dad's painting was part of the package."

Mr. Butters stuffed another hunk of cake between his lips, eyes unfocused.

"Grady knows you didn't do this," I whispered, giving his hand a quick squeeze before turning back to Amelia. "We'll figure it out."

"How?" she asked, abandoning her fork beside the barely touched cake.

Another familiar face arrived before I could think of an answer for Amelia.

Rose, the documentary's producer, walked inside with a man I recognized from the production team. She ran anxious fingers through her wild brown hair, then led him to a tall bistro table with a panoramic view of the seaside.

Amelia lowered her chin and whispered, "All those photos from Mitzi's dressing room were taken on the island, which means she had a stalker here, and I think that person killed her."

Her dad's head bobbed in agreement. "We can't let someone get away with this. Mitzi deserves so much better than what happened today. Tell us what to do, and we'll do it. Who should we talk to first?"

I leaned closer, contemplating the possibilities. "I'm not sure. Those photos could've been taken by anyone. Someone from here, or someone who followed her here. The luncheon was advertised online for weeks. The whole world had plenty of advance notice. I suppose we could start by interviewing the people we know with rental properties, see if anyone has a renter who gave them cause for concern." *Like what?* I wondered. *A wall covered in photos of Mitzi's face and a detailed plan to push her into a bee box?* Not likely, and there was another, larger hole in that plan as well. "Of course, there's no rule that says the killer stayed here at all. There are plenty of other towns nearby and on the mainland. The killer could've dropped by to do the deed at lunchtime and already be on a plane to Nantucket."

Amelia slouched.

"Be right back," I told her, then grabbed a couple of place settings and headed for Rose's table.

I squared my shoulders and worked up an appropriately pleasant smile. "Welcome to Sun, Sand, and Tea," I said, setting napkins and brightly colored biodegradable straws in front of Rose and the man. I'd moved to a more environmentally friendly approach to life after finding Lou, the seagull that hung out on my deck, wearing a set of plastic rings from a six-pack around his neck like the world's most dangerous necklace.

"Can I start you off with some iced tea?" I asked. "I keep twenty flavors on tap, all made in-house by me."

Rose looked weary. "Sure, and can we see some menus?"

I hooked a thumb over my shoulder, indicating the huge chalkboard hanging on the wall behind my service counter. I kept the daily menu items and tea flavors written there in big chalk letters. Traditional menus didn't work for me. I needed the freedom to change things up, and I usually worked with whatever ingredients were on hand instead of menu planning and shopping accordingly. The tea flavors were another story and changed less often. Locals had made their favorites clear, so I rarely took those away. I played with the remaining options, always looking for the next big hit.

Rose's brows rose behind thick bangs and dark-rimmed glasses. "Then I guess I'll have the iced ginger pear tea and the mango shrimp spring rolls."

"Perfect," I said, making note of her order on my striped green pad before turning to smile at the man seated across from her.

"Old-fashioned sweet tea sounds good to me," he said. "Maybe a few crab stuffed mushrooms…and I'd like to try your fresh berry bowl."

"Coming right up." I scribbled his order beneath Rose's, then paused before introducing myself. "You might not remember me," I began, lowering my voice and positioning myself between them and the handful of other guests behind me. "I'm Everly Swan. I own this café. I'm Clara and Fran Swan's great niece. I was there with them today."

Rose looked ill. "Of course. I'm Rose Long."

"I remember," I said. "We met briefly last night when I was decorating."

She looked me over more carefully then. "Of course. I remember now. Sorry, you look so different. Out of context I guess."

I smiled, certain she meant *out of jean shorts and a sweaty ponytail.*

The man extended his hand to me. "Quinn Farris."

"You two make up the production team," I said. "Plus a few volunteers."

"That's right," Rose said. "We're on a tight budget, despite a generous donation I secured after your aunts announced Mitzi Calgon was on board for the voice work. I'm still not sure how they pulled that off. Maybe you really are a magical family." When I didn't react, she moved on. "Any money not spent on production can be put directly into honeybee research and protection efforts, so we're working with a skeleton crew."

"Do you both work for Bee Loved?" I asked. "Or is your production company a separate entity?" My great-aunts had submitted a video application to Bee Loved, but that didn't mean Bee Loved employees were the ones making the film. They might've only been sponsoring and promoting it.

Rose pressed a palm to her chest. "I do, but Quinn works for Bio-Bee."

"Bio-Bee?" I parroted, turning to him for further explanation.

"Bio-Bee is a nonprofit start-up," he said. "I created it with some friends after college. We all wanted to study the American honeybee using science. Not just their anatomy and life cycles, but the intersocial connections and hive hierarchy as well as their impact on earth, human lives, health, and economics."

"He's the scientist," Rose said. "I'm the artist. We met in college. After graduation, I went to Bee Loved and joined a decade-old company selling bee swag with hearts to a substantial social media following. Quinn founded Bio-Bee. Now we get to team up again for an epic encore performance. Me with my creative mind and Quinn with his brilliant one. Two specialties. One goal. Educate the public to save the American honeybee."

Quinn watched a couple in pirate costumes enter the café, then shifted uncomfortably in his seat. "I had no idea Mitzi Calgon was so popular. I've never seen any of her work."

Rose shrugged. "I was a film student. I've seen everything. She was the only reason I secured such a big donation for film production."

"What happens to the documentary now?" I asked. "Will it be canceled?"

"No." Rose lowered her gaze to the table. "I think the show must go on. Right? As long as your aunts are still up to it, we can always find someone else to do the voice work later. We're here, so we should film while we can."

Quinn remained silent. Considering the options, perhaps. "We could head home, do some heavy PR work and wait for this to pass, then come back in the fall or something."

Rose shook her head resolutely. "Making another trip just wastes money. We're here now. We'll move forward as planned."

Quinn's jaw clenched and released, but he didn't argue. It was a tough call. I could see that, and I was glad I wasn't in Rose's shoes.

I took my leave and went to greet the pirate couple, then hurried back to the counter to prep the orders.

Amelia and her dad were hunkered around her phone as I filled fresh jars with ice and tea.

"What are you looking at?" I asked, sliding an old-fashioned sweet tea and iced ginger pear onto one tray, a strawberry mint and summer citrus blend on another.

"*Town Charmer*," Amelia said, eyes glued to the screen.

"Coverage of the luncheon?" I guessed.

I cranked the timer on my toaster oven, then popped in six mango shrimp eggrolls and a line of pre-stuffed mushroom caps.

"Nope," Mr. Butters answered.

"Then what?" I asked.

The Town Charmer was our local gossip blog, run by an anonymous but highly informed citizen. Most locals visited the site regularly. We all claimed it was a great resource for the weather and tide schedule, but the continuous feed of questionable and occasionally scandalous articles probably didn't hurt traffic.

The toaster oven dinged and I collected the food, quickly arranging the eggrolls onto a plate. I fanned them out from the center like a star or flower, then placed a dollop of sweet and tangy dipping sauce in the center. The mushrooms went in a circle on a smaller plate, a pile of finely diced tomato, cilantro, and onion in the middle.

I looked up and caught Amelia staring.

She turned her phone to face me, eyes glistening with unshed tears. A picture of Mr. Butters in full Blackbeard attire centered the screen. The watercolor painting from Mitzi's dressing room was in his hands. Beside that photo was a grainy shot of the evidence bags and Mr. Butters's painting in the hands of a cop.

"Read the caption," Amelia said.

"Charm Lawmen Search for Possible Stalker."

I glanced at Mr. Butters, who was working his way through Amelia's slice of rum cake as if he might find some comfort there.

The article went on to describe the photos of Mitzi, taken since her arrival in Charm late last night, and the creepy letter. The signed painting was described as "ominous and worrisome."

I grimaced as I prepped Quinn's berry bowl. The locally grown strawberries, blueberries, blackberries, and raspberries went into a dessert bowl with a dollop of vanilla yogurt at the bottom. I placed the bowl with the food and waiting teas.

Amelia snaked her hand out to catch my wrist before I lifted the tray. "Help us."

"Okay," I said, keeping the deliveries carefully balanced. "Give me a minute to drop these off and think about what to do. I'll be right back."

She released me on a ragged inhalation of breath.

I ferried two iced teas to the pirate couple, then moved on to Rose and Quinn. When the tray was empty, I tucked it under one arm and offered an encouraging smile. "Enjoy. If you need anything else, just holler."

"Actually," Rose began, her phone positioned between them on the table. "Is it true that you help local police solve crimes?"

"No," I answered quickly, hating the speed at which news traveled when it wasn't in my favor.

"Are you sure?" Quinn asked, one brow quirked. "The reporter who told us seemed pretty certain."

I shook my head and bit the insides of my cheeks. Not only did I definitely *not* help police with their investigations, I'd been asked repeatedly not to. "Reporters always seem certain about everything," I said. "Honestly, they're kind of a pain."

A bout of familiar laughter erupted behind me. "Really? I rather enjoy a good reporter."

No way. I spun on my toes to find Ryan, possibly the world's most annoying reporter, striding confidently through my café.

I needed to get louder wind chimes, or maybe I could just get Ryan a warning bell to hang around his neck.

I left Rose and Quinn to their food and went to greet my newest guest. "What on earth are you doing here?" I asked, grabbing him in a hug. Ryan made me crazy, but we'd shared a near-death experience once and that sort of thing creates a bond.

He hugged Amelia next, lifting her easily off the ground as Mr. Butters rose to greet him with a handshake.

Amelia beamed up at the somewhat attractive, obnoxiously overconfident reporter. "You're late."

"Late?" I asked. "You knew he was coming? Why didn't you tell me?"

Ryan smirked. "Everyone knows how much you enjoy a good surprise."

"Yes," I agreed. "A *good* surprise."

"Ha!" He arched his back in laughter. "I came to cover Mitzi Calgon's return to the spotlight after nearly a decade of living reclusively, but it seems I'm a little late."

"She wasn't a recluse," I said defensively, though I barely knew her. "She was retired. It's different." If she had been a recluse, I wouldn't have blamed her. Not with hordes of people following her around, dressed as pirates from a movie she'd made decades ago, taking her picture without her consent, and writing weird poems for her.

Ryan pulled his chin back in a look of disbelief. "Please. Actors love the spotlight. She'd obviously been hiding out for a reason, and now I guess we all know why."

I gaped. "Crass."

He shrugged. "I call them as I see them, and right now, I see a woman who knew she was in danger but came out of hiding to do a favor for a friend, and that favor got her killed."

"Get out," I said, pointing to the door, but only half meaning it.

He took a seat at the bar beside Amelia and smiled at me. "I missed that Swan sass. Lucky for you and Ms. Calgon, an extremely talented investigative reporter is now in town, and word has it that when I pair up with Everly Swan, criminals don't stand a chance."

"We're not teaming up."

"That's what you said last time." He winked.

Amelia patted his arm and smiled.

I cast a look toward Rose and Quinn's table and found them watching me. I'd just told them I didn't investigate things.

"Fine," I said softly to Ryan and the Butterses, angling my back toward the documentary production team's table. "I'll help clear up the confusion over whether or not Mr. Butters wrote that letter or took those photos, and I'll see what I can do about clearing his name as the killer, but that's it."

Ryan laughed again. Loudly. Drawing more attention. "And leave your grandmother's friend's murder unsolved? Yeah, right."

"How did you know…" I began.

Ryan tapped a finger to his temple, successfully ending my question. I'd nearly forgotten he claimed to know everything. "That reminds me. Let me see your phone," he said.

My hand went protectively to my pocket. "No."

Ryan tipped his head over one shoulder and made a get-serious face. "Come on. I found something you need for your blog, and I want to get it for you."

"You follow my blog?" I asked incredulously.

"Sure," he said. "I'm OneHotEnglishMuffin."

I gave him the phone for making me laugh. "What are you doing, Muffin?"

He ignored the jibe and tapped my unlocked screen a few times. "I've downloaded an app that all the big vloggers are using. Vlogs are video blogs."

"I know what a vlog is," I said, taking my phone back. "What does this app do?"

"It streams in real time. Not like those overedited, after-the-fact posts you put up. This is real. You hit one button, and the app begins to record. People want to see you working, flaws and all. Not watch you put dough in the oven, shut the door, pull it out, and it's done. That's not very realistic."

I grinned. "You watch my baking tutorials?" I asked, slightly shocked, mostly entertained.

"Of course." He folded his hands on the counter and frowned, as if he was offended I'd not expected as much. "Your followers want to see the flubs and follies, not a perfectly polished performance. They want to know you're real. Real people make messes and drop stuff sometimes."

I pocketed the phone with a grimace. I liked seeing online personalities as relatable too, but I wasn't ready to put my every flaw and incompetency online for the world to watch. And I'd completely forgotten about the footage I'd taken before the luncheon today. It seemed wrong to use any of that now, after the way things had gone. But it would be nice to offer my followers a little variety. "I'll think about it."

"That's all I ask," he said magnanimously. "Now, what can I do to get some of this rum cake I'm hearing so much about?"

❧

I stayed busy until the shop was empty and the clock on my stove indicated it was seven o'clock. Time to call it a day, though it felt more like a week since I'd gotten out of bed with the morning alarm. I flipped the deadbolt on the door, turned the sign to Closed, then headed to my deck to clear my head.

Balmy air kissed my face as I leaned against the handrail. I re-centered myself in the stillness, absorbing the blessed white noise of endless rolling waves, inhaling the uniquely seaside scent of sand, salt, and sunblock.

The house seagull, Lou, landed on the railing a few feet away with a gentle thud. Wings outstretched and chest puffed, he scrutinized me with one beady black eye.

"Ryan's back," I told him as a tear rolled over my cheek.

I hated what had happened to Mitzi. I hated losing a link to my grandma that I'd only just discovered. I hated that my emotions had a way of swelling until they leaked from my eyes even when I wasn't in the mood to cry. "I don't like how he looks at Amelia," I continued, complaining about Ryan, hoping to pull myself together. "I also don't like admitting he's a pretty good guy, if you ignore all the arrogance. He's not a bad reporter either. Probably a wise choice in an investigative partner, if I wanted a partner."

Lou settled his fully fluffed body over his feet until they disappeared. He wasn't much of a conversationalist, but he was a great listener. I appreciated that in a man.

"Do you think I should get involved in this?"

He cocked his head but didn't answer.

"Mitzi brought all my grandma's letters to Charm

with her," I told him. "More than two hundred. She must've been pretty important to Grandma for her to write all those letters, which makes me want to help. Mitzi was going to give those letters to me, but now they're probably in the evidence room at the police station. If I ask for them, Grady will assume I'm meddling again." I chewed my lip, an idea forming in my head. "Unless the letters aren't in evidence yet. In which case, they might still be in Wyatt's office at the nature center. I'll bet Wyatt would sneak me in if I ask."

If I went to look for the letters, not to snoop, and I happened to come across something that could help Grady find Mitzi's killer faster, that wouldn't be a bad thing. "I bet Grandma would want me to help her friend," I reasoned, "and surely Mitzi would want justice for what happened to her. I would, if I were her."

Lou made an ugly gull caw just as my phone gave a long buzz.

I frowned at the gull. "That was crazy timing. Did you know the phone would ring?"

I turned the device over and swiped the screen, ready to make a return trip to the nature center and try to catch Wyatt. I didn't recognize the number. "Someone left me a text message," I told Lou. "I hope it's not that lady reporter."

A close-up image of a honeybee nearly stopped my heart.

Lou made a repeated throaty caw sound as I read the three-word note below the photo.

Don't Bee Stupid.

CHAPTER
❧
FOUR

I can't believe you've been threatened already," Grady groused, looking somewhat defeated as he crossed the empty café to my side. His dark fitted T-shirt, blue jeans, and boots made him look more like trouble than the law. His haggard expression didn't help.

"Thanks for coming," I told him, passing my cell phone into his open hand and ignoring the way he looked in a cowboy hat and stubble. I lowered the volume on the small television I'd turned to the evening news while waiting for his arrival. I'd been hoping the local reporter who had harassed me earlier might've captured some useful footage—something that would lead to the truth about what happened behind the stage curtain today.

Grady tossed his hat onto the counter and leveled me with an accusing look. "Who did you talk to about what happened?"

"No one," I said, mentally running through the list of usuals. My great-aunts, Denise, Amelia and her dad, Ryan, and Lou... Plus, that television reporter had approached me, and I'd offered condolences or reassuring phrases to a couple dozen café patrons. "No one who would threaten me, anyway."

"Uh huh," he said, sounding wholly unconvinced. "Been asking questions about Mitzi? Maybe talking to the production team? Nature center staff? People from the crowd?"

"How do you know that?" I asked, suddenly suspecting Denise was a plant sent to spy on me for him.

"I know you, Swan, and this isn't our first rodeo." He rested the heel of one hand on the butt of an exposed sidearm on his belt and caught me in his signature cop stare. "Someone with a connection to your family was killed today. I'd have to be willfully stupid to think you aren't trying to get a lead on who did it. Do I look stupid to you?"

"I'm a victim here," I said, hoping to change the subject. I scooped a pair of empty jars off the rack and filled them halfway with ice, then set the cubes afloat in a flood of old-fashioned sweet tea, Grady's favorite.

He pursed his lips and rolled stormy gray eyes up to meet my gaze. "It's only been a few hours. The sun hasn't even set yet."

I glanced through my windows at an amber and apricot horizon. "It's getting close."

Grady sighed and rested a palm on the counter, my phone still cradled in his opposite hand. "Let's start over. First, I'm sorry you lost a friend today."

"Thanks," I said, feeling a lump form instantly in

my throat. "We'd just met, but she knew Grandma and we were going to talk about her tonight over midnight pancakes with my aunts."

"You'd never met before today?" he asked.

"No. I knew Mitzi Calgon was doing the voice work, but I didn't know she was doing it as a favor to my aunts or that Mitzi had known Grandma until today. It was a surprise my aunts had set up for me. They told me this morning."

Grady's expression eased. "I'm truly sorry."

"S'okay," I said, softening as regret registered in his eyes, the set of his jaw, and rigidity in his shoulders. Grady had an excellent blank cop face, but I was learning to look for the things he couldn't hide when I wanted to know what he was thinking. I'd begun to notice little things he probably didn't realize he did, like running the fingers of his right hand along his left jawline when he was contemplative or angry.

"How are you doing?" I asked, sincerely concerned. "You look exhausted, and I know it's not just from today."

"I am," he admitted, "and it's not."

I fetched a lemon cake from my pantry and placed it on the counter between us. The only thing Grady liked more than my family's old-fashioned sweet tea was my lemon cake. His eyes widened at the sight of freshly set icing hanging in thick white strips and droplets over the tangy curves. I took my time cutting and plating the slice, then slid it to him in offering.

"Want to talk about your thing?" Whatever it was.

"Not yet," he said, trading my cell phone for the cake and fork. "Why don't you go first?"

"You already know about the worst parts of my day," I said. "Also, Ryan's back," I smiled as his expression soured. Ryan tended to have that effect on people. Everyone except Amelia, anyway.

"Great."

"He said he came to get the scoop on Mitzi and her return to the spotlight but was too late."

"I don't like him being here right now. He fuels your fire for this stuff," Grady said, forking a bite of cake with unnecessary roughness.

"I fuel my own fire," I told him. But he was right. Ryan did get me going. "He called Mitzi a recluse and wanted to know why she'd been out of the public eye for so long, but she wasn't. Not really."

"She's seventy," Grady said. "She retired."

I sipped my tea and paddled the cubes around with my straw. "That's what I told him, but he's always expecting to uncover some big story. He thinks Mitzi staying out of the limelight for so long had something to do with her death."

Grady grunted.

"What's that mean?" I asked. "You agree with him? You think the photos and letter from her dressing room were part of a larger problem she was having?"

He chewed his next bite of cake more slowly. "All I know is someone put her in that box today. She wouldn't have gone willingly."

"She was allergic," I said.

He nodded. "I haven't seen an official report yet, but one look at the skin around those stings told that story."

I pressed my eyes shut as the image of Mitzi's swollen face reappeared in my mind. "Will you be able to find out who sent me that message?" I asked, forcing my eyes open once more and turning my focus to the threat I'd received via text.

Grady's frown returned, and he pressed the tines of his fork into the lemon cake. "I forwarded the message and the number it came from to Tech Services. We'll see what they can do with it."

I glanced at my device on the counter between us. "What if it was sent from a burner phone?" I asked. "Will they be able to see who the phone belongs to?"

"Depends on how it was paid for. But as long as it stays on, we can still trace it, and that's something," he said. "Chances it's still on are slim. More likely, the phone was purchased solely to send that text and is now at the bottom of the ocean."

"I hate pollution," I said.

Grady stifled a smile.

"What about Mitzi's phone?" I asked. "Have you gone through her calls and messages yet?"

Grady squinted at me. "We're trying, but the phone was password protected. Tech Services is working on it now. Why?"

I stepped closer, nerves buzzing and jangling in my core. "Mitzi got a call right before she went to lunch. She didn't tell me who it was, but she looked bothered by it and when I asked, she just said, 'small annoyances.' Maybe Ryan was right. Maybe she was avoiding someone, and he or she contacted Mitzi just before she died. What if you trace that call and find the killer?"

"Maybe," he said, before stabbing another bite of lemon cake. "What's most important is that you understand *I* will get to the bottom of whatever's happened here, *not you*."

I locked my hands on my hips and narrowed my eyes at him. "I thought you'd want to know about the call."

"I do. Thank you," he said. "Meanwhile, I've already requested a copy of her phone records, so you don't need to worry about that."

"Good." I sliced a second piece of cake for Grady and refilled his tea, then went to sit on the stool beside his. "Did you find anything useful at the nature center? Some kind of lead to get you started?"

He rubbed his left cheek with the fingers of his right hand. "No. There were too many people in that building today. Thousands of footprints. Fibers. Hairs. Whatever amount of materials we normally process from a crime scene, multiply that by a hundred. My men are combing surveillance footage from the police station right now because the nature center doesn't have any cameras." He gave a soft, humorless laugh.

"At least the police station is next door," I said, offering an extremely thin silver lining. The nature center and police station stood in tandem along the bay, sharing a parking lot and picturesque views of the sunset. "I guess we're lucky in that way." Most businesses in town didn't bother with surveillance. Cameras were expensive to purchase. So were maintenance and upkeep plans. Plus, crime was low in Charm. Most folks would just lose the money spent on security tech, not to mention the monthly bill for video surveillance storage on the cloud. I'd looked into all those things this year. Ultimately, I'd decided the only security measures in my budget were deadbolts and better judgment.

"It didn't help that some moron left the back door unlocked," Grady said, preparing to dig into the second slice of cake. "I suppose that was Odette, making her private phone call."

I wrinkled my nose. "It might also have been Wyatt. That was how he snuck Amelia and Mr. Butters in early without the crowd noticing."

Grady whispered a curse. "Well, if we've got that on camera, it's not going to help Butters's case." He rubbed the dark skin beneath his eyes, and I took notice again of the way he looked miserable and emotionally spent.

"Hey," I began carefully, drawing his eyes back to mine. "You haven't been around much lately. Denise says you travel on your days off and stay holed up in your office after your shifts. You want to talk about that?"

"Not really," he said. "I've just been busy."

"With?" I asked lightly, twisting on my barstool in his direction for a more direct look at his face.

Grady returned his attention to my phone screen. "I've been helping Olivia look for her husband."

An electric current of enthusiasm ripped through me at the candor in his response. Grady was opening up! Sharing his secrets. *Trusting me.* "How's it going?" I asked.

I'd researched Senator Denver the moment I realized she was Grady's late wife's mother. It hadn't taken long to learn her husband, a member of the CIA, had gone missing shortly after their daughter's death. Rumors suggested suicide over a broken heart. But there had never been a funeral.

If the senator's husband was alive, Grady could find him.

"How do you think it's going?" Grady asked, his lips twitching in the almost-smile I loved.

"You found him," I whispered, instinctively lowering my voice and leaning closer. "Holy cannoli. You found him! Didn't you? Was he alive? Is he hurt?"

"He was on assignment," Grady said. "That was all Olivia knew when she asked for my help. He's been deep undercover since shortly after Amy died." He paused, the way he always did after speaking his late wife's name. "But Oliva needed to reach him. So, I did."

I waited for more information, but Grady's jaw locked. Clearly, there was more to that story, but he wasn't ready to share it with me. He swiped my phone to life again, then turned the screen to face me.

I tapped my access code and released the device back into his care.

Grady stared at the three-word threat and honey-bee image. "Who could have sent this message?" he asked. "Who have you talked to about Mitzi's death? What did they say?"

I watched him for a long moment before speaking. "Are you mad at me?" I asked, confused and a little miffed by his accusatory tone. "None of this is my fault. I barely spent five minutes with Mitzi before she was killed. I don't follow her online. I'm not a fan of her films. I'm innocent here, and I have no idea who would have sent me that text or why."

Grady opened his mouth to say something, but the sound of my name drew our attention to the small television across the counter.

"Everly Swan," the overconfident voice drawled, "a native of this town and one-woman crime fighter, has assisted police in the capture and arrest of three killers since her return to our charming island little more than a year ago."

My jaw sank open in shock.

Grady made a low guttural noise beside me, then went to turn up the television's volume.

"I didn't talk to her," I sputtered. "I swear. She tried to get me to comment on what happened, but I refused. I just said, 'No comment.'"

The camera switched to a close-up of my face, the words Local Sleuth positioned above my name with a tiny magnifying glass beneath. My mouth was moving, but the voice was that of the news anchor.

"So, look out, local criminals. According to the statistics, your days of freedom are numbered."

Grady's face turned tomato red, then darkened to a purple nearing eggplant.

I giggled nervously and pushed my slice of cake in his direction.

CHAPTER

FIVE

I woke groggy the next morning thanks to a short and restless sleep. I'd dragged myself to bed after the nightly news, unable to keep my eyes open another minute, but the moment I settled into bed, my mind sprang to life. My thoughts raced in circles over my day, bringing back snippets of the things I'd seen, said, or heard in sharp flashes—there and gone before I could grasp them. I was caught in the flux. Too tired to make anything coherent of the fleeting images or ideas. Too lucid to fall asleep before the barrage stopped. It had been half past three the last time I'd looked at the clock. Two hours later, my alarm roused me promptly at five thirty.

I willed myself upright, stuffed my bare feet into fuzzy slippers, then padded across the large central living space of my home's second floor. I made it to the kitchen with a grateful sigh. Thanks to a little planning, the coffee maker had also woken at five thirty and had already begun to brew. I held the partially filled pot in one hand and shoved my favorite mug under the drip instead. When the cup was full, I replaced the pot, pressed the mug to my lips, and headed back across the living area to my deck windows.

I opened the curtains, squinting momentarily at the flood of May sun. Natural light filled the beautifully open space I'd been slowly refinishing. My walls were a soft and inviting gray. The wide wood trim was a fantastic white. My couch, chairs, and coffee table were arranged on a massive damask rug at the room's center, a floating island on the sea of highly polished, historic wooden floorboards. Standing there, beneath the ornate plaster ceiling and elaborately carved crown molding, it was easy to feel as if I'd fallen back in time. I tried to embrace that feeling anytime I faced a new decision on the necessary updates and changes. There was a definite and delicate balance between honoring the past and embracing the present.

Subtle movement caught my eye a moment before Maggie, a magnificent white cat, came into view. Maggie, like Lou, seemed to have come with the house. She'd looked ragged and a little feral when we first met, but she had reluctantly accepted a proper grooming since then. Lou lived mostly on my roof and decks, but Maggie had a habit of materializing and vanishing at unpredictable intervals, both inside the home and out. I tried not to look too deeply into it, but my aunts had a theory.

According to Aunt Clara and Aunt Fran, my

property had once been owned by a wealthy business-man who'd commissioned the home for his mistress, Magnolia Bane. When the man's wife found him cheating, she threw herself into the ocean, never to be seen again. When Magnolia realized what her love for the man had done, she flung herself from the widow's walk on my roof. The man, Lou Something-or-other, then moved into the home and slowly lost his mind to grief for the women. My aunts claimed that Lou's restless spirit still rattled around my home, or it had until I purchased the place, and one of the women from his earthly life had been reincarnated into a cat that never left. I didn't believe the story, of course, but I liked the names Maggie and Lou so I borrowed them for the gull and cat.

Maggie, the cat, wound around my bare calves and purred. I bent to scratch behind her ears and stroke her fur. "Any big plans today?" I asked.

She blinked luminous green eyes at me, and I had the distinct impression she was trying to tell me something.

"Are you hungry?" I asked. I went back to the kitchen and filled her bowls with kibble, then refreshed her water. She hopped onto the countertop and watched, but she made no move to eat.

"Why can't you talk?" I asked for the hundredth time since we'd met.

She lifted her chin at that, turned on her paws, and leapt onto the floor, tail held high. A moment later, she was gone.

I knew better than to look for her. Maggie apparently had an escape hatch around here somewhere that I'd yet to find. I just hoped a bat, rat, or baby alligator didn't find the access point before I did.

The fog rolled away from my sleepy mind as I poured a third cup of coffee. The familiar rush of adrenaline hit seconds later. Someone had murdered my grandma's friend yesterday. Mr. Butters was being linked to her death because he'd painted her a beautiful picture. Gossips were twisting facts, sensationalizing leaked details, and making up the rest. It wasn't right, and I'd promised Amelia I would help.

I went to shower, dress, and get started on my quest.

Halfway through blowing out my unruly hair, my little rubber fitness bracelet began to complain.

BE MORE ACTIVE!

"I'm trying," I protested, jamming my fingertip against the little button to stop the alert. Thanks to technology, the bracelet had become familiar with my routines and anticipated my morning walk. If I was late, or dared skip, I heard about it. I didn't like being told what to do, but I also missed the days when I could zip my pants without lying on the bed. So, I kept the bracelet.

I slid into size twelve navy blue yoga pants, wondering where my size six figure had gone, topping them with a white cotton sports bra, tank top, and tunic. I shoved socked feet into my most comfortable walking shoes and jogged down the steps to my front door.

Then I spent a minute on my porch, stretching my legs and adjusting my ponytail. A gentle breeze stirred briny scents of the sea into air already sweetened by my gardens. Roses bloomed in mass along my home's northern side, alternating colors and mixing with a dozen other beautiful blooms surrounding my gazebo. The gardens stretched the length of my home, front to back, winding whimsically along a cobblestone path to the place where my property ended abruptly. Time and weather had cut a jagged edge in the hill my home sat atop, leaving a sharp plummet to the sand and surf below.

I stepped off the porch and headed south, up my short gravel drive to the boardwalk. A handful of brightly colored beach towels and umbrellas were already sprinkled across the beach. The boardwalk was a popular pedestrian and bike path caught between the ocean and a narrow marsh. Ocean Drive, the main road along the seaside, was just across the marsh and provided access to beach parking and connected homes on the outskirts—like mine—to the rest of the town.

The boardwalk was to hikers and bikers what Ocean Drive was to cars and trucks. The sun-bleached planks had been set in place generations back and wound around the island's perimeter, breaking only where roads and inlets demanded. I used the board-walk to get my steps in each day as I battled against the twenty-five or so pounds I'd added since leaving home eight years ago. I'd made and lost headway in my battle with the bulge over the course of the last year, but the pounds were stubborn, and I liked cake as much as walking. So, I chose to focus on the fact I could climb the steps without seeing spots these days, and I called that a win.

When the boardwalk angled closest to Ocean Drive just beyond the widest stretch of beach, it was time for the planks and me to part ways. Startled briefly by a crane spearing a tiny fish from water in the marsh, I ducked under the lush branches of a leafy deciduous tree. Then I hopped across a set of large stones to the grassy roadside and straightened to an unexpected sight.

The road was lined in campers and food trucks. The air was scented with fresh fried doughnuts, various icings, and flavored coffee. My stomach growled in appreciation. The sidewalks teemed with people, many dressed in pirate costumes, and a parking lot normally reserved for Main Street shoppers was crammed with news trucks from as far away as Georgia.

I hurried across the street, then kept going until my great-aunts' shop, Blessed Bee, came into view. The yellow clapboard house was nestled conveniently between identical pink and blue houses: Sandy's Seaside Sweet Shack and Ice Cream Parlor on one side and Amelia's bookstore, Charming Reads, on the other.

Aunt Clara had stenciled honeybees flying broad loopy paths over the large shop window at Blessed Bee and the welcome mat had a hive on it. The overall look was one hundred percent adorable. I pressed my way inside and paused again to marvel at the number of shoppers.

Handmade organic products populated magnificent displays and floor-to-ceiling shelves but were now hidden by the crush of people. The interior walls were painted pale yellow with lots of white trim and crown moldings. A sky blue ceiling ran overhead, where Aunt Clara had painted fluffy clouds. The Blessed Bee products were handcrafted by Aunt Clara and Aunt Fran. Lip balms and face scrubs, suckers and soaps, all infused with pure organic honey drawn directly from their private hives and accented with dried herbs and flowers from their extensive gardens.

I slid carefully past a pair of women dressed as pirate brides, both angling their black armbands carefully toward a camera. They snapped pouty-faced selfies in front of a wall with a Blessed Bee logo and hive mural. The heartbroken expressions vanished once the final photo was taken.

I rolled my eyes and kept going.

The checkout line wound through the store. Everyone seemed to have a basket full of products. Good news for my aunts, though the likely reason for their added sales was a friend's murder.

My aunts finally came into view as I neared the checkout counter. Aunt Fran stood at the register, ringing sales and taking money while Aunt Clara bagged the items beside her and thanked folks for coming.

Rose, the documentary film producer, moved slowly along the perimeter, a small video camera in hand. She turned the device in an arc, taking in the crowd and details. When the camera landed on me, she lowered it to her side. "Hey, Everly."

"Hey." I went to stand with her while my aunts rang out the long line of guests. "This is a little crazy, huh?"

"Crazy good," she said with a grin. "I've been interviewing shoppers all morning, and most of them made the trip to Charm after hearing what happened yesterday. These folks loved Mitzi and want to support her life's final cause—American honeybees. They recognized the Blessed Bee logo from news footage and came here to buy products that will support the bees. I enlarged the donation button on the Bee Loved website, and money has been flooding in. It's amazing."

I frowned. "Really? Because it feels a little like the exploitation of Mitzi's death to me."

Rose pinned me with a look of shock and distaste. "Mitzi Calgon was a movie star. People who go into careers like that enjoy a spectacle. They *want* a spectacle. If they didn't, they wouldn't have chosen this life. Trust me. This isn't exploitation. This is capitalism."

I opened my mouth to heartily disagree, but the pirate brides I'd noticed earlier interrupted.

"You're that woman from the news, right?" the taller bride asked, arriving several steps ahead of her friend. "The local sleuth. Emery?"

I did a slow blink.

"Are you really looking into Mitzi Calgon's death? Do you think it was murder? Have you found any clues? Is that why you're here? Are you investigating?"

"Everly," I corrected, unsure how to proceed.

"It's Everly," the woman said, casting her voice into the air for all to hear. "The local sleuth!"

Several nearby shoppers moved in our direction, and others quickly took notice. Within seconds, a thick semicircle of bodies had formed around us, and my tongue seemed to swell in my mouth.

"I'm not investigating. I only came to see my aunts," I said, motioning to the counter. "I stop here every morning. It's part of my routine."

"But you are investigating," a stranger called from the back of the crowd.

Rose turned her camera on me, and the room went still.

I cast an apologetic look at my aunts, who appeared as off guard and stunned as I felt. I raised one hand to my ear in the universal sign for *I'll call you later*, then told the gathered mob, "No comment."

I marched into the back room of Blessed Bee, thankful no one was bold enough to follow, then exited into the rear alley as a volley of questions exploded behind me.

CHAPTER

SIX

I wound my way out front, deciding to check on Amelia and Mr. Butters before heading home.

Charming Reads was as packed with shoppers as Blessed Bee had been, and it took a minute to locate Amelia in the crowd. She was hunched between rows of shelves, stocking books along the far wall. I headed immediately in her direction.

Amelia had given her bookstore its name as a nod to our town, but Charming Reads absolutely lived up to its name. She'd applied her lifelong love of romance and fairy tales to every adorable detail. The French Countryside color palette she'd chosen for the walls and accent furnishings were a perfect fit for a seaside town. Muted blues, greens, and grays were offset with punches of brightly colored paintings, courtesy of her father. Ornate cherry bookshelves lined several walls, topped with custom wooden arches and details from beloved children's classics: an enchanted rose beneath a glass dome, a pair of bluebirds taking flight with a ribbon, a wand hovering above a bucket and mop.

Amelia spotted me at once. She wrenched upright with a wild expression. "Can you believe this crowd?" she asked. "It's insane, right?"

"Rose, the documentary lady, says it's 'crazy good.'"

Amelia made a throaty sound of disagreement, then puffed air into her long blond bangs. "I don't mind the extra sales, but the reason behind them is creeping me out. Half of these people are looking for books on local legends, Blackbeard, or the Outer Banks in general. I'm nearly out, and I can't get more without wiping out some other independent bookstore in the next town."

"Do it," I teased. "Spread the good fortune."

Charm was one of many small towns on the smattering of barrier islands most people called the Outer Banks. My aunts, Amelia, Mr. Butters, and I simply called it home.

"I guess if we're looking for a silver lining," I said, "at least having all these Mitzi fans in one place means it should be easy to get the scoop on what was going on in her life before yesterday. If she had a stalker before she got here, surely one of these people heard about it."

It seemed reasonable to assume that any fan motivated enough to make an impromptu trip to Charm following Mitzi's death was dedicated—and hopefully knowledgeable.

Amelia turned her attention to the cash register,

where her dad seemed to be holding court. "I know who we can ask. Come on."

I followed her to the front of the store and hugged Mr. Butters before turning to the group gathered in front of him.

"A thousand dollars," a short man with a white beard and black bandanna said, as if I hadn't interrupted them. "Make it just like the one from the news."

Mr. Butters lifted his palms. "I told you. That was one of a kind. I won't make another."

The little man stroked his beard and turned away to confer with the other men in the group.

Amelia leaned closer to me. "These guys are from the fan club Dad belongs to that I told you about. They caught sight of Dad's painting on the news and tracked him down to request a few for themselves."

"A thousand dollars for one painting?" I asked.

"Make it two thousand," the white-bearded man said. "With your signature."

Mr. Butters shook his head, congenially. "I won't do it. Not for any price. Out of respect for Mitzi. Maybe you can purchase hers somehow."

The potential buyer twisted his mouth into a knot.

"So they all know each other?" I asked Amelia. "From online?"

The little man turned and gave me a slow appraisal. Recognition lit in his eyes. "You're the Nancy Drew."

Amelia laughed.

"I'm not a Nancy Drew," I said. "I'm an iced tea shop owner. What about you?"

He passed me a business card. "Burt Pendle, attorney at law."

I examined the card. "Have you known Mr. Butters long?"

"Too long," Pendle said. "He used to be agreeable. Now he won't take two thousand dollars for one painting."

Mr. Butters grinned. "Burt and I have been in the Mitzi Calgon Fan Club since *Blackbeard's Wife* released. Back then the newsletters were mailed on paper and delivered by a postman."

Mr. Pendle laughed. "Sometimes the breaking news had already changed twice before we received our copies."

"Nowadays we get email updates and text alerts when something happens, but those are few and far between," Mr. Butters said. "Mitzi's been retired a while now. Not much activity on the news front. Until yesterday," he added gravely.

Grady had also called Mitzi "retired." I couldn't help wondering if that was the only reason she'd kept to herself lately. "Could there have been something else causing Mitzi to avoid the public eye?"

The men looked at one another, then at the group around them. Their collective gazes settled on a tall man in a black cape, boots, and gloves.

The man nodded slowly as he stepped forward. "Indeed. I have information confirming the arrival of several anonymous letters and poems in the weeks preceding Mitzi Calgon's death. However, the letters weren't the reason for her notable absence these last few years."

"What was the reason?" I asked.

Mr. Butters cleared his throat and extended his hand in my direction before sweeping it toward the tall man in black. "Everly Swan, meet the Canary."

The tall man extended a gloved hand to me. The black leather coordinated seamlessly with his dark pants and billowing cape. I wasn't sure if he was in costume or normally dressed this way, but he looked more like a crow or an actor portraying Jack the Ripper than a pirate. With a name like the Canary, there was no telling what he considered normal. "A pleasure to meet you," he said.

"You too," I agreed, though that was yet to be determined. "So, you kept tabs on Mitzi?"

He nodded. "It's my life's work."

Well, that was sad and exceptionally creepy. "How so?"

The Canary produced a thick manila file from beneath his cape. The cover was tattered along the edges, obviously well-worn and handled often, with a wide rubber band fitted around its middle. "It's my job to know what's going on with her first. Sponsors pay for that kind of information."

"And you've been doing this a while?" I guessed. I knew firsthand how difficult it could be to develop an online following. I couldn't imagine what it would take to stand out in the virtual crowd and secure sponsors for my content.

"I discovered the *Blackbeard's Wife* franchise in high school and instantly became Mitzi Calgon's biggest fan. I learned everything I could about her, and the hobby became a business. Now I run the single largest Mitzi admiration society on earth with hundreds of thousands of members worldwide. I keep insiders close to the source at all times, but they aren't there for gossip. They're there to keep track of her well-being. If she ever needed us, we'd be ready to step in."

I pursed my lips, wondering if he saw the irony in that statement. *Where had he and his worldwide admiration society been yesterday?*

"You say you keep insiders close to the source? Is Mitzi the source?" I asked. "If so, how do you manage to have someone near her all the time? That seems impossible."

He grinned mischievously. "Very few things are truly impossible. To answer your question, I keep a member of our society in her employ at all times. A driver, dog walker, gardener, maid, pool boy. You name it. There's always someone."

"And your insider can confirm the delivery of other recent letters like the one she received yesterday?" I asked.

The Canary nodded assuredly. "The letters began shortly after a public announcement was made about her involvement with this project."

"So the two are related," I guessed.

He shook a long finger at me. "Correlation doesn't

necessarily indicate causation, so we can't jump to conclusions."

I crossed my arms. "Any idea who the notes could've been from?"

"Her ex-husband is my best guess," he said quickly and apparently without thought, though I suspected he'd given the matter plenty of thought long before I'd asked. "The divorce didn't go his way, and he's mad. Also, Mitzi kept his daughter from another marriage on as an assistant, but she cut him off completely. That had to sting."

I rocked back on my heels, dumbfounded by the unexpected information. "Odette?" *The standoffish assistant was Mitzi's ex-husband's daughter?*

The Canary raised his brows, clearly pleased with my reaction to his scoop. "Surprised?"

"A little." *More like wholly confounded.* "I met Odette yesterday. She didn't seem very upset about what had happened to Mitzi. I assumed they weren't close or that Odette was new to Mitzi's team." A step-daughter was the complete opposite of that theory. They had to have known one another well. If Odette's father didn't feel he'd gotten his fair share in the split, that was definite grounds for hard feelings. Maybe even murderous feelings.

"There are plenty of others with a grudge against her," the Canary said. "When you're an icon like Mitzi Calgon, claws tend to come out on the jealous and the petty."

I suddenly wondered if the man had chosen his

unusual code name because canaries loved to sing, and he couldn't seem to stop. "Anything else I should know?"

He handed the thick file to me. "Everything you need to know is right in here."

A collective hush rolled around us, drawing my attention away from the folder and the man.

Onlookers had gathered near, much like the crowd I'd unintentionally drawn at Blessed Bee.

This time, I couldn't run. Not without thanking the Canary for entrusting me with his collection of secrets. "I'll get the file back to you as soon as I can," I vowed.

He waved a dismissive hand. "Don't worry about it. I have all those details and more saved on the cloud and various hard drives. Digital is the only way to go these days. Paper is far too destructible."

I slid the rubber band away from the folder and opened the file. Pages of documentation on Mitzi's schedule and outings were collected inside. Her orders at restaurants, the lengths of time spent in various salons and shops. Photographs of vehicles coming and going from the gate to her home. Newspaper articles, online printouts, and paparazzi style snapshots were stacked several inches deep. I lifted my gaze to the Canary, simultaneously thankful and somewhat afraid.

What sort of man saw this level of privacy invasion as any way to live? How had he made it acceptable in his mind? What differentiated him from Mitzi's stalker?

The Canary reached for the open file and flipped it shut. Keeping one hand on mine, he drifted closer, his steady gaze locked tight. "Not here," he said, his voice low and thick with warning. "Too many eyes. Too many ears."

I nodded, unable to find my tongue.

The Canary dipped his mouth to my ear and whispered softly, "Personally, I think her killer was a fan."

CHAPTER

SEVEN

I tucked the file of newfound treasures under one arm and shook the Canary's hand, then excused myself, letting Amelia and Mr. Butters get back to work. I had another hour before Sun, Sand, and Tea opened and approximately forty minutes before Denise showed up to work. I planned to make good use of those minutes.

Outside, the sun was bright and already warmer than it had been when I'd left my house. That was spring in Charm—brisk mornings and cool nights with days in between that made you think summer had already arrived.

I picked up the pace, both to push myself physically and to get home as soon as possible. I could cool off while I sorted the papers inside my new folder. I'd only gotten a brief look while I was in the bookstore, but there didn't seem to be any method to the madness. Just jumbles of old and new information mixed with photos from the past forty years. I wouldn't be able to get my head around the mass of information until I'd organized it a bit. From there, I'd weed out the irrelevant and focus on details that could lead to naming Mitzi's stalker. I couldn't help wondering if she'd reported the other letters she'd allegedly received to her local police department. If so, could Grady reach out to someone there for more information? I wasn't sure how to make the suggestion without appearing to meddle. Then again, sharing the things I'd learn from the contents of the folder might be worth ruffling a few of Grady's feathers.

I swung my hips, pumped my arms, and lengthened my strides into a speed walk. The folder lay securely against my forearm, held in place by my tightened grip. My heart pumped wildly as I sped over the historic, sun-bleached boardwalk. I checked my watch and gauged my estimated arrival time. If I sorted the file's materials until Denise arrived, I could sneak in a little reading when I went upstairs to change for my day. The trick would be to keep the file hidden from her view. It was better that Denise didn't know what I was up to. She might be tempted to tattle to Grady, and I didn't need that right now. I wanted to be the one to tell him about the folder—preferably after I'd had time to read it, since I suspected he'd take it from me once he knew it existed. Luckily, I was making good time toward home and would have a chance to get started before she arrived.

"Hey, Everly!" Denise called from several yards ahead, where her path intersected with mine.

I started, then groaned inwardly. *So much for my alone time.*

I forced a bright smile and reduced my speed. *No need to hurry now.*

It was strange how often I ran into Denise these days. We'd barely spoken for several months after she, Grady, and Denver had moved to Charm. Then, suddenly, she began popping up everywhere. I had made a mental note at Christmas to reach out to her more, thinking she might not have any friends here or may have regretted relocating to an island with limited romantic opportunities. Before I had the chance to follow through, she came to see me about a job. Now I rarely went a day without bumping into her. If the community weren't so small, I'd have thought she was following me.

"You're running really early," I said.

"Yeah." She lifted a disposable cup between us and gave it a shake. "I saw the food trucks when I took Denver to school, so I gave myself time to stop for a lemonade on my way to work. Check out their logo." She turned the cup until the words *Fresh Squeezers* came into view. Below that, two hands squeezed a pair of grapefruit-sized lemons. "Is it just me, or is the logo a little bizarre?"

I laughed. "A little. Yes."

Denise fell easily into step when I finally reached her. "What do you have there?" she asked, eyeballing the folder I'd been gripping to my chest and planning to hide.

"Files," I said, thankful for the simple truth. I wasn't any good at lying and whenever I tried, my guilty expression gave me away. "I'm not sure how busy we'll be today with all those food trucks available," I said, quickly changing the subject.

Denise wrinkled her perfect nose. "Yeah, right. In case you haven't noticed, you're kind of big news right now. I think there'll be plenty of customers for you."

I felt my lips curl downward. "Some guy at the bookstore called me a Nancy Drew."

Denise snorted delicately, wrapping thin fingers over her mouth and nose afterward. "I always liked Nancy Drew."

Who didn't? But Nancy was young and rich. She had a driver's license and spoke French. We both liked to cook, but my ability to see a clue and instantly understand how it fit into a criminal's endgame was nil. Nancy was brilliantly written.

Maybe my life needs a better writer, I mused.

"Have you learned any more about Mitzi's death?" Denise asked.

"Not yet," I said, feeling the folder in my arm grow heavier. "Have you?"

"No, but Grady was in his study half the night after he left your place. I thought something new might've come to light."

"Grady told you he'd been to my place?" I asked, my interest piqued. Exactly how much did Grady confide in her? Their relationship was a constant conundrum to me. A beautiful young woman, living with a ruggedly handsome lawman, sharing the responsibilities of raising his child and running his household. How had nothing romantic ever come from it? Or had it? How would I know if it did? Would I want to know?

Denise's breezy expression slipped slightly but refreshed in a heartbeat. "I don't normally ask him where he goes. It was just that he'd left so abruptly and seemed so upset. I worried something bad had happened, maybe another attack or worse. I was glad to hear he'd been doing some normal detective work for a change."

"He hasn't been doing normal detective work lately?" I asked.

Her smile widened a moment and she shot a quick sideways look in my direction. "You got me," she said, but she didn't offer to elaborate. "Nothing new for you, then?" she asked. "With the case, I mean."

"Not yet," I said carefully, wondering why she'd press the subject, a strange new sensation taking hold. Maybe I was being paranoid or the intensity of the past twenty-four hours had caught up to me, but I was suddenly unsure if Denise was making casual conversation or spying on me. And if so, was she spying for Grady? I opened my mouth to ask her directly, but a shadowy figure came into view on my front porch and temporarily stole my breath.

The silhouette was long and lean as it stretched upright and moved down the steps into the sunlight. "Howdy," Wyatt said in a low, teasing drawl. He removed his wide-brimmed Stetson and pressed it to his chest.

"What are you doing here?" I asked.

Wyatt met me halfway up the gravel drive and pulled me into a hug. He kissed my cheek and rubbed my back before releasing me. "Just checking in."

"Thanks," I said, and surprisingly, I meant it.

Six months ago, I would have kicked stones at him for touching me so casually after breaking my heart, but these days Wyatt and I were working on a new kind of normal. Platonic friendship.

Wyatt shoved long, tan fingers into the front pockets of his jeans as he looked at Denise. "Miss Cheveraux," he said, brilliant blue eyes twinkling.

She scanned him, unmoved. "Why are you waiting on Everly's steps? And what happened to your arms?"

The bruises I'd noticed yesterday were darker now and more profound. I'd asked the same thing and he'd blown me off. Considering they barely knew one another, she was sure to get the same...

"Rodeo," he answered.

I lifted and then dropped my palms. "You realize I asked you the exact same question yesterday?"

"You had enough to worry about yesterday," he said.

"I decide that," I grouched. "Not you." I marched stiffly up the front steps to unlock the door.

Denise followed with Wyatt close behind. "You're training for competition again?" she asked. "I thought you worked full-time at the nature center now."

"I do," he said. "I'm tracking and studying the island's wild mustangs, but the rodeo's not something a man just quits. Rodeo's in my blood."

I rolled my eyes until it hurt, then straightened my expression before sliding behind the service counter and beginning my morning prep routine.

"How long have you been riding?" Denise asked.

"All my life," he answered. "I don't know any other way to live. Injuries are just part of the package."

"It's a nice package," Denise muttered.

I was almost certain Wyatt's head became visibly larger.

"You can call me Denise," she continued. "Miss Cheveraux is a little much, don't you think?"

I thought whatever was going on between those two was a little much.

"Did you need something, Wyatt?" I asked. "You don't normally hang out on my porch."

Wyatt dragged his attention back to me as I busied myself checking tea levels and the brew times on each dispenser. I maintained a strict twenty-four hour rule from brew to disposal. Any longer than that and my teas lost their pizazz. "I was just checking on you, like I said. Yesterday was rough, and I wanted to be sure you were okay."

"I am," I said. "I don't have a single bruise."

Half his mouth kicked into a lopsided grin. "You've always worried too much about me. I'm tougher than I look, and I'm a quick healer, you know that."

"You are until you aren't," I said, my voice unintentionally sharp and cold. The torrent of fear ripping through me brought a stunning realization with it. *I still worried about Wyatt.* I still cared about his safety and well-being. And why wouldn't I? We'd been together for years, and before things had gotten rocky, he'd been my rodeo, my life's goal, and my light at the end of each day.

Wyatt reached for me as I went to check on available ingredients in the fridge. He caught my hand in his and squeezed. "Truth is, I'm here because I'm thinking of giving it up, and I wanted to know what you thought."

I stopped to examine him. "You're thinking of giving up the rodeo?" I asked, not for a second believing that was what he'd meant. Then I saw the storm clouds of regret gathered in his dark blue gaze. "Wyatt. Why? You just said it's in your blood."

"I'm thirty-two," he said. "I've never hit it big. Not once. Not everything that's in our blood is good for us."

I felt his grief in my bones. "Thirty-two isn't old. This is all you've ever wanted."

"Maybe it shouldn't have been," he said. "I fooled around and made a life for myself here and I like it. When the Wild Bunch came looking to ride, I went back, no questions, but when I got thrown…" He glanced away, shame coloring his cheeks.

"What happened?" I gripped his hand tighter in encouragement, praying a fresh injury hadn't resulted in the discovery of something awful or life threatening.

"It hurt," he said flatly. His jaw worked side to side as if he'd admitted to something horrid instead of something rational. "For the first time in my life,

I didn't want to get back in the saddle. I wanted to come here, get some iced tea, and take a walk on the beach. Or maybe a nap. The thing I'd enjoyed more than anything else was suddenly…scary."

"Being thrown from a bull is scary," I said. "You've nearly died that way. More than once."

I knew. I'd been there each terrifying time. I'd been with him in the sawdust waiting for medics, begging him to open his eyes. I'd been in the ambulance praying we'd reach the hospital in time. I'd been in the waiting rooms, my heart in my throat. Through surgeries and comas, broken bones, and everything in between. "Of course you were scared."

"But I never was before," he said, releasing my hand. "Something changed."

Denise moseyed in our direction, and I sucked in a breath. The moment had been so intense and so intimate, I'd forgotten she was there. "You were afraid this time because now you have things to lose," she said, not hesitating to insert herself into our conversation. "Something did change, Wyatt. *You.*"

That hurt, and I grimaced at the thought. Wyatt hadn't had anything to lose before, because I hadn't counted.

Denise braced her palms against the counter and cocked her pretty head. "Before, all you cared about was winning. You were focused on the prize. The money. The buckle. The glory. You probably would have paid any cost for it. Maybe even your life."

Wyatt went pale. The words had struck a nerve. Could they have been true? Would he have died for the glory? For one perfect ride?

"Good news is," Denise said, "horses will always need to be ridden, loved, and cared for. People will always need to be taught about those things, and you are more than qualified to do all of it. You're needed here. Now. You're happy, and getting hurt could ruin that for you. That's why you're scared. You're not a coward. You're growing up."

"Ugh." He made a sour face at her, then dragged his defeated gaze back to me. "Did you hear that?"

I smiled. "Yes, I did."

I picked up a piece of chalk and an eraser and went to work adjusting the daily menu while Denise and Wyatt talked. She poured him some tea and made him a sandwich. I was relieved by the thought of him never riding another angry bull, and I wondered what that meant.

"I read all about you when you showed up last year," Denise told Wyatt.

I paused my chalk mid-stroke to listen.

"That couldn't have been good," he said. "Was it?"

"It was interesting," she said. "You had a long streak of severe injuries, then suddenly you didn't. I found that odd."

Wyatt glanced my way, and I turned back to the menu board. He'd accused my family's curse of caus-ing his injuries while we were together because after the breakup, he'd seemed to thrive. "My ego was too big in the early years," he told Denise. "I liked to get the crowd going, so I took chances I shouldn't have. I quit getting hurt when I started concentrating on the ride instead of the show, if that makes any sense."

"It does," she said.

I put the chalk down and tried not to wonder if I'd been his bad luck charm.

Denise pulled her phone from her pocket and gave the screen a quick look. "Excuse me. I have to take this."

Wyatt smiled at me as Denise moved away. "I know what you're thinking."

"I doubt it."

"You're wondering if a three-hundred-year-old rumor is true. You think it was somehow your fault that I stunk at being a decent boyfriend and cowboy."

I rolled my eyes. "Lucky guess."

"It wasn't," he said. "Not a guess and not your fault. You're always ready to take the blame, and you assume responsibility for everything. It's nuts. Do you want to know how I know the Swan curse is nonsense and loving you doesn't stop a man's heart from beating?"

A cascade of tingles shimmied over my skin. I wanted that proof more than I wanted to get skinny by eating lemon cake and truffles. "Yes."

"Because here I am," he said.

The air thickened and electrified around us. Was he saying he loved me now? That he'd loved me then? Did it matter? Did I care?

Denise cleared her throat and I nearly jumped over the counter. "That was Grady, checking in on you," she said. "He spends a lot of energy on that front."

I turned to her, thankful for the reminder. I had an important question to ask. "Is Grady the reason you came here looking for something to do while Denver was in school? Did he send you?"

Shock raced over her face, then vanished in the span of a heartbeat. "Yes."

"Yes?" I parroted. I hadn't expected her to confirm my suspicion. I'd assumed I was wrong—or that she'd lie if I wasn't.

Her ruby lips curved into a soft smile. "The minute I expressed an interest in part-time work, Grady suggested your shop. He thought you were overworked and could use the help. Plus, he thought I could use a friend, and he said you would make a good one."

I slumped back against the counter. Denise hadn't been sent to spy on me. She'd been sent to help.

Wyatt rose fluidly from the barstool, his tea jar and plate empty. He repositioned his hat on his head, gave a silent, two-finger salute and sauntered out.

I wondered when my life had gotten so complicated.

෯

By eight o'clock, I'd changed into my most comfy cotton shorts and an old T-shirt. I pulled my legs onto the gazebo bench beneath me and faced the distant ocean, a sea of flowers blooming between us.

The setting sun at my back cast an amber glow over the world before me, giving the flight of fireflies in my garden a magical feel. The breeze was warm, the ocean magnificent. It was the most peaceful moment I'd had all day, and it seemed fitting I should finally get to open the Canary's file and satiate my curiosity in solitude.

I lifted the thick manila folder onto my legs and worked the rubber band away, then thumbed through the papers inside. Some of the pages read like a scientific review. "Subject remained inside today with the exception of a morning swim." Other pages read like voyeuristic diary entries. "It's Christmas Eve and the driveway is packed with cars and lined in twinkle lights. Laughter and music spill out each time the home's door opens, but I've yet to spot Mitzi amidst the merriment. I hope she's enjoying the party. It's been so long since she's had one."

There were a number of printed articles on the topic of Mitzi's association with the Bee Loved project. Some called the upcoming voice-over work "beneath her" and claimed her involvement was "an obvious cry for attention at her advanced age." Others commended her for using her influence to save the planet, one honeybee at a time. I got dizzy just reading the constant back-and-forth of opinions on her life.

I paused to review a stack of pages detailing company statistics on both Bee Loved and Bio-Bee, then stared open-mouthed at snapshots of my great-aunts, the island, *and me.*

A rustling of leaves caught my attention, and gooseflesh rose on my arms. A moment later, Maggie strutted away from the bushes, her white coat shining in the moonlight.

I shut the folder, stomach tumbling over the photos of my aunts and me. I struggled to recall when I'd worn the outfits in the photos. How long ago were they taken? Where had the Canary gotten them? I rubbed sweat-slicked palms over my thighs and tried to re-center myself in the moment.

Maggie walked past my bench, tail high.

I patted the space at my side.

She sniffed the air, then leapt gracefully onto the gazebo's edge across from my seat. She walked the handrail, green eyes luminous as she examined the night.

The gentle snap of a twig caught my ear, and Maggie's tail bushed out. She exhaled a long venomous hiss, and my limbs went rigid.

We weren't alone in the garden.

I set the folder aside, freeing my hands to defend myself if necessary. I was prepared to run, but before I could turn or stand, something hard and blunt pressed against the nape of my neck. I prayed it wasn't the barrel of a gun.

"Don't move," someone growled in my ear. The low and menacing sound sent ice splinters down my spine. "Hands up."

I obeyed slowly. Making no sudden moves. Giving the attacker no reason to get violent. Begging my brain to come up with a plan.

My world went black as a bag was pulled over my head. My senses screamed for orientation and fear rang in my ears. Would I be abducted now? Killed where I sat? Thrown off the jagged hill at the edge of my garden and into the raging surf below?

A wild shriek rent the night, and Maggie's bushy fur dusted my arms as she flew past me. Her sharp predator nails scraped loudly against the wood of my gazebo.

Retreating footfalls sounded behind me, growing quieter and more distant as I ripped the bag away from my head and scanned the world for signs of danger.

But there was only me, my gardens, and an otherwise empty gazebo.

The file I'd set beside me was gone.

CHAPTER

EIGHT

I waited in my foyer for Grady, mostly because my shaking noodle legs refused to carry me any farther. I pressed my back to the locked door for support but slid down until my backside hit the floor. It seemed like a good enough place to wait, so I dragged my knees to my chest and rested my forehead on them while I caught my breath.

Memories of the stranger's breath in my hair and on my cheek sent goose bumps over my chest and down my arms. I gripped uselessly at the back of my neck, trying to erase the phantom sensation of whatever had been pressed there. I didn't want to know what that had been.

I wanted to forget.

The timbre of the whisper was scorched into my mind and playing on a loop, only occasionally sticking to the original script. More often than not, the voice told me all the ways it would hurt me. The bag pulled over my head had felt like the end—an abduction I wouldn't return from. The scent of the stifling fabric clung in my nostrils, suffocating me even as I sat in my foyer.

What if the attacker came back?

A heavy hand landed against the door at my back, and I screamed.

"Everly!" Grady called, giving the door a series of heavy raps. "Open up. It's me. Are you okay?"

"No!" I yelled back. "I'm freaking out!" I scrambled to my feet and yanked the door open with trembling hands.

Grady stepped inside, then pulled me into his arms before kicking the door shut behind him. "Are you hurt?"

"No," I said, shamelessly clinging to him. "I'm just all shaken up." I buried my face in the curve of his neck and curled my fingers into the fabric of his shirt, attempting to steal a little of his strength and resolve.

He ran one hand up and down my back, then reached behind him to flip the deadbolt on my door. "Why don't we go upstairs?"

"If I let go of you, I might cry or melt into a puddle of panic and self-pity," I warned.

"I'll take my chances," he said.

When I didn't let him go, he lowered his mouth to my ear. "If you can't walk, I can carry you."

An image of my bathroom scale darted through my mind and pride loosened my grip. I knew, logically, that size didn't matter and weight didn't determine worth, but there was no logic in pride. I stepped back, then led the way upstairs.

"Couch," Grady said, catching me by the elbow as I reached my private living quarters and turned for the kitchen. He pointed me in the other direction. "You sit. I'll serve. You're probably in shock. You need water."

I collapsed onto my couch and pulled a decorative pillow into my arms. "You don't have to do that," I said, watching him fill a glass with ice, then pull a water pitcher from the fridge. Someday I would get a refrigerator from this millennium for personal use. Something stainless steel with automatic water and ice dispensers.

"I came to help. Let me help," he said, snagging a legal pad off my island and heading in my direction.

I flopped back against the couch cushions. "Why is it that every time my life starts to chug along and resemble normal, something horrible happens and it all goes pear-shaped?"

"Here," Grady said, taking a seat at my side and passing me the water. "Drink." He set the notepad on the coffee table. My favorite pen was attached by its cap.

I accepted the water and gulped half its contents before stopping for air. "Wow. I was really thirsty."

Grady flashed a penlight in my eyes.

I swatted it away. "Hey. Knock it off. I'm fine. Just a little parched."

He caught my hand in his and pressed two steady

fingers to my wrist, rudely taking my pulse without asking. I decided I'd allow it since he'd been kind enough to come to my rescue and bring me water. Plus, the toe-curling current of electricity his touch produced was a guilty pleasure of mine. Hopefully, he'd attribute my staccato heart rate to the recent scare.

Too soon, Grady released me in favor of his ringing phone. "Hays," he barked, brows crowded tight. "Get it to the lab. Keep me posted." He disconnected and tossed the phone onto my coffee table.

"They found my folder?" I guessed, trading the glass for the notepad and pen. I knew the drill. Grady needed a written statement. I didn't want to go to the station, so he'd accept whatever I wrote here. I poised the pen over the paper, then glanced at him, still waiting for an answer.

A question blazed in his eyes. "No. There was a pillowcase in your gazebo. Probably the bag you felt pulled over your head. You want to tell me about the folder?"

I balanced the notepad on my thighs and reached for my glass to finish the water. Our knees bumped as I moved.

Grady scooted back several inches, creating a distinct line between us and successfully ruffling my feathers.

The move felt a little like rejection, and it reminded me that he'd been making me feel like that a lot lately. "What's been going on with you since Christmas?" I asked. Normally, I wouldn't have been so direct, but what if I'd died tonight? I would never have had the answer because I'd been too timid to ask. I set the empty glass aside and crossed my arms, waiting for him to change the subject or leave—his usual response to direct questions about his life outside my view.

"I don't see how that's relevant," he said. "Is there some reason you don't want to tell me about the file you just mentioned?"

"You kissed me," I said suddenly, boldly, both shocked and proud of myself for the candor. Neither of us had mentioned the kiss after that night, though it had been the subject of local gossip for weeks to follow. "You kissed me at Christmas, and then you bolted." I pressed on. "You've been distant and weird ever since, and I want to know why. Whatever it is, just tell me so I can stop wondering, and don't worry about upsetting me. I have an excellent imagination. Believe me, whatever I've thought of is probably worse than whatever you need to say."

His mouth opened, then shut. He shifted, and did the mouth thing again, but no sounds came out. He rubbed his palms down his jean-clad thighs, then gripped his knees.

"Talk," I demanded.

"I've already told you," he said, forcing his eyes back to mine. "I'm working on a project for Olivia. That's it. And it has nothing to do with you." His expression flattened and his eyes dimmed. He hadn't made a single move, but Grady was retreating. Leaving me alone in the conversation. And I hated it.

"What you're doing has everything to do with me," I said, wanting to reel him in and make him see how important it was to have someone to confide in. Spectacular Christmas kiss aside, Grady and I were supposed to be friends. As far as I knew, I was the only friend he'd bothered making on the island. "Denise told me that you asked her to work at my shop," I said. If that wasn't proof that he believed in friendship, then I wasn't sure what was.

His eyes widened, then narrowed. "What do you mean?"

"I mean," I said—bristling at his clipped tone— "you thought it was important that she have a friend. So, why don't you think you deserve the same? And why am I good enough to be her friend but not yours?"

Grady exhaled slowly, tension easing from his brow. "Right. No, of course," he said. "I need to open up more. Hazard of the job."

I squinted at him, lips pursed. Clearly, I was missing something bigger. From the look on his face, he had no intention of telling me anything tonight.

I wanted to scream.

"What was in the folder?" he asked, like a dog with a bone.

My stomach flopped. "It was a manila file folder about three inches thick, worn at the edges and held shut with a big rubber band."

"I didn't ask for a description," he said. "What was inside the folder? Don't say paperwork. Tell me about the content, point, and relevance of the papers instead."

I cringed. This was the part where he would be a lot less happy with me. "I ran into Mr. Butters and a few of his friends today. One of them gave me the file."

"Go on," Grady said, grinding the words out. "A file that contained…"

"Information on Mitzi's life."

Grady's eyes slid shut for one short beat. He opened them to glare at me. "You have a three-inch thick folder of information on a recent murder victim?"

"Had," I said, feeling a lot less bold than I had a moment before.

He pushed onto his feet and began to pace angrily in front of my coffee table. "Why would you have that? Why did this man give it to you? Why did he have it? And why on earth didn't you call me immediately upon receiving it?"

I watched as he stormed in a narrow ellipse. "The guy calls himself the Canary. He had the information because he's a celebrity gossip blogger who specializes in Mitzi Calgon. He's in Charm because of her." I stopped to think about that. Did the Canary say he had come to see her? Or that he'd come after her death? Maybe he hadn't said at all. If he hadn't come as a result of her death, then why would he have all that information with him? Why had he printed it if it was stored on the cloud as he'd said?

"What?" Grady snapped, having paused his

mini-procession. "What are you thinking? It had better begin with a list of the folder's contents."

"You're awfully cranky," I said. "I was the one attacked tonight."

I ignored the vein that began to throb in his forehead and did my best to answer his questions. I hadn't read the entire file, but I gave him a rundown on everything I could remember. "The Canary said Mitzi's ex-husband wasn't happy with whatever he got in the settlement," I added. That hadn't been in the file, but it had been weighing on my mind. Divorces could get messy, especially when a substantial amount of money was involved. "The Canary also said the assistant, Odette, is the ex-husband's daughter. That had to make for a complicated work environment."

Grady rubbed his chin. "I've put a couple of calls in to the ex."

"Did you know about Odette?" I asked, sensing the answer was written in the creases of his brow.

"She didn't mention it when we spoke at the station."

I whistled the sound of a falling missile. "I'd say that puts Odette and her dad on the possible suspects list. His recent divorce and her personal assistant role gave them both means and motive. If not as a pair, then one or the other." The proverbial light bulb flickered and my jaw dropped. "What if you can't reach the ex in Beverly Hills because he's here?"

Grady didn't answer.

So I kept going. "The fans here are pretty intense too. It's possible that one of them snapped."

Grady let his eyelids droop into a droll, unimpressed expression. "Why don't you rein that in, Swan. Let's stick to facts over theories. Actually, I'll stick to the facts, and you stop creating theories." Grady checked his watch, then moved toward the door. "Careful what you say about crazed fans. Your friend Mr. Butters fits that description, and he isn't exactly looking innocent right now."

"Be serious," I scoffed.

"I mean it. I know he's a Charmer and your best friend's dad, but it's hard to believe that painting and creepy note weren't given as a set. Add the fact that several equally disturbing surveillance photos were found with them and I have to ask myself if I'm overlooking the obvious suspect because you like the guy so much." He puffed out a long breath. "Heck, I like the guy too, but that doesn't mean he didn't kill Mitzi Calgon, accidentally even, then attempt to cover it up with the bees."

I crossed my arms and narrowed my eyes, having nothing nice to say about that load of hooey and certain I'd say something I'd regret if I opened my mouth.

Grady mirrored my miffed expression, returning my silent attitude with practiced precision. "I'm going to make another pass outside, then head over to the station. Are you about finished with that statement?"

I wrote a few more simple sentences in ink, trying to stick to facts. Since I didn't have many, the statement was short and sweet. I tore the paper free and carried it to him. "This is everything I can remember."

He read the page silently, his lips moving as his gaze slid over the words. A moment later, he looked up. "I almost forgot to ask. How are your aunts holding up?"

"Better than me," I admitted. "Mitzi was a friend of my grandma's, and I had a million questions for her. We were supposed to have dinner and trade stories, but instead she was killed by my family's bees. I'm starting to feel as if Wyatt was right. Maybe the Swan family isn't cursed. I think we *are* the curse."

Grady smiled. He found my family's alleged curses and my continuous preoccupation with them amusing.

"Don't try to convince me otherwise," I told him, wallowing low in self-imposed misery. "I'm having a moment."

"Maybe do that later," he said, "because Mitzi didn't die from bee stings. So the family bees are off the hook."

"I saw her," I said. "Swollen and smeared in honey."

"She was drugged," he said. "The coroner found the injection location in her neck. He missed it initially due to the discoloration and swelling of her skin. Likely, she was drugged and then dragged to the demonstration box."

"Where she was stung to death," I pointed out. "Because she was allergic."

"The coroner believes it's more probable that the

sedative from the syringe interacted fatally with the prescriptions she took on a regular basis for blood pressure, cholesterol, and anxiety. It was the drug combination that stopped her heart, not the bees. The stings added insult to injury, so to say, but it's doubtful she would've survived the sedative, regardless of what happened next."

I took a minute to process that as I followed him down my private staircase to the foyer.

Grady tucked my written statement into his back pocket, then gave me a curious smile. "This probably isn't the right time to ask, but how are your baking tutorials coming? Denver and Denise have baked the chocolate-dipped peanut butter cookies about three times already, and I'm ready for a change. If I have to keep adding miles on the beach every morning so I can eat the sweets and praise my son for his baking skills, I'm going to need a little more variety as motivation."

I tried not to imagine Grady running on the beach every morning or wonder what time and where. "I'm almost out of easy-to-explain recipes so I've been dragging my feet. My aunts will have more in the archives. I just have to make the time to find them." I definitely wasn't trying out the new app Ryan installed on a complicated recipe. Too many opportunities to embarrass myself.

Grady stopped on my porch and looked me over. "You going to be okay?"

"Yep." I answered too quickly, torn between not wanting to be alone and not wanting to be needy.

He lingered a moment, and my traitorous mind began to think of the days when mistletoe had hung in my doorways. Maybe that had been the reason he'd kissed me. It was his duty. He'd practically been bound by tradition and manners.

Maybe I should rehang the mistletoe.

"I'll wait until you lock up," he said, stepping further onto the porch.

It took a minute for the words to breach my daydream. Then I snapped into action and closed the door in his face. "Good night," I called through the window without bothering to pull back the curtain and reveal my heated cheeks. The deadbolt gave an audible snap, then Grady headed into the yard.

I went upstairs, locked my bedroom door, and crawled into bed.

Grady's truck revved to life a short while later. I pulled the blankets to my chin and pretended he wasn't leaving. I hadn't been injured tonight, but I had been terrified and emotionally violated, which felt the same in my head.

My phone lit and buzzed on the nightstand.

I yanked it to my chest, praying it wasn't another killer honeybee on screen while simultaneously seeing a consolation prize. Another threat would bring Grady back, and I wouldn't have to be alone.

The message was from Grady. Short and sweet.

Stay safe, Swan.

I managed a small smile and whisked off a return message before taking time to consider it.

You'd be lost without me?

His answer was nearly instant.

Yes.

The little word heated me through. I stared at the phone, wanting more. It buzzed again, and my smile widened.

Who would make me lemon cake?

I laughed. It wasn't the first time Grady had made a comment like that, and the fact he'd remembered our little joke made it all the sweeter.

CHAPTER

NINE

I still can't believe it," I told Denise the next morning, pressing a nearly empty mug of coffee to my
lips. "I slept like the dead, despite everything. I'm all
amped up right now, but I slept like a log."

"Uh huh," Denise said, wiping big wet circles over
the counter at Sun, Sand, and Tea. "How many cups
of coffee have you had so far?"

"I'm not sure." I glanced at the nearly empty pot.
"A few." Plus, I'd had three before making my way
downstairs. "How many have you had?"

She draped the rag over the edge of the sink and
pressed a hand to one hip.

"None."

My eyes widened and a giggle burst out of me, star-
tling a pair of guests seated at a small table near the
counter. "Sorry," I said, turning my back to them and
covering my mouth. "It's just that my heart is racing,
and I've got all this energy."

"Caffeine," she corrected. "What you have is too much caffeine." She took the mug from my hand and replaced it with a bottle of water. "You're going to crash and regret it."

My bracelet beeped and I shook my arm until it thought I was running. "Did Grady say anything about me when he got home last night? Do you know if the police made an arrest?"

"No, and I don't know," she said. "Have you remembered anything else that might help them catch whoever did this? Any idea if the whisperer was a man or woman? Could you tell by the whisper? Did you smell cologne or perfume?"

"All I could smell was my gardens and the sea. Then the fabric softener on the pillowcase." I shivered, then brightened. "The police will be able to track the pillowcase to its owner, right? Whoever owns it was my attacker. I'll bet the lab can pull hairs or fibers from the material that lead to an arrest."

"Maybe," Denise said.

I puzzled over my word choice for a minute. "What if the police find whoever put the pillowcase on my head but can't arrest the creep? Is that possible?"

"I don't know," Denise admitted with a frown. "Do you know you're marching in place?"

I stopped. Marching had become a defense mechanism against the fitness bracelet when it shamed me. I swung my hands behind my back and wiggled my wrist some more. The longer I thought about what happened, the madder I got. "I can't believe I was ambushed and robbed in my own gazebo."

"What about the stolen folder?" Denise asked. "Is the superfan who gave it to you expecting it back? Have you told him that's no longer possible?"

Her words hit like a lightning strike, sending a fresh surge of energy through me. The Canary would know who'd want to steal the folder!

"You're brilliant!" I stripped off my apron and checked the clock. "I've got to find the Canary. Maybe he has an archnemesis who'd want the materials for competing blog fodder or snappy headline materials."

Denise swung her arms open like an umpire. "Wait a minute. Grady's already on that. You shouldn't get any more involved in this than you already are."

"Easy for you to say," I said, hanging my apron on a hook behind the counter. "No one's sending you killer bee threat texts and putting bags on your head." I slammed my mouth shut. "I'm sorry. That was rude. It's the coffee and the emotions. I didn't mean it."

Denise shot me a colder look than I'd ever seen on her pert, youthful face. "Everly." She stepped close in a slow, predatory move.

I stepped back.

Her jaw locked. She glanced at the smattering of guests enjoying iced tea and finger foods. "I can't pretend to know what you're going through or how you're feeling," she said, the sugar in her tone not quite matching her posture, "but I can promise you that letting Grady handle this is the right thing to do. He's working hard, and you're his first priority. Right behind Denver, of course," she amended. "Regardless, you're safer as Grady's second priority than anyone else's first. In case you're forgetting, he's a highly trained military operative and former big-shot U.S. marshal." A mischievous smile curled her lips. "He's got this covered. You can relax."

"I didn't know Grady was a highly trained military operative," I said, drawn to the new information. He'd mentioned his time served but always in passing and never with any amount of detail. I tried to imagine the man I'd begun to think of as my personal island cowboy wearing night-vision goggles and tactical gear, but I couldn't. To me, Grady was a loving single father, a grieving widow, and the figurative, though badge-holding, guy next door. "Sometimes I forget he had a life before Charm."

Denise's gaze jumped with the sound of my sea-shell wind chimes. She smiled at the newcomers, then slipped away to greet them.

I gave the menu a long look and checked the available supplies. Most of the lunching guests had ordered shrimp tacos, and I didn't want to run out of an obvious hit if I could avoid it. There was plenty of shrimp and the cabbage slaw I liked to serve it with in the refrigerator, a hearty stack of flour tortillas on the counter, and enough minced garlic cloves to protect the world from vampires, but I didn't like the level of my garlic-lime sauce. We'd be out soon if I didn't replenish now.

I squeezed the juice from a dozen limes while

Denise spun through the café taking orders, refilling drinks, and ringing folks out at the register. From there, I added generous amounts of garlic, mayonnaise, and hot sauce until I was out of all three. I mixed the ingredients thoroughly, then swiped a dollop from the end of the spoon with my finger. I stuck the spoon into the sink and the finger in my mouth. My eyelids fluttered at the taste. "That's amazing," I told myself. But it wouldn't last long if the crowds kept up. It was definitely time to visit Molly's Market for a few things.

I filled a pair of take-out containers with fruit salad, tucked a few fresh baked croissants into a bag with my homemade jam sampler, and headed for the front door. "I'll be back," I called, waving an arm overhead at Denise.

Several patrons returned my wave.

Denise didn't look happy to see me leave.

I hit the boardwalk with a skip in my step, mind racing over last night's events and wondering full throttle if the lab had taken a look at the pillowcase from my gazebo yet. Since I couldn't exactly drop by the police lab unannounced and expect answers, I decided to look for the Canary instead. First, I routed myself in the direction of my aunts, per my usual. We'd traded texts and quick phone calls but hadn't had a decent private conversation since Mitzi died. I wasn't used to the silence between us and I wanted it to end. From there, I'd hit up Charming Reads and ask Mr. Butters where I could find the Canary.

I crossed the marsh on a fallen tree trunk and hopped into the grassy area beside Ocean Drive. Three steps later, I stopped cold at the sight of my personal nemesis, Mary Grace Chatsworth. Since I'd last seen her, she'd dyed her hair platinum blond and attached herself to the town's stand-in mayor, Chairman Vanders, like a barnacle on the hull of a big, slow ship. But I'd recognize her ghoulish scowl anywhere. Plus, the air temperature around her was naturally twenty degrees cooler.

I sidestepped the duo, trying not to wonder why she was clinging to Vanders's arm and whether or not it was a hostage situation on his part.

Vanders had been the town's head councilman for ten years before our mayor was killed last Christmas. Now he was filling the role until the fall election, when Mary Grace planned to run against Aunt Fran for the job.

Mary Grace lifted her lips into what was probably intended as a smile but came off more like a snarl. She thrust a large white envelope in my direction.

"No, thank you," I said, uninterested in whatever she was selling.

"Everly Swan!" she snapped, stamping one foot and glaring. "I'm trying to be nice. Now, take this darn thing!"

Nice? I nearly laughed. Mary Grace wasn't nice. As a child she'd spread the rumor that the real reason my dead mother wasn't around was because she'd left me to become a circus clown. The day her family left the island, I nearly threw a party. Grandma stopped me, or it would have been epic.

I returned Mary Grace's seething gaze. "I don't want it," I said, confident in the decision.

A moment later, curiosity reared its ugly head. "What it is?"

"It's a wedding invitation, of course," she said.

"Whose?" I asked, baffled.

"Mine," she scoffed, craning her head back to look up at Chairman Vander's smug face. Mary Grace shook her head as if something was unbelievable.

She was right. I was having a hard time believing anyone would marry her. I opened the envelope and skimmed the fancy font. "You're marrying Chairman Vanders?"

She rolled her eyes and huffed. "Where have you been? Under a rock?"

I considered the tall man at her side. "Blink twice if she's holding you against your will," I whispered.

"Very funny," Mary Grace deadpanned. "We're having a destination wedding, then a formal reception when we get back. We're on the gift registry at every shop in town to make gift selection more convenient."

"Always thinking of others," I said, a touch of sarcasm in my tone.

"You're welcome to bring a plus-one to the reception, if you can talk anyone into it," she said before breaking into obnoxious laughter and dragging her man puppet away.

I gawked until they were nearly out of sight, then

eyeballed the closest trash bin, wondering if I could make a clean basket or if the envelope would touch the rim going in. Ultimately, I decided to hang onto the invitation. My aunts were highly likely to attend the ridiculous party, obviously contrived to gain gifts, so I'd go with them. There was strength in numbers, after all. Plus, if we didn't go, it might look like we were boycotting or being petty. And since Aunt Fran and Mary Grace were opponents in the upcoming mayoral election, there could be trouble. I should be present to mediate a confrontation or call the police if needed.

I turned back in the direction I'd been headed and crossed the road toward Blessed Bee. The line was out the door again, so I decided to try the bookstore first, then double back to check on my aunts.

Amelia was tidying shelves near the register when I ducked inside. She smiled when she saw me. "Perfect timing. I need to talk to you, and I think most of our crowd finally went in search of food."

"What about you?" I asked. "Hungry?"

Her stomach growled at the mere mention of sustenance. Luckily, I'd anticipated that.

"You still like my fruit salad and croissants with jam, right?" I asked, lifting the bag in her direction.

"Bless you," Amelia said, taking the bag behind the counter to unpack it. "You are a goddess."

"I try."

Mr. Butters crossed the room with a broad smile. "Tell me that's a Philly steak on a hoagie bun with loads of melted Swiss."

"Nice try," I said. "I heard all about your doctor appointment last month. You have to watch your cholesterol."

He shot his daughter a grouchy look, then popped the top on a take-out box. "No one will serve me a hamburger in this town now."

Amelia grinned. "I made a few calls."

Mr. Butters dunked the pointy end of his croissant into the little container of jam, then bit into it with gusto. Paint speckled the backs of his hands and the cuffs of his rolled shirt sleeves, hanging loosely around his forearms.

"Have you been painting?" I asked.

"All day," Amelia said, answering for him as he chewed. "Once potential buyers realized he wasn't going to make any replicas of the painting he gave Mitzi, they started asking for similar pieces with dates added to his signature so they can prove he painted them while the investigation is going on."

"And they're all asking that I don't recreate their commissioned works so they can own a one-of-a-kind piece as well," Mr. Butters added, finally swallowing the hunk of croissant. "I've gotten more orders this morning than I've had all year, and these buyers are willing to pay top dollar. I hate the circumstances, but when you're an artist, you've got to strike while the iron's hot."

"How hot is it?" I asked. "Have the police been in touch since the luncheon?"

"Yes," Mr. Butters answered softly, then finished

the croissant with a crestfallen stare. "I'm not sup-posed to leave town, and Detective Hays suggested I speak to an attorney in case he finds a problem with my alibi or timeline on the day of the murder. I've spoken to Burt Pendle about it. He says I shouldn't say anything else on the topic without him present."

I set my hand on his briefly and gave it a pat. "I'm sorry. I wish there was something I could do to help." I knew firsthand what it was like to be accused of murder in Charm, and living under Grady's scrutiny as a suspect was the pits. I turned my attention to Amelia. "Is that what you wanted to talk to me about when I walked in?"

She bit her lip and nodded. "There's more. Dad wasn't with Wyatt and me the entire time after we entered the nature center that day."

"What?" I yipped. "Why not?" Tension wrenched the tightly bunched muscles along my shoulders. "Why didn't you tell me sooner?"

"We forgot. In all the confusion and commotion, it just slipped our minds," Amelia whispered.

Mr. Butters hunched over the counter and stuffed the end of a second croissant into his mouth. "I forgot my reading glasses in the car," he said forlornly. "I wanted to be able to read the program, so I ran out to grab my glasses. When I came back, Wyatt and Amelia weren't in the hallway, but it only took me a minute to find them."

"We were in the big storage closet near the rest-rooms," Amelia said. "Wyatt's organizing the space to make room for his materials on the wild horses, and he came across some old children's books he thought I might want for the Little Libraries," Amelia said. "I agreed to pick them up after the luncheon, but you know how that went. Anyway, we were only there a minute. When we walked out, Dad was in the hall, and we all met up with you a few minutes later."

I let my head drop forward with a groan. "That's the exact time frame when Mitzi went missing." I dragged my chin up and fixed my gaze on Mr. Butters. "I don't know how long it would take to see Mitzi and drug her, then drag her into the bee box behind the curtain, but would you say you were alone long enough to have done that?"

His shoulders rose to his ears and his face went sheet white. "Maybe?"

I pressed the heels of my hands to my closed eyes. "Surely someone saw you going to get your glasses. The parking lot was full of fans who should be able to provide you with an alibi." I dropped my hands away to see his face when I didn't hear an answer.

Mr. Butters raised his brows. "Sure. Lots of folks saw me. I had to wade through the crowd to reach the car, but no one spoke to me, and I was dressed as Blackbeard. With a beard and hat and everything. Just like dozens of other people."

I stifled a deeper, longer groan. "It's going to be fine. What did Grady say?"

The Butterses exchanged a long look.

"You told Grady," I stated, willing the words to be true.

Amelia stepped closer to her dad and linked their arms. "Not yet. We wanted to talk to you first. You know him better than anyone, and we know this makes Dad look guiltier. Giving a false statement. Withholding information. It's going to make a bad situation worse, and it was an accident."

I jerked upright and scanned the room for listening ears. "Shh," I whispered. "That's the sort of thing that can be overheard and mistaken for a confession. Call Grady." I motioned to the phone on the desk. "Make sure he doesn't hear it from anyone else. It's not great that you didn't tell him sooner, but if you explain it to him, he'll understand."

Mr. Butters nodded. "We just remembered at breakfast this morning. We were rehashing everything we heard and saw, hoping for a clue to help him find the killer."

I pointed again to the desktop telephone beside the register. "Tell Grady."

Mr. Butters lifted the handset.

Amelia released her dad and returned to her meal. She forked a pile of diced fruits and eyed me, tipping her head toward her dad. "I can't listen to that conversation without developing an ulcer. So, what's going on with you? Any luck sorting through all that paperwork Skeet gave you?"

"Who's Skeet?" I asked.

"I refuse to call a grown man the Canary," she said. "I demanded his real name. Turns out it's Skeeter Ulvanich. Skeet for short."

I wrinkled my nose. "I'm not sure that's any better."

She shrugged. "Did you read the file?"

I gave a long sigh, shored up my nerves, and relayed my recent ambush for her. "So," I wound the story down, "I was hoping to talk to the Canary about who might've wanted the file badly enough to come after it, scare me half-to-death, and take it from me." I gave the sprinkling of shoppers a careful scan. No signs of the Canary. "Any idea where he is?"

Mr. Butters disconnected his call, then turned to us, scratching his head. "I had to leave Detective Hays a voicemail."

"It's okay," I assured. "He'll call back or stop by."

"Have you seen Skeet?" Amelia asked her father.

"Not since he left here yesterday."

"Any idea how long he's staying in Charm?" I asked.

"Can't say," Mr. Butters said, stuffing another wad of croissant between his lips. "A couple of days, I'd guess."

"Was he in town when Mitzi died, or did he come after he heard about her death?" I asked.

Mr. Butters gave a helpless shrug and an apologetic smile. "I'm not sure."

I bit the insides of my cheeks to keep from screaming in frustration. "I only have a couple hours before Denise has to pick Denver up from school, and I have to take over at the shop. I need to find him before then, if possible."

Mr. Butters chewed slowly. "If he's still in town,

he's probably out collecting clues or evidence. He's a snoop by trade, right? Maybe check the location you'd be right now if you were investigating too."

"I *am* investigating," I said. "I'm here and he's not."

Mr. Butters thought about that for a second. "Well, he probably wouldn't be looking for himself like you are. So, where would you be if you weren't looking for him?"

Amelia laughed, then dipped a piece of croissant into her jam. "Dad said *probably*."

I sighed. "If the Canary has ever gone looking for himself before, I don't think I want to know."

"Maybe talk to Ryan," Amelia suggested. "He knows everything about Mitzi. He was studying her life for weeks before coming here to interview her. Since that opportunity vanished, he's been out there nonstop, trying to break the case."

I puffed my cheeks in defeat. "Fine. I'll look for Ryan."

She beamed. "Great, and since you're headed out…" She reached under the counter and produced a massive shopping bag of books. "Will you fill the Little Libraries on the boardwalk for me? I'm having trouble getting away from this place, and I'm sure the Little Libraries are in serious need of fresh books by now. If you can fill them today or tomorrow, I would owe you forever."

I dragged the heavy bag off the counter and over my shoulder. "Okay, but don't get too happy about me teaming up with Ryan. You seem to like him for some reason and the last time he and I worked together, it didn't end well."

I turned on my toes and headed out. Now I had two men to locate before school let out.

CHAPTER

TEN

I made my way into Blessed Bee with a fifteen-pound bag of books on my shoulder and fought my way to the register. Surprisingly, and unlike yesterday, Aunt Clara and Aunt Fran were chatting alone. None of the dozens of shoppers were in line to make purchases. Instead, the shoppers were gathered around Rose, who was taping interviews with locals and Mitzi fans.

I counted my blessings for the chance to squeeze my aunts without an audience, then dropped the bag of books on the counter before circling around to hug them. "How are you?" I asked. "I've missed you." I reveled in the feel of their thin arms around me and the scent of their perfumes in my nose.

Aunt Fran was first to break the hug. She pulled back for a look into my eyes. "I think the better question is how are *you*?" I'd called my aunts early in the morning to recount the uglier points of my night.

Aunt Clara rubbed my back and stroked my hair. "I'm just glad you're okay."

Aunt Fran didn't look happy at all. "I hope to high heavens that detective of yours catches whoever's doing this before you get hurt again. It's ridiculous that you consistently find the killer before he does."

I laughed. "If you mean that I consistently bumble into the killer's clutches while Grady follows legal channels to prepare a case and make an arrest, then yes. That is ridiculous."

Aunt Fran narrowed her eyes.

I changed the subject. "So, what's with all the interviews?" I motioned to Rose and her crowd of anxious interviewees.

"She's taking advantage of all the unexpected people," Aunt Clara said. "Asking folks questions about bees, testing their knowledge on various aspects. She says it will help her home in on which topics need to be covered most thoroughly in the documentary."

"Mostly, she's trying to convey that honeybees aren't killers," Aunt Fran said.

The memory of Mitzi in the demonstration box returned unbidden, and I did an involuntary full-body shiver in response.

"I'm eager to start filming footage for the actual documentary," Aunt Fran continued. "All the production team has done since that nightmarish luncheon is tape the crowds and do mass interviews like this."

Aunt Clara reached for her sister. "The crowds won't last forever. I'm sure all these nice folks have real jobs and family responsibilities they'll need to get back to eventually."

I gave Rose a long look. She seemed happy, enthu-siastic even. Was it possible that she'd drugged Mitzi in an attempt to create hype around the film? It was hard to imagine the pretty brunette as a cold-blooded killer, but the drive to succeed had made many people do things they wouldn't normally. The drugs would have been enough if Mitzi had lived and made a spec-tacle of herself. Any scandal involving Mitzi Calgon guaranteed national coverage. "Do you know when you'll begin filming?" I asked my aunts.

"Tomorrow," Aunt Fran said. "We're supposed to take a walk through our gardens and visit our hives before we come to work."

Aunt Clara's face lit up. "You should stop by for breakfast. We're serving pancakes to the crew before the walk."

"I'd like that," I said. "I wanted to take a look in your archives anyway. I've run out of easy-to-demo recipes for my blog." I checked the time on my watch, then hoisted Amelia's bag of books onto my shoulder. "I've got to run, but I'll be there for breakfast." I kissed Aunt Clara's cheek, then Aunt Fran's, before hustling out the door.

The books were heavy and my time was limited, but I was still hoping to find the Canary before I headed home. Mr. Butters said I should check wher-ever I'd be if I was investigating. That was a no-brainer.

Twenty minutes later, I flashed my annual pass at the nature center welcome desk. The midday sun and stifling humidity had drawn sweat from places I didn't like to think about and plastered my hair to my cheeks and neck.

I pretended to look at nature displays while catching my breath after the half-mile speed walk, making my way toward the rear hallway of private offices. If I was caught by the center's security, I planned to claim I was innocently looking for Wyatt.

The hall was quiet. A flimsy line of crime scene tape ran across the partially open doorway. "Knock knock," I whispered, hoping no one would answer. When no one did, I peered down the hallway in both directions. The door wasn't sealed, so someone must've been working on the crime scene. So where were they? I set the bag of books outside the door and ducked under the tape. Mr. Butters was wrong. The Canary wasn't here. But since I was, it couldn't hurt to have a quick look around as long as I didn't touch anything.

I stole a pen from the mug on Wyatt's desk and used it to poke around. I'd learned that from watching Grady. This way, I wouldn't get my prints on anything.

From what I could see, Mitzi's things had been removed, presumably relocated to the police station's evidence locker. What remained was a sparse and tidy office. I hooked the pen in the handle of a desk drawer and dragged it open. Nothing interesting inside. I repeated the process, uselessly wishing I'd come across the letters from my grandma that Mitzi had promised to me.

A creaking sound nearby turned my limbs to stone.

My eyelids fell shut, and I listened hard for the sound to come again.

"Hey! What are you doing in there?" a deep voice growled. "That's a crime scene!"

I spun around so fast I lost my footing and knocked against the desk for balance, palms raised in surrender. Then, I threw my pen at Ryan's laughing face. "You stink!" I gasped, both thankful and aggravated to see Ryan where I'd expected to find a police officer. "What are you doing here?"

He moseyed away from the wall where he'd tucked himself behind the door when I crept inside. "I was taking photos before you interrupted." He pointed to the professional camera hanging by a strap around his neck. His hands were covered with blue disposable gloves and paper hospital booties were stretched over his shoes.

I pressed a palm to my ribs, where my heart was attempting to break free. "You can't publish those pictures," I said. "It wouldn't be right. It's the exploitation of an old lady's murder."

Ryan rolled his eyes. "I'm not going to sell the photos. I'm going to print and study them for clues after I get out of here. We don't have much longer before the crime scene team returns."

I glanced at the open door. "Where are they now?"

He smiled. "I paid the sandwich shop to set up a buffet in the employee break room, then asked the nature center staff to let the crime scene folks know lunch was being catered. No charge."

Food. The world's oldest motivator. Anyone who doubted food's power had obviously never eaten anything worth the time.

Ryan aimed his camera and took a picture of my feet.

I dropped my gaze to find a small strip of black-and-white snapshots near my toes, like the ones taken in photo booths.

"They fell from the desk when you knocked into it," he said.

I picked the photos up on instinct, regretting my lack of gloves immediately. Then, I realized who was in the photos. "Grandma."

Ryan stepped closer, craning his neck for a better view. "She's beautiful."

I smiled, mesmerized by the youthful face looking back at me. I'd recognize Grandma's eyes anywhere, but her cheeks were round and full, her hair curled into the careful style of the times, and her mouth open in laughter. She was barely more than a girl. "I never knew her like this." My earliest memories of my grandma included her shocks of gray hair, crow's feet, and laugh lines. I recognized the woman beside her as Mitzi Calgon. Until this week, my only memories of Mitzi were of her at this age in *Blackbeard's Bride.* Since the women were together, the photos must've been taken in California before my mother was born. "Grandma was younger than me here. Maybe eight or nine years younger."

"You look just like her," Ryan said.

I pulled my gaze from the photo and gave him an awkward smile. "Thanks. You realize you accidentally called me beautiful."

"Wasn't an accident," he said confidently. "You're quite striking, when your personality isn't getting in the way."

"Back at you," I said.

Ryan laughed. "Come on." He tipped his head toward the door. "We need to go. The crime scene team can't eat forever. I've gotten enough photos to get us started."

"Us?" I asked, slipping back under the tape.

He shouldered the bag of books I'd left at the doorway. "Sure. Partners, right?" He offered me a fist to bump as we moved away from Wyatt's office.

I considered his intent and my options. "Why are you really doing this?"

He shrugged. "I have a curious mind. Plus, I want to help Amelia and her dad. I really like her, you know. I'm not playing games or being cheeky. She's a special lady."

"She's my best friend," I said defensively.

Ryan threw a long arm across my shoulders. "Precisely. And I believe the Spice Girls said if I want to get with her, I've got to get with her friend."

I scoffed. "You admit you're using me to get closer to her."

"Of course. Your opinion means everything to Amelia."

I sighed, unable to find the energy to be offended.

"You really can't publish those pictures," I said. "Selling them is just icky on your part and publishing them now could do serious damage to the investigation."

He wiggled his waiting fist in front of me. "I'm keeping them until the case is wrapped, then I plan to sell a comprehensive insider's account of the whole ordeal, start-to-finish, for top dollar. Maybe even parlay it into another book deal."

I suppressed the urge to smack him. I'd forgotten he turned our last run-in into a book and then sold the manuscript to a major publishing house. I had no doubt he'd return to the scene of the crime, i.e., Charm, for his book launch and related hoopla, whenever that took place. Lucky for him, the object of his affection owned the town's only bookstore.

I bumped his fist reluctantly.

He opened his fingers immediately and made a goofy explosion sound.

I had no idea what Amelia saw in him.

"I heard about what happened to you last night," he said as we approached the center's front door. "I'm sorry about that."

My steps stuttered. "You heard? Already?" How was that even possible? I'd only told Grady, my aunts, Denise…and Amelia.

"*Town Charmer* covered it this morning," he said, dropping his arm off my shoulders. "Whoever runs that website has mad skills for collecting information. I'm thinking it's a mole at the police station."

I didn't want to think about who ran the town

gossip blog. I'd lost too much time on that subject when I first moved home and learned the blog existed. "I'm fine, but the file I'd been reading was stolen."

He arched a questioning eyebrow. "What sort of file?"

"Details about Mitzi's life. A guy named the Canary gave it to me. I was hoping to run into him here. Any chance you've seen him?" I asked, raising one arm overhead. "He's about this tall, dresses like the Count of Monte Cristo."

Ryan's eyes were wide. "You met the Canary? *The Canary* is in Charm?" He pressed the front door open, and I followed him outside.

"You know who he is?" I marveled back.

"He's only a god in my world," Ryan said, "nearly as all-knowing as the person behind the *Town Charmer*."

I snorted, not sure if he was joking.

A breeze from the bay fluttered the bottom of my photo strip.

"Is that writing?" Ryan asked, attention fixed on the pictures caught between my fingertips.

I turned the strip over. Faint blue ink was scrawled across the white backing. *To my beautiful maid of honor with love, Hazel.*

Breath caught in my throat. "Her maid of honor?"

"May I?" Ryan asked, snapping a photo of each side of the photos, then pressing them back into my palm. "She never mentioned a husband?"

"Never." I filled him in on my aunts' theory about a possible movie star cowboy, Grandpa.

He shook his head, eyebrows high. "Your family wins the trophy for most interesting." He tossed my bag of books onto the seat of a familiar red convertible. "I'll give you a ride home. It's hot and you look miserable."

"Amelia let you drive her car?" I asked, already climbing inside.

"Sure," he said. "It's faster than walking, and she doesn't need it right now. I'd do the same for her."

I buckled up, unimpressed. "You're only driving me home to win points with her."

Ryan rounded the hood, then slid smoothly behind the wheel. He wiggled his eyebrows before pushing classic black Ray-Ban sunglasses over the bridge of his nose.

I spent the drive home and the entire rest of my day staring at the little strip of black-and-white photos every chance I could. Once Sun, Sand, and Tea was closed, I took the photos upstairs with me and kept them close as I typed a blog post and fumbled awkwardly with the new app Ryan had installed on my phone. Instead of baking, I went live with a two-minute "Hello" video to let folks know I was considering the possibilities of a future livestream. A dozen people had followed me within the hour, but I wasn't sure it was the way to go for my tutorials, no matter how simple they were.

I climbed into bed at eleven and propped the photos against the lamp on my nightstand.

"Well," I told the images of Grandma and Mitzi as

I turned out the light, "I really should have taken you to Grady and confessed my trespassing, but I'm not ready to let you go."

I felt confident I had Grandma and Mitzi's support, so I rolled onto my side and stared at them in the dark. "I miss you, Grandma," I whispered.

And I'd do anything I could to get justice for the woman who'd meant so much to her.

CHAPTER
ELEVEN

I woke well before dawn when Maggie ran across my bed and nearly caused me to have six consecutive strokes. The house had been empty when I'd gone to bed, and I hadn't seen her since she'd chased off whoever had stolen my folder from the gazebo. When she raced from the room, I followed her and found her in the kitchen. I worked some quick magic and rewarded her for saving my life, if not my file, with some boiled chicken and mashed carrots. I had hot tea and enjoyed the unique stillness that only occurred when I knew everyone else in town was probably asleep. In those moments, it was as if I were the only person on earth. While I'd never actually want to be the only person on earth, I loved the strange sensation of utter peace.

My home was lovely in the wee hours, not off-putting or frightening like many rambling old homes could be. Maggie joined me as I curled onto the couch, covered my legs with a knitted throw, and balanced my laptop on my knees. "How about a little research since we're awake?" I suggested.

Maggie stretched and yawned, then rolled onto her side between my throw-covered feet and purred.

"I'll take that as a yes," I said, typing Mitzi's name into a search engine. I began to read everything I could about her life, watch interviews with her, and stalk the social media attached to her name, likely maintained by someone who wasn't Mitzi at all. Somehow I couldn't imagine the woman I'd met at the nature center sharing photos of her meals or pedicures. They probably weren't even Mitzi's feet in the photos. From there, I fell down a digital rabbit hole and didn't find my way out until the first amber rays of sunrise drew my attention to the sea.

I set the laptop aside and went to watch the sun from my deck. Maggie was long gone. I hadn't noticed her leave.

Brilliant shades of a new day crept over the horizon and into my home, lighting me slowly from toes to nose as I watched from the patio doors.

Despite all the research I'd done, I still hadn't come up with anyone who'd want to kill Mitzi Calgon. There were plenty adoring fan sites that bordered on obsessive and creepy, but no one in particular had stood out to me as potentially dangerous. Mitzi's divorce had been a hot topic across the board. Bloggers reported extreme hostility on both sides regarding the division of property over the last ten months. No wonder Mitzi had been willing to get away for a while. Possibly the most shocking thing I'd learned about the split was that the divorce wasn't final. She and her nearly ex-husband, Malcolm Pierce, were fighting valiantly as he continued to seek more of her estate. And for all the boo-hooing he'd been doing, Malcolm Pierce wasn't exactly living in poverty. He'd had plenty of money when they married and had made a ton since. He owned real estate all over the West Coast, commercial and residential alike, as well as a handful of small and medium-sized corporations and other businesses.

It seemed strange to me that Mr. Pierce continued to seek more from the divorce when he had so much already. Records showed the couple had elected for a prenup prior to marriage, guaranteeing each partner would retain whatever had been theirs at the time of the vows and divide all assets gained during their marital years in the event of divorce. So, what was the guy's deal?

The fact Mitzi had died before the divorce was final made me wonder if killing her had been the perfect answer to Mr. Pierce's problems. Now, he'd likely inherit everything.

I switched from tea to coffee as the sun finished its ascent, then dressed for my day and went downstairs to visit with Lou and wait for Denise. Lou was ripping a crab limb from limb on the deck when I arrived, so I decided to give him some privacy.

I ran through my morning tasks. Cleaning. Food prep. Menu adjustment and double-checking the balance in the cash register. When I went to get the mail, Denise was already coming my way.

"Hey," I called. "You're super early." I hadn't expected her for another hour, and she looked amazing per her usual.

She smiled back. "I just couldn't wait to get out into the day. It's so beautiful here. Like living in a postcard." Denise's Tiffany blue silk tank top illuminated her eyes. The pleated white skirt accented her long, tan legs and athletic figure. The fact she'd paired bare feet with canvas tennis shoes reminded me that she was much closer to twenty than I was to thirty. "I hope it's okay that I'm here already. I thought I could help you with the morning prep and we could talk more about the Mitzi Calgon case." She whispered the last part of her statement, then gave the world around us a quick look, presumably for prying eyes or ears.

I pulled my lips to the side, unsure how to respond and feeling like her comment was part of a setup. Possibly something Grady concocted to gauge my involvement or teach me a lesson. I flipped blindly through the letters from my mailbox before responding. "I thought you wanted me to stay out of Mitzi's murder," I said, glancing briefly into Denise's eyes before turning back for my house.

She fell easily into pace at my side. "That would be best, but I poked around a little last night, and I can see how you could get drawn in."

"What do you mean?" I held the front door, then followed her through the foyer and archway to Sun, Sand, and Tea.

She stopped at the service counter and chewed her

lip for a long moment, looking almost guilty for whatever she was about to confess. "I was posting some pictures of Denver to Instagram last night, and I saw a few photos of old friends in my feed. It made me wonder if Mitzi's assistant, Odette, might have an account."

I moved in closer, attention rapt. "And you found her?"

Denise nodded. "If her Instagram is a true reflection of her reality, Odette lives a wild life. Nightclubs, parties, travel, men. Scrolling through her account was like viewing still shots from some rich-kids-gone-wild reality show."

I weighed my options on how to respond. If Denise had been snooping, then she couldn't judge or tattle on me for doing the same. *I hoped.* "I don't suppose you got the feeling she needed money? Maybe badly enough to hurt her former stepmom to get it?"

Denise slid her purse from her shoulder and tucked it under the counter. "No. Honestly, it looked like she was loaded."

"Her dad's married to Mitzi," I said, watching Denise's blue eyes widen. "His name's Malcolm Pierce and he and Mitzi were in the middle of a complicated divorce when she died. Now he's likely to inherit the kingdom. I did a little research too," I admitted. "Mitzi never had children of her own, and I didn't see any mention of another next of kin. It would make sense that her estate go to her husband in the event of her death, unless she's legally arranged something else. I couldn't find a definitive answer on that."

Denise looked as if I'd grown a second head. "I thought I did something great by looking through some social media profiles. How did you learn all that?"

"Most of it is public record," I said. "I picked up a few skills while looking into some other deaths. Details on Mitzi's personal life were more accessible than most because of her celebrity status, but we had a ton of fabrications to weed through. Sometimes the outlandish headlines were based in small, uninteresting truths. Other times, they were blatant slander or speculation."

Denise took a seat at the counter and rested her chin in her palms. "Anything else?"

I only hesitated a minute before pulling the strip of photo booth photos from the back pocket of my jean shorts. "I found this. It's not related to the case, but it's my grandma and Mitzi when they were your age, and I can't stop looking at it."

Denise took the photos carefully from my hand and ran the pad of her thumb across the aged material. "Wow."

"I know."

"You look like your grandmother," Denise said with a wistful smile. "I wish I could have met her."

"Me too. You would have liked her," I said.

"She and Mitzi look so proper and demure." Denise smiled at them. "The online photos of Odette are nothing like these." She returned the pictures to me with a sigh. "I guess the world has changed a little since then."

"No doubt." I poured us each a cup of tea and plated a pair of croissants with jam for us to share. "If Odette's life is such a party, and her dad and Mitzi were splitting up, I wonder why she agreed to be Mitzi's personal assistant. I only met her briefly, but she didn't seem to like the job. I didn't get the impression she and Mitzi were close."

"Maybe she wanted to spite her dad," Denise said. "Rebel against him for something he did. Make it seem like she was choosing Mitzi over him."

"Or…" I lifted a finger. "She might be working with her dad as a spy or something worse."

Denise grimaced. "That took a dark turn."

I shrugged. "I'm trying to think of every possibility."

"Everly?" Wyatt's voice arrived with the sound of my wind chimes.

I jumped and Denise spun on her stool.

Wyatt raised a palm waist-high in timid greeting. He moved cautiously into the café when we didn't respond. "Is it too early to order a little tea and toast?"

Considering the café didn't open for an hour, and despite the fact I hadn't deadbolted the door, the sign in my window clearly said CLOSED. I was leaning toward, *Yes. So please go away while we talk about potential murderers.*

Denise was on her feet before I could say anything. "Coming right up." She strode around the counter and grabbed a loaf of freshly baked bread on her way to the toaster.

I looked from her to Wyatt. "What's up?" I asked.

"Just checking in," he said. "How are you holding up?"

"Oh, you know me," I said, unwilling to admit I had no idea how I was doing—though *curious* topped the list of my current emotions. Why had he really shown up an hour before I opened? Surely he had toast at home. Did he know I'd been poking through his office yesterday? I might've owed him an apology for that.

"I do know you," he said. "That's why I'm asking."

Denise returned with toast, sweet tea, and jam. "This is nice," she said, delivering Wyatt's order, then sampling one of the croissants I'd plated for us to share. "A quiet little breakfast between friends."

"Breakfast!" I bonked the heel of one hand against my forehead. "Sorry, guys. I've got to go. I'm supposed to be at my aunts' house for pancakes." Apparently waking up in the middle of the night wasn't great for my clarity of thought. I grabbed the big bag of Amelia's books I'd abandoned behind the counter last night and shot an apologetic look to the friends staring back at me. "I swear I don't mean to keep running off and leaving you alone. The food's all prepped and ready to go," I told Denise.

"Perfect. Don't worry. I've got this," Denise said, motioning widely to the café. "Have fun. We'll finish our talk later?"

I gave her a thumbs-up, and I was off.

"Hug your aunts for me," Wyatt called behind me.

I hurried down the boardwalk toward the first of

two Little Libraries in my area. They were in opposite directions from my place, so I decided to hit the one farthest from my aunts' house first, then double back.

Hot summer sun beat against my skin and glistened off the gorgeous ocean waves. I watched gulls swoop and call in the cloudless blue sky. I couldn't help wondering if one of them was Lou and if he'd left any pieces of his breakfast on my café's rear deck. I suspected most of my lunch guests would find bits of mutilated crab unappetizing.

I checked my watch and said a prayer of gratitude when the first stop came into view. Amelia's Little Libraries had become a staple in our community and were easily the cutest things on the boardwalk. She had several more throughout the town and all were heavily frequented. The Little Libraries were made from upcycled materials and worked on a need-a-book, take-a-book premise. Some were designed to look like giant birdhouses, others like big wooden tomes. All were whimsically painted and held a great selection of books.

I set the bag at my feet while I opened the little door. I arranged the handful of remaining books to make room for more, then stocked the shelves in a tidy fashion.

The bag was seventy-five percent lighter when I finished. Amelia had been right about the Little Libraries being low on stock.

I'd barely gotten the bag back on my shoulder when a pair of familiar figures rounded the bend ahead. I recognized them both in seconds: Quinn from the documentary and the Canary! My heart jolted and I swung an arm overhead. "Canary!" I called as they moved in my direction.

The pair of men stopped thirty yards away.

"Mr. Canary!" I called again, hiking Amelia's book bag higher on one shoulder and loping their way. "It's me, Everly Swan. Do you have a minute?" My strides faltered when the expression on his face turned to panic.

"I need to talk to you," I said, regaining myself quickly and increasing my speed. "I only need a minute."

The Canary's mouth opened, then shut. His brows rose dramatically, and then he ran.

CHAPTER
❧

TWELVE

I ground to a stop beside Quinn and dropped the bag of books between us. "Why would he do that?" I rasped, gripping the stitch in my side and wishing I were in better shape.

"He's a weird guy," Quinn said, watching as the Canary vanished around the bend behind them. "How do you know him?"

I groaned and let my head fall back as the pinch between my ribs faded. I snapped upright as a more important question occurred to me. "How do you?"

"I don't," Quinn said. "He recognized me from the documentary team and wanted to know if I had an insider's story he could use for his blog. When I said no, he asked if I had anything of Mitzi's that he could have for his private collection. I told him that was creepy. I mean, why would I have any of Mitzi's things?" He wrinkled his nose. "Why does he?"

"He's a superfan," I said, hoping that was true, and that the Canary wasn't actually her stalker. Or worse, one and the same. Maybe he was the one who'd sent her the letters. If so, why had he shared his file of information with me? Nothing made any sense. I rubbed my face in frustration. "I wish he wouldn't have run. I really need to talk to him."

Quinn looked unabashedly baffled. "Why?"

"Never mind." I sighed and turned back in the direction I'd come. I was far too tired to get into that whole mess at the moment. Instead, I worked up a smile and hoisted the bag of books back onto my shoulder. "Any chance you're going to my aunts' place for pancakes and some filming?"

Quinn smiled. "That's where I was headed when the Canary saw me."

"Well then, we can keep each other company."

We walked in companionable silence most of the way, stopping to unload the rest of the books into Amelia's other Little Library on the boardwalk. My few feeble attempts at small talk didn't get us any further than his occasional question about my life growing up on an island with beekeeping great-aunts. Neither of us mentioned Mitzi, but the elephant in the room between us was huge and likely the reason we couldn't seem to connect. I still wasn't sure how I felt about Rose's decision to press on with the documentary so soon after Mitzi's death. It just didn't seem right, but maybe that was my Southern manners talking. I would have been far more comfortable bringing her family casseroles and helping around their house while they took time to grieve.

I picked up the pace when Aunt Clara began sending texts to ask if I was coming. Apparently, the pancakes were done and beginning to cool.

"There it is," I told Quinn when the family homestead came into view.

My aunts lived in the home where I'd grown up, the same home where they'd grown up, and where their moms and grandmas had grown up. The property had been handed down through the generations since a Swan woman founded the town centuries prior. One day the lot of it would be mine, and that was the saddest thing that would ever happen to my world. It would mean that I was officially alone.

"Cool house," Quinn said, marching eagerly up the flagstone walk, his nose and chin high—probably pulled along by the rich, buttery scent of Aunt Fran's signature pancakes.

I smiled, admiring the dark gray colonial saltbox with a neat black roof, window trim, and door. Emerald green grass ringed the home and outbuildings where I'd once run barefoot, chasing robins and butterflies. Wildflowers pressed against the scalloped wooden fence and tidy cobblestone paths that wound through carefully tended gardens.

A trio of strangers stood near a tripod in the gardens. They each had a steaming mug in hand. Various props leaned against a card table holding an open laptop and a basket of muffins.

The home's front door popped open, and Aunt Clara stepped out. "Good morning!" she called, waving furiously and bracing the door with her hip. "Come in! Come in!"

I stepped inside and waved to Rose, seated on a three-legged stool at the massive center island. The kitchen was as warm and inviting as always. A black kettle still hung from a chain in the oversized fireplace, which had long ago served as an oven. These days it mostly boiled water with essential oils and herbs picked from the gardens to sweeten the air.

Bouquets of flowers, handpicked by my aunts, dangled from the rafters where they were hung to dry. The leaves and buds would soon be added to soaps, potpourris, candles, and any number of organic products sold at Blessed Bee.

I helped myself to coffee while Aunt Clara welcomed Quinn into their home and Aunt Fran set two more places at the table. "Who are the people in your gardens?" I asked.

Aunt Fran waved me to my seat. "Stagehands," she said. "Rose invited a few of Mitzi's fans to work on set today."

"It's perfect," Aunt Clara cooed. "The fans are so happy to be involved in Mitzi's final product that they didn't want to be paid, and the money saved on wages can go directly to bee research or film production."

"Smart," I said, offering a smile to Aunt Clara, then Rose.

Rose didn't notice. Her plate and mug were empty, her expression unusually sour. Her attention seemed fixed on Quinn.

"Swan for mayor," he said, peeping through the open doorway to my aunts' sewing room/office/campaign headquarters just off the kitchen. "Cool. Which one of you is running?"

"You know this," Rose said at the same time as Aunt Fran answered, "Me."

Quinn's gaze slid over Rose to land on Aunt Fran. "Exciting stuff. Best of luck with that. Thank you for breakfast." He accepted the plate and took a seat at the table beside the garden-facing window. "This was very kind, and it smells delicious."

"And yet you were late," Rose said.

Aunt Fran cast Rose a wayward look, clearly bummed at the change of topic. Campaign details and strategies were among her favorite discussions these days. She'd already declared that the moment the documentary filming ended, the three of us Swan women were diving directly into campaign madness. And we would stay there until the election.

I tried not to think about that. Campaigning would involve far too many run-ins with Mary Grace Chatsworth and her man candy, Vanders. I shut my eyes and shoved the memory of their pending nuptials from my mind.

Aunt Clara took a seat beside me at the table. "We were just talking about Mitzi before you arrived. Did you have a chance to get to know her, Quinn?" she asked.

He shook his head. "No. We didn't cross paths

much. Rose handled all the details and organization of the trip and Mitzi's role here."

"Because you weren't around," Rose said, covering her empty mug with a palm when Aunt Fran tried to refill it. "Where were you this morning? We were supposed to meet here and set up together. Instead you're late and I had to set up alone."

I forked a hunk of pancake and dragged it through a puddle of Aunt Fran's elderberry syrup. "He was detained on the boardwalk by a superfan," I said. "That's where I ran into him."

Quinn's expression relaxed a bit, and he went back to his pancakes with gusto.

"Did either of you know Odette well?" I asked, dragging my attention from Rose to Quinn. "I didn't realize when I met her that she was Mitzi's stepdaughter. Did the two of them get along?"

"Odette's high strung and entitled," Rose said, still looking sour. "She's young enough to be Mitzi's granddaughter, but she was her stepdaughter, and that made for lots of snickers and gossip, which she hated. The age difference made it nearly impossible for them to agree on anything. Plus, she's the only child of a millionaire. She wasn't the easiest person to get along with, but Mitzi made it work."

"What didn't they agree on?" I asked, biting my tongue against the urge to say, *specifically.*

"Money, mostly," Rose said. "How much she should be paid. How many hours she should work.

How she should spend her earnings. All of that." She slid off her stool and carried her plate and mug to the sink. "We need to get started or Clara and Fran will be late to open their shop."

I checked my watch. I wasn't sure how long they planned to film in the garden, but I needed a few minutes in the archives. "I'll be right out," I told my aunts. "I want to take a look at the old cookbooks before I head home."

"Take your time," Aunt Clara said, planting a kiss on my forehead.

"See you in a bit," Aunt Fran called, holding the front door for everyone to pass.

"Quinn?" I asked, before he stepped outside. "You mentioned that funding for this project came in after Mitzi got involved. What happened?"

"Initially, we planned to do some crowdsourcing and online auctions to come up with a budget for filming. Then Fran told Rose about Mitzi's willingness to get involved, and once Rose confirmed it, people got a lot more interested in helping." He rubbed his eyebrow. "Rose said an investment company called to offer her a big check, and that was that. No more need for fundraisers. I guess the investor heard Mitzi Calgon was involved and figured there was no way to go wrong by backing this film."

"Do you remember the investor's name?" I asked, a flutter of excitement building in my core.

"Not offhand, but I can ask Rose." He gave an

apologetic smile. "Ocean Pacific Something, I think. I'll ask."

"Thank you," I said, stepping back so he and Aunt Fran could catch up with Rose before she became any more irritated.

I returned to the table and finished my pancakes in solitude, watching the foursome in the garden through the kitchen window. I savored the homemade syrup and remembered why I didn't serve breakfast. My best efforts couldn't touch Aunt Fran's pancakes or secret recipe syrups. I pushed Rose's opinion of Odette around my mind while I pushed the remaining breakfast around my plate. When I didn't get anywhere with my ruminating and the plate was empty, I washed it in the deep farmhouse sink, along with all the other dishes that had been stacked there.

Outside, Rose stood behind a large camera on a serious-looking tripod, making hand gestures while my aunts spoke to one another from a pair of red rocking chairs positioned among the blooms. Aunt Fran made a stuffed bee fly through the air, and Aunt Clara held a bouquet of flowers. I assumed this was a segment on pollination. It reminded me of the presentations they frequently gave for children, and I wondered what sort of documentary Rose was making. Quinn wandered in the periphery, brows furrowed in concentration, while a set of folks I didn't recognize extended boom mics and light reflection materials in my aunts' general direction.

I dried my hands and headed for the archives

with surprising gusto. I hadn't realized how much I'd missed spending time there. I nearly jogged down the hallway leading from the kitchen to the first-floor guest room and bath. I made a right past the stairs to the second floor and crossed into one of the oldest parts of the home. The archives were in what had once been the main living area. With time and the help of many skilled craftsmen, the Swan home had grown from a one-room cabin to more than four thousand square feet of history and charm. I only wished the nooks, crannies, and hallways could tell me the things they'd seen.

I slowed in reverence and anticipation outside the aged wooden door, then turned the knob slowly as excitement built in my chest. The scent of old books hit me the moment I pushed the door wide. I hopped down three wooden steps into the sunken space and took a minute to enjoy the dry heat and familiarity. The ashy scent of ancient pages and crumbling leather called to me. Dust particles floated like silver confetti in the light, a party just for me. I rocked my heels on the creaky knotty pine floorboards and enjoyed the slow complaint of the hinges as I pushed the door shut.

Hundreds of books sat on shelves pressed against the walls, as well as on bookcases pressed back to back and anchored to the floor and ceiling like aisles in a bookstore. If more of the books had been penned by real authors instead of ancestral Swans, we could've called the room a library.

I knew exactly where to look for recipes. I'd been doing it all my life, but this time, instead of seeking a challenge, I needed something simple. Something I could showcase on my blog and followers couldn't ruin. If a viewer was willing to give it a try, I wanted them to find success, not discouragement.

I ran my fingertips over the old covers, pulling dessert books lovingly into my arms. I started with books from Grandma's generation, then slowly moved deeper into the room…down a makeshift aisle of older tomes, selecting one or two books from each set of shelves until I reached the last row. My favorite row.

Against the rear wall, farthest from the door and window, protected from extreme temperatures, light, and humidity, were the handful of handwritten texts—journals that had withstood the tests of time, including house fires and tropical storms that flattened almost everything else on the island.

I carried my selections to the armchair in front of the window and sat in the warm light, then opened the oldest book on my lap. I could take the others home with me, but the oldest books were too fragile to travel. The ink on their pages was nearly too faded to read. Aunt Clara was slowly, painstakingly, copying the recipes into new books while the words were still legible so generations after us could enjoy them too.

The book practically fell open to the rum cake recipe everyone loved so much. I took a picture of the faded cursive script and notations so I could enjoy them later. Then I added a few more photos of breads and cookies that might work for my blog before returning that book to the stack at my feet and selecting another.

The sound of footfalls reached my ears from somewhere outside the archives, and I paused to see if they were coming my way. I supposed Aunt Clara or Aunt Fran could have forgotten something or come in search of a couple extra hands. When the floorboards groaned outside the archive door, I stilled and waited. A sensation of unease rippled over me, and despite the wall of bookcases between myself and the door, I felt exposed. "Hello," I called, my knees officially knocking.

The door creaked open, then slammed shut a heartbeat later. There hadn't been enough time for anyone to come in. So, what had happened? "Hello?" I tried again, inching my way to the end of my row.

Something heavy scraped the floorboards outside the door.

"Aunt Clara? Aunt Fran?" I peeked around the bookshelves, unsure what I'd heard or what it meant. "Anyone there?"

My phone buzzed with a text and I swiped it to life, heart hammering and throat painfully dry. Another unknown number lit the screen. Another image of a honeybee.

Bee smarter or bee sorry.

A low buzzing caught my ear, and I spun to face the window. Two honeybees bumped the glass from inside, crawling along the pane.

Breath caught in my throat, and my stomach flipped.

Mitzi's swollen face and unseeing eyes flashed in my mind, and I made a run for the exit.

I reached the short flight of steps in three panicked leaps, then climbed them in one. I turned the knob and slammed against the unmoving door. Tears stung my eyes as I wiggled and twisted the knob. Something was blocking the door. Holding me inside.

I screamed as a bee buzzed past my head.

Honeybees were everywhere. They crawled near my feet and hovered over my head—swooping and zipping through the shrinking space. Fear heated my body from the inside out. Panic stole my breath.

Someone had dumped a bunch of bees inside the room with me, and they'd blocked the door so I couldn't leave. Panic overtook me as I pounded my palm against the door and screamed. "Help! Help me! Please!"

A bee flew into my hair, and I lost my balance on the old wooden steps while swatting it away. I tumbled off and collided hard with the floor. Tears rolled hot and heavy over my cheeks as the bees zigzagged overhead. I didn't know how many there were, but I felt them on me. In my hair and on my clothes.

I was locked in a giant bee box, just like Mitzi.

CHAPTER
THIRTEEN

Thirty minutes later, I sat on a chair in the kitchen with my head between my knees, occasionally brushing invisible bees from my arms, face, and hair. It had taken what seemed like forever, but eventually reason had broken through my mortal fear and I remembered the cell phone in my pocket. I didn't need to scream and pound the door and roll on the floor like a nut. I could sit up and dial help.

I'd dialed Grady.

He told another cop to call my aunts. I'd caught him at the office and refused to let him hang up, just in case I didn't make it out alive. The bees had begun to gather on the window, but whoever had dumped them into the room with me could easily have something else planned, after all.

Thankfully, nothing else had gone wrong, and the next voice I'd heard was Aunt Clara's. She and Aunt Fran had only beaten Grady to me by a matter of minutes, which was saying something, considering he'd been at the station when I called and they'd been in the yard.

The kitchen hummed and rattled around me now, awash in a flurry of activity. My great-aunts alternated between fussing over me and making sure the unexpected house full of people were all feeling welcomed. I measured my breaths at the table where three late-arriving superfans of Mitzi's awaited their turn in questioning. Apparently, Rose had offered a second shift of fans the opportunity to work on the documentary for free. The additional fans had shuffled in after I'd planted myself in a chair, and I didn't bother looking up to greet them. My face was almost certainly puffy and red from fear and tears. The little makeup I'd bothered with was probably smeared from my chin to my forehead, and I couldn't bring myself to meet anyone's eye like this, or to care about being rude.

I stared at the five pairs of shoes accompanying mine beneath the table. I recognized Rose's trendy red Converse and Quinn's hipster rubber-soled moccasins. The others were new: two sets of white run-of-the-mill sneakers and a pair of black boots.

The front door opened and closed continually behind me as local law enforcement and crime scene personnel buzzed in and out. There was only one reason that releasing bees indoors would bring a crowd of uniforms. Grady believed the person responsible for this was also responsible for Mitzi's death.

I peeked in the direction of a familiar voice speaking with Aunt Clara. A kind and attractive EMT named Matt Darning finished the proffered cup of tea with a wink and sincere smile. He leaned against the wall and turned his attention to me, stubbornly refusing to leave until I let him look me over. I hid my face in the crook of my arm on the table, not quite ready to deal with the inevitable. Matt had helped me last summer when I'd been attacked at my home following a wedding/murder combination, and he'd visited Sun, Sand, and Tea a number of times since. His sandy hair and soulful brown eyes gave him the look of someone who should be on a surfboard instead of wearing a stethoscope, but he did both well.

"Mr. Pendle?" a man asked.

I rolled my cheek against my arm and peered up at the officer standing beside our table. Brayden Castle gave me a reassuring nod when our eyes met. In high school he'd been a cocky upperclassman who hadn't given girls like me the time of day. Lately, however, his job had required him to help me on a number of unfortunate occasions. *Karma, am I right?*

"I only have a few questions," Brayden said to someone seated opposite me. "Then you can call it a day."

'What?" Rose said. "We can't call it a day. We were just getting started."

"Ma'am," Brayden said calmly, "if you turn that camera back on inside this house, I will take it from you. This is an active investigation following the invasion of a family's home. This is *not* fodder for your film."

"Thanks," I whispered, feeling distinctly more

confident. I didn't hide my face again, but I lacked the energy to lift my head or straighten my posture.

The chair across from mine scraped over aged floorboards and a familiar little man met Brayden at the end of the table. "Burt Pendle?" I asked, suddenly putting the name Brayden had called with the face before me. "We met at the bookstore. You're a friend of Mr. Butters."

"Yeah, so?" He seemed startled and a little wary.

"So?" I repeated, forcing myself upright in the chair. "What are you doing here?"

He lifted his palms and shoulders in an exaggerated silent response.

"Right this way, Mr. Pendle," Brayden directed.

Leave it to an attorney not *to answer my question*, I thought. Hopefully, Brayden would have better luck.

I swallowed my pride and scanned the other faces at the table but only recognized Rose and Quinn. Rose had a death grip on her camera, though it was on the table instead of at her eye for a change.

Quinn leaned on his elbows. "I swear this whole project is cursed. We need to go home, regroup, and make a new plan."

Rose spun on him. "We're not going home. We might have to turn this bee thing into a true-crime film, but we aren't leaving."

"The film's not cursed," I said, hung up on the way everyone had to default to that word. "Someone's trying to force me to stop asking questions about what happened to Mitzi. Nothing more."

Rose swept an open palm in my direction, eyebrows high, gaze locked on Quinn. "See?"

Aunt Clara strode into view with a water pitcher and refilled the glass I'd drained after emerging from the archives. "Feeling any better?" she asked, her voice as soothing as any balm.

I took the glass and drank greedily. "A little."

Brayden released Mr. Pendle and called for the next free laborer to meet him in the sewing room/ campaign headquarters for questioning.

Mr. Pendle tipped his hat at me on his way out the door. "Take it easy, Everly," he said. "Be safe."

I shuddered at his word choice.

Ryan passed Mr. Pendle in the doorway. "Hello, all," he sang, a peppy little kick in his step.

I rethought the reason for my chill. "What are you doing here?" I asked.

He feigned offense. "Checking on you, of course. I came straightaway once I heard what happened."

"How can you possibly know about this already?" I asked.

"I was at the nature center when I saw your detective and a pair of cruisers tear out of there." He winked. "I followed. I took the liberty of checking the property lines while the chaos died down in here. You have a beautiful garden."

"Why, thank you!" Aunt Clara beamed and pulled him to the table. "Would you like something to drink? I've ground fresh coffee and lots of organic leaves for teas."

"Coffee sounds wonderful, thank you," he agreed.

"Everly?" Grady's voice cut through the white noise to my ears.

I sprang upright, nerves strung tight. "Yes." Had he found something? A clue about who'd done this? A culprit? *A killer?*

He cast a questioning look at Ryan, who'd crossed the room behind Aunt Clara to help with the coffee.

I hurried in Grady's direction and nearly launched into a tackle hug.

He took my hand before I could embarrass myself and pulled me into a small parlor in the narrow hallway off the kitchen, then closed the door.

A half dozen really good reasons for closing the door rushed to mind. My favorite possibilities included a proclamation of his earnest romantic feelings for me, an encore of our Christmas kiss, and a request to check my body for honeybee stingers. I hadn't been stung, but I was willing to let the man check.

He moved his back to the door and crossed his arms.

I followed his gaze to Matt Darning and his EMT tackle box. "Jeez," I said, equal parts relieved and disappointed none of my wishes had come true. "Really? An ambush?"

"Absolutely," Grady said. "After what happened to Mitzi, there was no scenario where you left here without a medical evaluation."

I flopped onto the velvet Victorian settee at the

room's center and waited while Matt opened his medical supply kit and knelt before me. "I'm fine," I told him.

"You look great to me," Matt said, taking my hand in his and checking my pulse. "But the detective insists, so we should probably do what he says."

I flicked a glare at Grady, catching his gaze on my hand in Matt's.

"Never a dull moment with you," Matt said. His smile was endearing, even if his words weren't. He pressed a stethoscope to my chest. "Your heart's racing. I suppose I can't blame you there. How many fingers am I holding up?" He waved a peace sign before my eyes and winked.

"Two."

"Did you hit your head when you tumbled down the steps?"

"No."

"Twist your ankle?" he asked.

"No." I slid another heated gaze in Grady's direction, my cheeks hot with embarrassment. "You told him I fell down the stairs? I told you that part in confidence."

Grady shrugged.

Matt probed my head with skilled fingers. "No bumps. Any tender spots?"

I pulled away from him. "I told you, I'm fine."

Matt nodded. "I believe you." He pulled a two-pack of aspirin from his pocket and uncapped a mini bottle of water from the medical kit. "You're in good shape. No signs of serious injury or concussion. That's going to win me a lot of money back at the station. I knew you could make it another month without injury." He laughed as he offered the water and pills.

I stared, unsure if he was kidding but unwilling to ask in case he wasn't.

"You did fall, though," he said, "so once the adrenaline works its way through your system, you're probably going to be a little sore."

I took the pills and downed the water.

"If you get home and anything changes or you have a question, call me." He handed me his card, then closed his supply kit.

Grady rolled his eyes and opened the parlor door.

"Do you really think they take bets on my well-being at the station?" I asked Grady as Matt vanished into the hall.

"I'd rather not guess," Grady said, looking down the hall in the direction of the archives before closing the door. He made his way to me on the settee. "Your family library is pretty amazing," he said. "I've never seen books as old as that outside a museum, or known anyone with such strong ties to their lineage. People spend thousands of dollars trying to trace their family histories. You've got it all documented in one room."

"I'm lucky," I said. "Speaking of luck," I segued lamely, "have you spoken to the Canary or located the folder that was stolen from my gazebo?"

Grady shook his head. "No."

"I saw him today," I said. "He was on the boardwalk

by the Little Library near public beach access. I called out to him and he ran away. I have no idea why."

Grady ran his fingers along his jawline. "When I find him I'll ask."

"Thanks." I deflated against the uncomfortable back of the antique love seat. "Have you spoken with Odette again or Mitzi's ex-husband?"

"Yes," Grady said. "Turns out they're both in town and staying at the inn on the bay.

I straightened. "Her ex is here? Why would he come to Charm? When did he arrive?" Before or after Mitzi's death?

"He says he came to support the project and after what happened, he's not leaving without her. Apparently, he funded the documentary so he's feeling some grief-induced guilt. As if the show might not have gone on without his money and therefore she would still be alive."

I shook my head at Grady. "He didn't fund the project. An investment group gave Rose the money."

"Yeah. *His* investment group," Grady said.

I stopped to ponder that. "He funded the project that brought her here, then he followed her. Odette could have let him in through the back door, and he could have killed Mitzi to get his hands on the whole of her estate before the divorce was final."

Grady stood, all hints of concern for my well-being gone. "Stop."

"I'm just giving you something to think about," I said. "Don't you agree it's weird that the man who's had her tied up in court for months over division of assets flew across the country to support her in a small voice-over project?"

"Leave this alone, Everly," Grady warned. "You've had two threats in four days, and I'm only one person. I'm spread too thin to keep an eye on you and solve this case while trying to protect everyone else I care about."

"What?" My ears rang. Did he just say everyone *else* he cared about? As in he cared about *me*? Possibly as more than a citizen whose safety he was sworn to protect?

I took a moment to enjoy the swell of pride and possibilities in my chest—until another idea shoved its way past the first. "What do you mean, you're trying to protect everyone you care about? What's going on?"

He averted his eyes and gripped the back of his neck.

I went to join him near the door, crossed my arms, and peered up at him. "You just said we need protecting, Grady." I waited for his cool gray eyes to find mine. "From what?"

CHAPTER

❦

FOURTEEN

I walked home from my aunts' house in a huff, declining Grady's offered ride after he'd refused to elaborate on why he thought we were in danger. Denise must've heard about it from him or sensed my mood because she didn't press the subject when I told her everything was fine. I'd stayed busy prepping menu items and refreshing the teas while she was there to tend tables, but once she'd gone, everyone in the café began to look vaguely dangerous. Any one of them could've killed Mitzi and locked me in a room with bees. The notion made me sweat, so I called it a day around four thirty.

I flipped my sign to Closed the minute the café was empty, then tried to breathe. Whoever had trapped me in the archives was either incredibly bold or incredibly desperate. I wasn't sure which was worse. The culprit had marched into my aunts' home while multiple potential witnesses were right outside. That kind of behavior took a lot of nerve or a seriously powerful motivation. I supposed that getting away with murder was plenty inspiring, but I couldn't help wondering if there was more to it.

I grabbed my laptop and read everything I could find about Malcolm Pierce, his marriage to Mitzi, and his businesses. His web presence was split; half of his social media profiles were private and the other half were clearly run by members of his company and used for marketing. Frustrated with my inability to find anything to support my theory that he'd killed his wife to cut through the red tape of divorce, I switched gears and went through Odette's social media. Denise was right about Odette's extensive online profiles. She'd documented her travels, parties, shopping, and everything she'd eaten for the last ten years in great detail, usually with photos. Every additional post made her life appear more impossibly glamorous and increasingly surreal, like a montage from a movie.

I stopped on a set of pictures taken on the island. One contained her frowning face beside the Welcome to Charm sign. She'd edited the photo with a hot pink squiggle through the word Charm and the word Mayberry finger-drawn above it. Other recent photos included gorgeous scenery with captions complaining about the lack of traffic and abundance of elbow room on the beach. She wasn't impressed with our small population, lack of couture clothing shops, or nightlife, either. I fought against the irrational urge to respond to her posts with all the reasons Charm was wonderful. I assumed the effort would be lost on her, and I'd be revealed as the cyberstalker I was.

I set the laptop aside and checked my phone for messages. Grady had promised to call if he found a lead on who'd locked me in the archives. I didn't have any messages, but my thoughts moved quickly to Grady's strange and worrisome comment about protecting the people he cared about. From what? And why? My temperature rose in remembrance. What kind of person says something like that, then refuses to elaborate? Was it possible that Mitzi's killer was threatening him too? Trying to stop everyone from looking too closely at the murder? Perhaps suggesting Grady's family was in danger if he didn't leave the investigation alone?

I stared at the phone screen, certain that calling Grady was no use. He would only tell me what he wanted to tell me, and if he wanted to tell me something, he would've called. The icon for my new livestream app caught my eye. Ryan was apparently right about my followers wanting to see me bake in real time because I'd only made one short video, and I'd accumulated several dozen followers.

I pressed the icon and jumped at the sight of myself in selfie mode. My cheeks were pale, my lips were bare, and my mascara had migrated to the hollows beneath my eyes. No wonder the café had emptied fairly quickly after Denise had gone. I looked like an extra from a zombie movie. But I needed to add another video to my feed or followers might drop me before I'd ever really gotten started.

I made a trip to the café's small bathroom and splashed water on my face to work the remnants of melted makeup away. The look didn't suit me, but plenty of Mitzi's fans wore the dark smudged makeup intentionally, choosing to imitate her look from the movie's infamous death scene. After visiting enough fan sites, it had become clear that *Blackbeard's Wife* was real for her superfans, and Mitzi Calgon was merely a character she played outside that world. Much scarier than my creepy undead appearance, if anyone asked me.

I rubbed goose bumps from my arms as I recalled the amount of personal information in the folder stolen from my gazebo. What if the Canary had crossed the bridge from obsessed superfan to delusional stalker and had given me the file to throw me off his tracks? What if he'd regretted the decision once the moment had passed, and he'd wanted the file back? How could I be sure he hadn't retraced his steps after running away from me, then followed Quinn and me to my aunts' house? He might've worried that I'd recognized his voice from that night in my gazebo and wanted to scare me into shutting up.

I ran a tinted bee balm gloss around my lips and rubbed a wet paper towel under each eye, then finger-combed my hair before checking my image in the camera again. Not great, but Ryan said people wanted to know I was real. They wanted authentic and imperfect. Well, I didn't know two words that could describe me better. "Here it goes," I whispered, hovering my thumb over the little Go button.

I squared my shoulders and worked up a smile. "Hey, y'all," I said to the camera, forcing pep into my voice and hoping to look like less of a hot mess. "I'm back with some good news. I've raided the official Swan Family archives and returned with lots of ideas for our next bake-along. That's right," I said, pausing for effect. "A bake-along. As in I'm going to work with you in real time, and we're going to make something unbelievably delicious together. So, press your aprons and prep your cookie sheets, then stay tuned!"

I held the smile, undecided where to go from there. I wasn't ready to bake. Hadn't even chosen a recipe. But it was too soon to cut the live feed. Some folks were probably just tuning in. "Since we'll be working together," I said, off the cuff, "I'll select a few possible recipes and create a poll on my blog. The recipe with the most votes will be the one we work on next." I nodded, the smile becoming genuine as a new realization settled in. My followers and I were slowly becoming an online baking community.

"Until then," I said, another bout of improv erupting, "you might like this trick I learned from my great-aunts. I call it salad on-the-go and it's great for a quick, healthy snack or lunch. Easy to pack for a picnic or take to a covered dish." I hurried to my fridge, camera bobbing in my hand. "Hang on." I propped my phone against a row of clean mason jars, then grabbed an armload of ingredients and spun back to line them on the counter.

"Ready? Take some sturdy romaine hearts and line them up." I arranged a row of leaves in the camera's view, then popped the lids off several containers of chopped veggies. "Add diced tomatoes, bell peppers, cucumbers, and anything else your leaf can hold, then sprinkle on the feta cheese, drizzle with dressing, and enjoy." I lifted a gluttonously overfilled romaine leaf, feeling smart and fancy. Then I winked obnoxiously at the camera like a cheesy commercial actress. The ingredients toppled down the front of my shirt before I could take a bite, splatting against my chest and plopping on the floor while dressing slid into my bra.

I bit back a curse as my eyes found the still-streaming camera. I forced a smile, snatched my phone off the counter, and crammed my thumb against the End button without saying a proper goodbye to anyone out there watching my personal humiliation.

I wiped the veggies off my chest and floor, thankful the bulk of falling foods had hit my skin instead of my shirt. I wouldn't need to change, but I'd be picking olives from my cleavage for days. I wet a rag and rubbed it against the material of my shirt, removing physical evidence of my faux pas. If only I could delete the livestream...or at least edit my idiocy from the end.

No more impromptu streaming! I was far too clumsy and ridiculous for a live feed. I required editing.

The front door opened, and I froze. It wasn't time for my aunts to come, and I'd turned the Closed sign over. "Hello?" I called, tucking myself behind the half-open bathroom door, phone in hand for quick emergency dialing.

"Everly?" Denise's voice relieved me to the core.

I released a gust of held breath and felt my head go light.

"Why are you closed? Is everything okay? It's not even six," she said, stepping cautiously through the archway, her back angled to the wall so that the entire café before her and the foyer behind her would be visible or in her periphery. The calculated move struck another nerve in me, and I watched her with deep curiosity.

"I'm here," I said softly, stepping into view.

Her posture changed slightly, becoming more natural while clearly still on alert.

I wasn't sure where Senator Denver had found Denise, but I would've bet my family recipes it hadn't been with any kind of actual childcare organization.

"Everything okay?" she repeated.

"Mm hmm. Just getting through the day," I said. "My aunts are coming for dinner, but the café was empty so I decided to close early."

"I don't blame you," she said. "You need a little time for yourself. It's been a bad week." Denise made a lap around the room, pretending to look out the windows while her gaze traveled over every square inch of the café. "I'm glad your aunts are coming."

She peeked behind the counter, then opened the pantry and shut it. "Have you seen my sunglasses?" she asked casually.

"No."

She headed into the former ballroom and I followed. When she turned back abruptly, we nearly collided.

"Find them?" I asked.

She smiled, looking significantly more at ease. "I guess I'll check my car again. How about you? You want to talk about it?"

"About losing your sunglasses?" I asked.

"No. Your morning," she said. "You've been on my mind since I left today."

"I'm okay," I said. "Really."

Denise moved around me to peer through the nearest window. A moment later she turned and marched purposefully back toward the foyer. "I'm glad you're feeling better. I think I'll go check my car for those glasses."

"Okay." I dragged the word out, wondering if she realized how hinky she was behaving. "I guess I'll walk you out."

"Nope." She lifted a flat palm in my direction like a traffic cop, then smiled sweetly. "I've got this. You probably have lots to do before your aunts arrive. I'll leave you to it, and I'll just see you tomorrow."

I nodded in silent agreement, but curiosity pulled me along in her wake. I watched as she jogged down the porch steps and turned for my gardens. "Well,

what do you know?" I said. "There are my aunts now."
I waved an arm overhead in greeting as they moved up
the boardwalk in our direction.

Denise smiled and waved when they approached,
then rushed us all inside while she brought up the rear.
"I just had a wonderful idea. I'll serve dinner so Everly
can get off her feet and visit."

I let my aunts pass me in the foyer, then turned
back to Denise as she approached the open front door.
"I'm glad you've decided to stay for dinner, but you
don't have to serve us. We're off the clock. Join us. Be
my guest."

Before Denise could respond, Ryan popped into
view on the porch behind her, waving a Chatsworth-
Vanders for Mayor sign in one hand and wearing a
goofy grin on his face. "Put your hands up," he said,
lifting the opposite fist in the air.

I didn't have time to read the sign before Denise
spun on him, cranking his arm behind his back and
smashing him facedown with grace and precision.
She pressed one knee into his back, and Ryan made a
gurgling sound as the breath left him.

"Holy yikes!" I yipped, falling onto my knees
beside them. "It's Ryan," I said, latching onto Denise's
arm. "It's okay."

He sucked air as she shifted off him.

Denise's face turned dark shades of red as Ryan
flopped onto his back and lifted the sign. An enlarged
photo of Mary Grace and Chairman Vanders centered
the blue border. Their joined hands lifted, showcasing

her giant engagement ring beneath the stupid slogan Hands Up for Progress.

"Put your hands up," Ryan said, a pained smile on his face, "for progress."

"I'm so sorry." Denise offered a hand to help him up, but Ryan's narrow-eyed expression clearly stated, *I'll pass.*

She took a step back. "Right. Of course." Her cheeks glowed scarlet as she moved down the steps.

Ryan stretched to his feet, then helped me up.

My mind was too busy sorting the blurred images of Denise flattening a man twice her size to think of getting up on my own.

I stared at her as she retreated. The hairs on my arms stood at attention. "Where'd you learn to do that?" I asked.

"College," she said swiftly, well-practiced. Her feet hit the ground, and she took a step backward. "Mandatory self-defense training, freshman year. I guess it took."

Ryan chuckled, dusting himself off. "I guess so."

My aunts moved onto the porch with us, looking puzzled. "What happened?" Aunt Clara asked.

I kept my eyes on Denise, unwilling to be distracted. "I don't think you've ever told me where you went to college," I said. "Was it in Virginia?" I hated to be rude or pushy about personal details, but now that the proverbial can of worms had been breached, I might as well get it open.

She released a long breath, shooting another

remorseful look in Ryan's direction. "I'm really sorry. I get jumpy when men tell me to put my hands up. That's all. I should go." She turned and left before I could pose any follow-up questions, but I was certain she hadn't perfected a full-body takedown during freshman self-defense training.

So why had she lied?

CHAPTER

❧

FIFTEEN

R yan joined my aunts and me in the café. I handed him a bag of frozen peas for whatever body parts might be hurting, then turned to my aunts, who looked a little shell-shocked.

"I'm so glad you're here. Thank you for coming to dinner." I wrapped my arms around them and squeezed.

Aunt Clara patted my cheek. "We would never miss a chance to visit with you."

"Or eat your dinner," Aunt Fran added, wiggling free to assess my expression. "How are you feeling? And what the heck just happened on your porch?"

"I'm edgy and a little sore," I said. "Also, I think Denise is a trained spy or assassin of some sort hired to act as a nanny unless the need to protect her charge arises, at which time I'm mostly certain no one will ever see that person again. Can I get you a cup of tea?"

Aunt Clara's mouth fell open.

"I can see it," Ryan said, arranging the peas over his shoulder.

The trio followed me to the counter. I went around to the business side and found a pair of aspirin for Ryan in the first aid kit I kept on hand.

Aunt Fran made her way to the tea dispensers. "I'll pour the drinks. You make the food. I'm starving and not in a very good mood."

"Deal." I pulled supplies from the cupboards and refrigerator. "How do scallops and asparagus sound?" Hopefully good because I didn't have a backup plan or the brainpower to think of one. My mind kept replaying Ryan being flipped off his feet. It was emotionally confusing because I liked seeing shock on his smug face for a change, but I hated that he'd been hurt, even if it was only a little.

Aunt Fran set two full jars of tea on the counter, then turned back to fill two more. "Anything you make sounds like heaven," she said.

Aunt Clara and Ryan each grabbed a barstool and added their agreement.

"How are the rum cake orders coming?" Aunt Clara asked. "Are you still taking orders?"

I grimaced. "No." I'd removed the Order button from my website while I was online researching for the Mitzi case. "I've got my hands full until Grady catches this killer and my life gets back to normal. After that, I'm thinking of only making rum cakes available seasonally, like the holiday cookies." I loved the added praise for my work and exposure for my brand, but I was only one person. Even with Denise helping at Sun, Sand, and Tea most mornings, I barely kept up with my life. I couldn't afford to hire more help, and the small savings I'd accumulated needed to go to home repairs or expansion efforts.

Fran rubbed my back. "You'll figure it out."

I hoped she was right and changed the subject before I got depressed. "Were you guys able to get any good footage for the documentary today?" I asked my aunts as I prepared and heated my pans.

"Some," Aunt Clara said, "but it was hard to concentrate on Rose's directions after what happened to you. Our hearts just weren't in it."

I smiled. "I'm okay, but thanks for worrying about me." I tossed scallops into a heated pan to brown and ran the asparagus under cold water. "How did things go before I was locked in the archives?"

"So-so," Aunt Clara said. "Rose spent a lot of time prepping her free help on what was expected of them."

Aunt Fran took the stool beside her sister and rolled her eyes. "It was a lot of wasted time if you ask me." She set the next pair of iced teas on the counter, one in front of each of us. "Rose is more interested in the fans' reaction to Mitzi's death and their appearance here than she is in saving honeybees. It's as if she doesn't even care that they'll all be gone soon if we don't do something to help them."

Aunt Clara patted her sister's arm. "I'm sure Rose will get to that part of the filming soon," she said, not looking sure at all. She turned her gaze on me, brows high.

"Was the store as crowded today?" I asked,

assuming she wanted a new subject. I didn't blame her. Aunt Clara and I did our best to avoid uncomfortable topics and situations. Aunt Fran usually let us.

"The store was fine," Aunt Fran said flatly. "I want to know about you."

"Me too," Aunt Clara said. "And don't say you're fine again," she added before I could get the words out.

I settled the asparagus into an empty pan, then loaded the scallop pan with butter to brown. A monsoon of thoughts and emotions raged through me as I turned the asparagus and added the lemon cream sauce I'd whipped up earlier while reading online.

"Well," Aunt Fran pressed. "Tell me you have some kind of lead on Mitzi's killer."

"What?" My eyes widened and I craned my neck for a look at her, while trying not to burn my meal. "I thought you didn't want me to get involved."

"We don't," Aunt Clara said.

"But we know you," Aunt Fran said. "You're involved and you're in danger. Now, we don't care who finds this lunatic as long as they do it fast and you aren't attacked again."

I exhaled a sigh of relief, and Ryan lifted a thumbs-up in my direction. "I feel the same way," I said. "I spent most of the afternoon doing online research. I read everything I could about Mitzi's ex-husband, Malcolm Pierce, and his daughter, Odette. Then I read a bunch of fan sites. It was interesting but I didn't learn anything useful."

Aunt Fran got up again. She came around to help me plate the scallops and asparagus. "You'll find something. You always do, and we're here to help if you need us."

"Me too," Ryan said. "Don't forget what an excellent team we make."

"We were never a team," I said. "We were both captured while investigating the crime individually. It was kind of a train wreck."

"Individually," he said. "That was the problem. This time we'll avoid all that mess and work together from the start."

I removed the pans from the heat and gave them each a little shake to keep the contents from sticking. "Have you had a chance to review the photos you took in Wyatt's office?" I asked.

"Absolutely," he said. "At least fifty good shots."

"And?"

Ryan cleared his throat. "I didn't see any obvious clues, but now that I have the photos, I can refer to them as things come up."

I rolled my eyes. "Uh huh."

Aunt Fran lined the counter with dishes. I followed with the scallop pan, shoveling tender, buttery morsels from my pan onto the waiting plates.

"Everything smells delicious," Aunt Clara cooed as the scents filled the room. "You are a truly gifted chef."

"Thanks." I savored the compliment and allowed it to fill my sails. Much as I enjoyed food, compliments about the food I made were my true sustenance. A single praise like hers would buoy me for hours. "Tell me more about Rose and the taping. Do you think she's still making the honeybee movie?" I left the thought unspoken, but wondered: *Could the whole thing have been a guise to raise money for the film she really wanted to make—a documentary on the aftermath of a celebrity's murder?*

"She taped a little on the way to Blessed Bee," Aunt Fran said, ferrying completed plates to Aunt Clara and Ryan. I followed with plates for Aunt Fran and me.

Aunt Clara frowned. "A bunch of fans showed up when we were leaving for the shop and followed us to work. They nagged Rose for spots on the documentary crew, and she ate up the attention."

"That's what she filmed for the rest of the day," Aunt Fran said. "Fans. Not us."

"Rose says the reason for the extra publicity on this film is unfortunate, but it'll lead to more people viewing the honeybee film, and that means more awareness. So it would be unwise not to take advantage," Aunt Clara added.

I speared a scallop with my fork and dragged it through a sea of browned butter, enjoying the warm, rich scents as they mingled in the air. "Do you think it's possible Rose could have planned this?" I pushed the bite into my mouth before saying more. I wanted my guests to have a chance to answer. I was positive Ryan would have an opinion on the matter.

Aunt Clara looked alarmed. "What do you mean?"

Ryan's smarmy expression said he knew exactly

what I was getting at. "Everly wonders if Rose is the sort of person who'd murder for this kind of attention. It certainly stands to further her career if she's any good at documenting all this. While everyone is telling the mainstream reporters to butt out and show respect, Rose is positioned deep in the mix and welcomed here."

"And honestly," I said, "I'm not sure how much she cares about the bees. I get the impression she's more of an artist than a bee-saver. Maybe this documentary was supposed to be her big break into the world of filmmaking."

Ryan lifted his tea and paused, seeming to consider my theory. "The industry is brutal. Aspiring producers and directors need some extreme luck or a miracle to make it in the business."

Aunt Fran set her fork aside. "Are you saying we've been spending our days with a murderer?"

"No." I nibbled on a bite of asparagus, enjoying the tang of lemon I'd added to the cream sauce. "Maybe," I adjusted, rethinking the theory. I turned to Ryan. "If the industry is tough to break into, then working with Mitzi could have been Rose's big break."

He nodded. "Any professional connection to a star of Mitzi's caliber would be priceless for the networking and name-dropping alone."

"Would chronicling the aftermath of Mitzi's death be enough to propel Rose's film career?" I asked. "Or would Mitzi have been more important to her alive?"

"Oh dear," Aunt Clara said, setting her fork aside and resting a palm on her middle.

"Sorry," I said. "I know this isn't exactly the most dinner-appropriate conversation, but I have to get this out of my head before it explodes.

She nodded warily, waving a forgiving palm. "I'm fine. Go on."

Ryan set his nearly empty tea jar aside and lifted his fork. "So, the killer could be Rose. Who else?"

"Mitzi's ex-husband," I said. I filled them in on what little I knew about the pending divorce, his investment in the film, and his recent trip to the island. None of it was a smoking gun, of course. For all I knew, he'd wanted to reconcile.

Aunt Fran frowned. "It's always the spouse."

Ryan dotted his mouth with a napkin. "It's certainly a possibility. I've tried to talk with Mr. Pierce and Odette multiple times, but they won't answer the door for me," Ryan said. "They keep the curtains drawn, and they only leave when they have to. They get food delivered twice a day, usually salads or seafood from the diner on Bay Street. I've tracked them to the morgue and police station, but they're very good at ignoring and avoiding reporters." He gave a wry smile.

"Your cargo shorts and flip-flops didn't fool them?" I asked.

"Not for a minute. After all those years with Mitzi, they can probably smell my interest a mile away."

"Are you sure they're still here?" I asked. "I was just attacked this morning, so if they've left the island, I can mark them off my suspect list."

"They're still here," Ryan said. "I watched Odette

answer the door for a delivery at four thirty. A large pizza and another salad. Too much for one person unless she's planning leftovers for the rest of the week. Maybe I'll try knocking again in the morning."

"No, don't," I said. "Until we know what's going on, there's no reason to kick the hornets' nest."

"You don't want to get them worked up?" Ryan tented his brows. "You really don't understand journalism at all, do you?"

I ignored the jibe and swallowed my rebuttals about him knowing anything at all. "Any chance you've seen the Canary? I'd really like to know why he ran from me today."

Ryan shook his head. "Sorry."

I finished my tea and the last of my asparagus. No one I'd asked had seen the Canary since he'd run away. So was he long gone, in hiding, or neither? Normally a six-foot man who dressed like a villain from Victorian England would've been easy to spot, but all the *Blackbeard's Wife* fans made a perfect camouflage for him.

Aunt Fran carried her empty plate to the sink. "Thank you, Everly. This was just as delicious as it smelled, maybe better, and the conversation is never dull."

"Thanks." I beamed. "Can I pack the leftovers to send home with you?"

"Already on it," she said, selecting to-go containers from my cupboard. When she turned back to face us, her attention stuck on Ryan. "I've been meaning to ask where you found that catastrophe of an election sign you had outside."

"On the courthouse lawn. I saw them on my way over here and stole one for Everly. I thought she'd get a kick out of it," Ryan said.

Aunt Fran turned to me then, scowling.

"I didn't get a kick out of it," I said. In fact, I'd nearly forgotten about the dumb sign. "Mary Grace is the worst, and Chairman Vanders isn't any better. I can't believe they're getting married. Are they running for office together too?" The idea was beyond horrific. "Getting married is probably their harebrained attempt to become a political power couple." I imagined them in coordinating suits at campaign rallies and suppressed the urge to gag.

"They might not be wrong," Aunt Fran said. "Two is often better than one, and some folks like Vanders for mayor while others prefer Mary Grace. Now they'll get both sets of votes. What about Senator Denver?" Aunt Fran asked. "Is she still running?"

I bit my lip. I wasn't sure. "I'll ask Grady the next time we talk."

Aunt Clara collected my plate, then Ryan's, and took them with hers to the sink. "We should go to the Chatsworth-Vanders wedding reception together."

"I'm in," Ryan said.

"You won't even be here," I said.

"I will," he retorted proudly. "I'm Amelia's plus-one."

I spun my stool until I faced him. "Why would

you fly back here from New York just to attend the reception of two morons?"

"For Amelia," he said slowly, then wiggled his eyebrows.

I shut my eyes against whatever his eyebrows were implying.

"You know," Ryan said, "dragging Blessed Bee into a murder investigation, even peripherally, could have been terrible for your business and your reputation."

"But it's not," Aunt Fran said. "Business is booming. We're low on everything."

"But," he said, lifting a finger, "it could have gone the other way. People could have been turned off by the bees that stung their heroine to death and boycotted your products until you went broke," he said.

Aunt Clara bristled, nearly dropping the stack of plates she'd been rinsing. "Our bees did not sting her to death."

"Hear me out," Ryan said. "This makes the second murder in under six months with you in close range. It could have made for some really ugly press. Maybe even incited some questionable feelings toward you as a mayoral candidate. Anyone with motivation could have attempted to use this to create doubts about your character before the election."

Aunt Fran crossed her arms. "You think Mary Grace killed a beloved silver screen icon to make me look bad?"

He shrugged. "Not necessarily. I'm just asking questions. Floating possibilities. And you're right about your bees not killing her." He moved his gaze to Aunt Clara. "I spoke with the coroner's assistant yesterday and confirmed that she was given a sedative before being dumped into the demonstration box."

I nodded, seeing where he was going. "Grady told me the sedative interacted with her prescription medications and killed her, but that wasn't public knowledge. And I read everything I could about Mitzi last night. There wasn't any mention of her bee allergy, either."

"So the whole thing could've been a fluke," Ryan said. "Assuming the person who injected her didn't know about her prescriptions or hadn't predicted the results of mixing them with the sedative, and most wouldn't, her death could've been a horrible accident."

"Or," I suggested, "We've just limited our suspect pool to those in Mitzi's inner circle. People who had personal knowledge of her health conditions. A spouse and personal assistant, for example."

"Don't forget the Canary," Ryan said. "He knew everything about her."

That was true enough. Hadn't he told me he kept one man on the inside at all times?

Aunt Clara shifted on her seat, looking paler than usual. "But if the injection was expected to kill her, why bother dumping her with the bees?"

Ryan shrugged. "To cover the fact that they knew the sedative would kill her? Maybe to try to cover the needle's injection site? And if the killer didn't antici-pate the interactions of the medication, the sedative could have simply been used to get her into the box."

"But why?" my aunts asked in near unison.

"Stings are painful," Ryan said, "and being found doped up and covered in honey is humiliating. Maybe she had an enemy who wanted to punish or ruin her."

I considered that a moment. "What if this wasn't about Mitzi at all? What if someone had just wanted to ruin the show and ended up a murderer?"

"Awful," Aunt Clara said. "How could anyone live with a truth like that?"

My guess was that the culprit would run. *Or hide.*

CHAPTER

SIXTEEN

I fell asleep on my couch, waiting for the nightly news. One minute my mind was racing over possible suspects, stolen files, and bees in the archives. The next minute my phone was buzzing on the coffee table and I was dragging my eyes open, trying to remember why I was on the couch. My heart seized at the sight of Grady's number on the phone screen. He rarely messaged me without a prompt, and I could only imagine what new and awful thing had happened now.

I swiveled upright and grabbed the phone to read his message. Was someone else dead? Were my aunts in trouble?

Are you awake?

Kind of, I thought. *Now that he woke me.* I rubbed sleep from my eyes and raked shaky fingers through my tangled hair.

Yes.

I lied, panic and curiosity already winding me up.

Grady's response was immediate.

Can I come up?

"Up?" I asked the empty room. *Not over?* As if he was already... *Oh no.* I ran to the window over-looking my front porch and spotted his truck in the driveway. *Shoot!* I made a mad dash for the bathroom and attempted to brush my teeth and hair at the same time. It was the adult equivalent of rub your head and pat your belly, and I wasn't any better at it today than I had been twenty years ago. My brush was momen-tarily stuck in my hair as a result. I let it hang there while I rinsed and spat, then went back to freeing the brush. I ran a washcloth over my face and balm across my lips, then grabbed an elastic band on my way to the steps, wrangling my wild hair into a ponytail as I fumbled to the foyer on sleepy legs.

I greeted Grady with a cautious smile, unsure if the news he'd come to deliver was the sort that warranted one. "Come in."

He followed me back up to my living quarters, and I set a kettle on for tea.

"Make yourself at home," I said. "Are you hungry?"

His mouth said "No" but his stomach growled, giving away the lie.

"Okay," I said, pulling sliced ham and cheese from the refrigerator and selecting a loaf of fresh baked bread from the pantry. I hit the preheat button on my oven before turning to face him. "What's up?"

Grady's gaze jumped from my bare legs to my eyes when I turned. He had his black cowboy hat in hand, held close to his chest, and for a moment I thought someone else really had died.

"Grady?"

"Denise told me what happened today. With Ryan," he added for clarification, as if anything else Denise had done today warranted a late night face-to-face.

"And you're here why?" I asked. To apologize for his au pair's behavior? Explain it away? How was that his responsibility? And why did he think the event needed further discussion—unless there was more to the story, as I'd suspected.

"A couple reasons." He watched me for a long beat before speaking again. "We know Mr. Butters separated from Wyatt and Amelia before the luncheon. He was caught, alone, on the security feed from the police station camera."

My pulse leapt. "He forgot, or he would've said something sooner. He left you a voicemail. I was there. I heard him."

Grady furrowed his brow. "Doesn't change the fact he omitted a very important piece of personally damning information during questioning in a murder investigation. And while you're thinking it's nice he called as soon as he remembered, he now has no alibi for the time of Mitzi's death. And taking a day to get his story straight is right out of a criminal's handbook."

I narrowed my eyes at him. "Mr. Butters didn't do this, and any amount of time you're wasting looking at him is time lost for locating the true killer." I felt my head begin to bob in a slow nod. "This is exactly why I get involved. I know him. These people. This town. And I have a sixth sense about folks. My aunts always say so."

Grady's lips twitched as he rubbed his forehead.

I could practically hear his thoughts. My great-aunts believed all sorts of things and none of those were true either.

"I'm just letting you know because you've got a personal interest in the Butterses. But that's not why I'm here," he said. "You mentioned before that I haven't been myself lately, and I feel as if I owe you an explanation."

A bubble of anticipation replaced the anger coiling in my stomach, and I bit my lip against an upbring-ing of Southern manners that demanded I tell him he didn't owe me anything. Which he didn't. But Grady had come to tell me something private. Something personal. He wanted to bring me into his confidence, and I was desperate to know anything he wanted me to know, plus a long list of things he didn't. "Go on."

Grady ran his fingers along the line of his jaw. "Olivia didn't really come to the island to be closer to Denver."

Well, that was a letdown. I'd thought I was going to have my suspicions of Denise's true identity con-firmed. Russian spy? MI6? Covert operative for a foreign dignitary? Avenger? I reset my thoughts to Olivia while assembling an award-worthy sandwich and smearing garlic butter across the top. I slid the masterpiece into my oven on a cookie sheet, then turned to face Grady directly. "So, why did she really come here?" I asked, hoping it hadn't been to drag him back to Arlington as he'd suspected before.

Grady's jaw popped and locked. He set his hat on the island between us, looking torn and unsure.

"You can tell me," I said, locking his conflicted gray eyes with mine. "I won't tell anyone, and I'd really like to know what's been going on with you. I worry."

"I know," Grady said. He released a steadying breath. "Olivia was contacted by her party's next presidential hopeful last year. He asked for her backing on a significantly controversial bill, and she agreed."

The teapot whistled softly, and I nearly knocked it off the stove. "What kind of bill?"

Grady took a seat at my kitchen island and folded his hands on the counter. "She didn't say, and I didn't ask. I assumed it was run-of-the mill petty politics."

In complete confusion, I poured two mugs of steaming tea, then returned the kettle and set the drinks on the island. "So, you're saying Senator Denver moved to Charm because she was asked to support a controversial bill? Maybe I'm still asleep, but isn't it more important that she be in DC where she can support the thing, whatever it is?"

"I thought you said you were awake when I got here."

I rolled my eyes. "Let's focus, please."

He scrutinized my face for another long beat before moving on. "There's been a complication with her agreement. The truth is that she moved here to be closer to me, and she bought Northrop Manor for its Fort Knox–grade security potential. Plus, the additional buildings on-site that are suitable for housing an extensive security detail."

"I thought those were for her household staff," I said. That had been his story at Christmas.

"There's plenty of room for household staff in the manor. It has twenty-six rooms."

Olivia had made up a cover story to move here, all because she'd agreed to support an unpopular bill and her party's next presidential candidate? I sipped the tea and pretended to process calmly while my insides screamed WHAT AM I MISSING? My mind was officially boggled. "I still don't know why she needs to be near you or why she needs the extensive security."

Grady gripped his cup without lifting it, running the pads of his thumbs along the handle. "It's because she's been receiving death threats since she was announced as a supporter."

"And she wants to be near you so you can protect her too?" I guessed.

He gave a small, defeated laugh. "She wanted me to find her husband using connections I made during my time with the Marshals Service. Everything Olivia does is about Olivia, and there's always more to what she says than is on the surface. It's the reason she and I never got along, and the one thing that caused a wedge between Amy and me. Amy refused to see her mother as anything less than perfect. Wouldn't acknowledge her selfishness or manipulation."

He rolled angry eyes in my direction, and I saw the thing he wouldn't say. Now Amy was dead, and he was stuck here, dealing with her mother, for the rest of his life. Only now, he had to do it without Amy as a buffer. He was angry with her for leaving him like this—and ashamed of himself for being angry with her.

"And you found him," I said, turning the conversation to what I hoped was a happier topic. A small measure of relief moved through me as I spoke the words. I didn't know the man in question, but I loved Denver, and I wanted him to have a grandpa. "That's good news."

Grady sucked his teeth. "Saying he'd gone missing was all part of the cover story. Apparently, he and Olivia stayed in touch somehow. She says they passed infrequent messages via some system they'd used when they were both in the military. She told him about the threats, and he wanted to be here to protect her. He started skirting protocols because he's worried about her. He lost his focus and that made her worry about him. Losing focus could get him killed. She knows it, so she asked me to find him and promise him I would personally assure her safety so he could refocus and live to finish the job at hand. Apparently he wasn't taking her word for it."

I wanted to smack her. Moving here "to be closer to her grandson" had all been an elaborate façade?

Part of a bigger plan. A means to a selfish end. What was wrong with people? "When did you find him?" I asked, presuming that was somehow one more part of Grady's mounting stress.

"In January. And if I could find him, then someone much more dangerous could as well."

My cheeks heated with unexpected anger as I yanked the oven door open with unnecessary force and liberated the hot ham and cheese sandwich. "Let me get this straight," I said, moving the sandwich to a plate and garnishing it with chips and a pickle wedge. "She put you and her grandson in danger so she could keep herself and her husband, a trained CIA operative, safe? Now you and Denver are living unprotected lives while she lives in a fortress with a full security detail?"

"I'm not exactly untrained and helpless," he said, looking severely offended. "I know how to protect myself, and there's nothing I wouldn't do to keep Denver safe. You know that."

"I do, but you can't be everywhere at once. You're only one person, and you've got too much on your plate already." I pulled my lips to the side, suddenly seeing his point about not being able to protect everyone he cares about. I took a steadying breath, then offered an apologetic glance. "I didn't mean to insinuate that you're helpless."

The truth was, I didn't know much about Grady's background except that he'd been a shooting star at the U.S. Marshals Service until Amy died and he eventually moved here with Denver to regroup and heal. He'd mentioned his military service in the past, using careful and vague references, but I understood. Protecting people was in Grady's blood. It was his passion, and he was good at it. My heart softened as the depth of pain and frustration on his face fully registered. "Here. Eat," I said, sliding the plate in his direction. "There's lemon cake afterward if you have room."

"Thanks, Everly," he said, his voice low and gravelly.

I sighed, searching for peace and positivity in the solemn moment. It occurred to me then that the senator had a literal team of security at her disposal, but she'd moved here so Grady could watch over her and help find her husband. I suddenly suspected I didn't know the half of Grady's skills and capabilities. I watched as he let his eyes shut while he chewed, lost in the gooey, salty bliss. "So," I asked, going for casual since he'd voluntarily told me so much already, "where'd you find your father-in-law?"

"That's classified," he said, eyes popping open as he struggled to form the words around a mouthful of sandwich.

I frowned and stole a chip from his plate.

Grady wiped his mouth and narrowed his eyes on me. "How are you holding up after your second attack this week, by yet another deranged lunatic?"

I licked salt from my bottom lip, in no mood to talk about me when I could finally learn more about him. "I'm fine, but I don't think you're allowed to call them deranged or lunatics," I said with a teasing grin. "They're people too, so you have to be sensitive."

"Is that right?"

"Sure. Even homicidal wackadoos have rights."

Grady snorted a short laugh, then finished off his sandwich. "I think you're the wackadoo," he said. "How the heck do you keep getting wound up in these things?"

"Small island?" I guessed.

He deflated and flicked a warm expression in my direction. His gaze ran steadily over me before settling back on my eyes. "Maybe I'm the wackadoo," he said, almost to himself. "What kind of lawman gets involved with a crime magnet?"

"You mispronounced delightful iced tea shop owner," I said, smiling stupidly at the idea he thought we were involved and the wonder at how lovely that would be.

He smiled. "Okay. Since I brought it up, have you uncovered anything on this investigation of yours that you want to share?"

"Maybe," I admitted, recalling my discussion with Ryan about the sedative and bee stings. "Do you think there's a chance Mitzi's death was a tragic accident? Maybe the killer hadn't meant to be a killer at all. Someone could have administered the drugs hoping to embarrass her or ruin the documentary but not kill her, and it went horribly wrong."

"It's possible," Grady said, "but she died, and whoever did it, whatever their intention may have been, is the only one to blame for a life lost. That person needs to face the consequences. And before you feel too badly about a possible fluke, remember that drugging someone is a crime, and Mitzi was given a heavy sedative intentionally and by injection. It wasn't sprinkled on her food or put in her drink. Someone got close to her and jammed a needle in her neck. It was a planned attack and the results were deadly."

A shiver rolled down my spine as I imagined the scenario playing out. Mitzi's shock, the pain of injection, the confusion as the drug took over, her fear as she was hauled toward the bees. I never wanted to know what that felt like. "Were you able to find out who called her that day?" I asked. "Or anything more about the number leaving text messages for me?"

"Yeah," he said. "Three numbers. Three disposable phones. We were able to track their purchases to an Eagles Beachwear and Souvenir shop in Hilton Head."

"Can you track them?" I asked, feeling buoyant for news of a solid lead.

"No. Each phone dialed one number. One time," he said.

"And now they're probably at the bottom of the ocean," I concluded.

"Sounds about right." Grady straightened and shifted on the stool at the bar. He pulled his phone from his pocket and frowned at it. "I've got to go." He wiped his hands and mouth on a napkin, then left it on the empty plate.

"Wait." I set a hand on his arm, effectively

anchoring him in place. "What about Denise? You said you heard what happened with her and Ryan today, but you didn't explain. What was that about?"

He stretched onto his feet and took my hand in his as he towered over me. I had to turn my chin up to keep his eyes in view.

"I was just looking for an excuse to see you. I knew it was late, but you'd be curious enough to let me in." His lips curved into an impish grin. "Sorry."

Heat flooded my chest as I squeezed his hand in mine. "I will always let you in, Grady Hays." My voice was too breathy. The chemistry thrumming between us too intense. "You don't have to have a reason to visit."

His gaze darkened and moved to my mouth. Then he released my hand and took a step back. "I have to go."

I nodded, unable to speak.

I followed him down the steps and back through the foyer. "If the topic ever comes up," I told his back as we made our way to the front door, "you can tell her I didn't believe for a minute that she'd learned to flip grown men like that in a mandatory freshman self-defense class."

Grady chuckled. He turned back as he opened the door. "That's what she said?"

"Yes, as if I were a complete idiot."

Grady laughed again. "Trust me. No one thinks you're an idiot, especially Denise."

His phone buzzed in his pocket and his smile fell.

He took it out to glare at the screen. "I've really got to go."

I walked him onto the porch. "I don't even know where she went to college," I called as he wrenched his truck door open.

Grady climbed behind the wheel and started the engine. He hung an elbow out the open window and smiled. "She went to Georgetown."

⟍◦⟋

I practically scurried out the door the next morning after a few awkward minutes of conversation with Denise. It was evident in the strain of her smile and set of her chin that she was still feeling uncomfortable about the way we left things after she'd taken Ryan down. I could understand. She'd done a crazy thing and hadn't given a true explanation, but I believed she was sorry, and that was all that mattered. She had instinctively responded to a perceived threat, and if Ryan had been an attacker, Denise would have saved us all. Hard to be mad at that. Plus, everyone was entitled to secrets, whether I liked it or not.

I excused myself as soon as politely possible and headed out to look for Ryan. He'd put a bee in my bonnet yesterday about the possibility of Mary Grace and her fiancé attempting a stunt to make Aunt Fran look bad and accidentally killing Mitzi in the process. I wouldn't put anything past either of them, and together they were twice as dense, so I figured it was worth following up. Also, Ryan had seen Odette answer the door and collect a large pizza, but that didn't mean her father was there or even still on the island. I wanted to pinpoint his whereabouts during my archive fiasco as well. I needed to eliminate someone from my crowded suspect pool before it overflowed. And more than anything, I needed to direct Grady and the local PD's attention away from Mr. Butters.

I followed the boardwalk until it curved close to Ocean Drive, then I hopped across the fallen log over the marsh and onto the grassy shoulder to survey Main Street. The streets were awash with morning sunlight, food trucks, and faces I didn't recognize, likely Mitzi fans. I didn't see the Canary, and I wasn't sure what I'd say to Odette or her father if I saw them, so I directed my path toward the courthouse instead. Chairman Vanders was the acting mayor until our fall election and spent his days in the mayor's office. I suspected I'd find his scheming fiancée with him.

I paused when a pair of silhouettes at the edge of the courthouse came into focus. A couple, I thought, before recognizing Mary Grace as the woman. I'd never seen the man before. I reconsidered my plans to ask Vanders where he'd been when Mitzi died, and I watched Mary Grace instead. She stood close to the guy, whoever he was, face-to-face along the alley-side of the building, their faces nearly cloaked in shadow. I drifted closer to listen in, but they began to move.

I lingered in the shade of an ancient oak until they reached the next block, then I followed. I could always come back to visit Vanders after I figured out what Mary Grace was up to. The pair strode briskly toward the bay, chatting fervently, their voices low. My mind raced with questions. Who could the man be? Not a local. Had she and Vanders hired an outside campaign manager? Was the guy her secret boyfriend? A hired gun? *A cleaner?* All the big bosses on crime shows had one of those. An unassuming person who scrubbed crime scenes and swept criminal misdeeds under the rug. This guy looked the part. Tall and lean with broad shoulders in a classic black dress shirt and trousers. His dark hair was slicked back with product and his eyes were covered with wide, dark-rimmed sunglasses.

They jaywalked across Bay Street and ducked into a newly renovated historic home. A promotional sign in the front yard announced it as the work of a local construction and design company. Were they meeting someone else? Had I stumbled onto a clandestine encounter? I dashed across the street at the crosswalk, then slipped into the house a minute behind Mary Grace.

The home's interior was lavish. I paused to enjoy the subtle, spa-like quality. Soft music wafted from hidden speakers. Sunlight filtered through an abundance of beveled glass windows, bouncing and glinting rainbowed beams across the walls. Marble floors stretched out before me to the base of a cantilevered staircase, and I moved in its direction. Elaborate tapestries adorned doorways and intricately detailed molding outlined the ceilings and the floors.

Mary Grace's soft voice pulled me deeper into the home. "Precisely," she whispered. "We need a plan. Cleanup won't be easy, and it has to be handled properly, thoroughly, and preferably without notice."

Breath caught in my throat. Had I been right? Was Mary Grace behind Mitzi's murder? I hunched low and crept closer, listening hard for something substantial I could take to Grady and have her arrested.

"Get in and get out," Mary Grace said.

"Got it," the man replied. "I'll make arrangements now."

The room fell silent and I took another step, angling for view around the threshold.

Mary Grace looked immediately at my face.

"Everly?" she asked, her expression pinching in confusion. "What are you doing?"

The man glared. "Were you listening to us?" He took a step in my direction. "How long have you been there? What did you hear?"

I straightened, hoping to look braver than I felt. "I heard everything, and I've already called Detective Hays," I lied.

"Who?" he asked, still scowling.

Mary Grace cocked a hip. "What did you hear?" she repeated his question, emphasizing every word.

The man looked at Mary Grace with disgust. "I

can see what you were talking about. These people are nosy."

"Yeah, and this one's the worst," Mary Grace said. "And she's clearly lost her mind if she thinks the police care about my reception plans."

"You do realize stalking is illegal?" the man asked, slowly, as if there was something wrong with my IQ.

Mary Grace chuckled, then sneered. "She can't help it. She's from a really messed-up gene pool. No men. Just inbreeding and hocus pocus."

I let the dig on my gene pool slide while I ran over the conversation going on in front of me. "You're a wedding planner?" I asked the broad-shouldered man in black.

He looked at me as if I were something stuck to his shoe. "What did you think I was?"

I swallowed a lump of humiliation in my throat.

Mary Grace narrowed her eyes. "Good question. What did you think we were talking about? Why were you following me? What's wrong with you?" Mary Grace snapped. "Did you forget to take your medication this morning?"

I opened my mouth and nothing came out. I was eleven all over again and humiliated by her sharp tongue, dull wit, and harsh words. I had no comebacks. No reasonable explanation. Just nausea and panic. So, I did the only thing I could do.

I lifted my chin, turned on my heels, and headed out the way I'd come in.

I knocked into Ryan, waiting on the home's front

porch, red-faced and teary-eyed with laughter. He performed a dramatic slow clap for me as I climbed down the front steps.

"Shut up," I said, picking up the pace as I headed for home.

CHAPTER

SEVENTEEN

I was certain I would die of embarrassment. I'd had no idea Ryan was following Mary Grace too, and I'd gotten between them, or I could've left him to it and spared myself the humiliation. Instead, I was heading home to lick my wounded pride, and he was off to look for Malcolm Pierce and Odette. Ryan and I agreed to catch up later and share what we'd learned so far. I hoped he had more than I did, because all I had was a pile of unsubstantiated theories, about a million questions, and a deteriorating attitude.

"Welcome to Sun, Sand, and Tea," Denise called as I crossed the foyer to the café. "Oh, hey Everly!" She smiled when she saw me. "That was fast."

"Yep. Fast," I muttered. Too bad the repercussions of my outing would last for Mary Grace's lifetime. "How are things here?" I asked, rounding the counter to pour a tall glass of strawberry basil tea and chug it.

Denise joined me at the dispensers, an apologetic

expression on her pretty face. "I'm truly sorry about what happened with Ryan last night. I didn't mean to hurt him or freak you and your aunts out. And I lied to you."

I opened my mouth to tell her not to worry, but I changed my mind at the mention of a lie. I put the tea jar to my lips instead, hoping she'd expound on the last part.

"I didn't learn hand-to-hand combat in a mandatory freshman self-defense class," she said.

I felt my eyes widen. *Did she just say hand-to-hand combat?*

"I spent years training," she continued. "I was a victim once, and afterward, I vowed never to be one again. I guess I'm a little on edge with another murderer in town."

"I think we're all a little on edge," I said, dying to know every detail about the time Denise had been a victim—and if the years of hand-to-hand combat training had been in the military—but instead, I offered a small smile. "I didn't hate watching Ryan get tossed around."

Her shoulders sagged in apparent relief. "I thought you liked Ryan. You saved his life last year."

"Yeah, but he's cocky, and I hate that in a person," I said. "Also, he's got his eye on Amelia and she really likes him, so I worry. I'm not convinced he's capable of caring for more than his career." I watched her for a long beat before adding, "I don't want him to break her heart."

"Careers are important," she said. "Time-consuming and often hard to balance with a personal life."

It sounded like something she knew from experience. "Well, with moves like yours, you can always be an undercover bodyguard if au pair work gets too dull."

Her smile dimmed before returning. "Meanwhile, no one will get anywhere near the Hays men on my watch."

I laughed—because I didn't doubt it.

A pair of rising voices caught my attention above the gentle din of afternoon chatter, and I immediately spotted the small commotion. Rose and Quinn were huddled around a laptop screen and vehemently disagreeing about something.

I eased past Denise. "I'll be right back."

I crossed the café quickly, eager for a look at the screen. They noticed my approach and paused the video. "Fancy meeting you here," I said brightly. "Everything taste okay?" I nodded to the empty plates before them. "Ready for a little dessert? Maybe some refills on your teas?"

Quinn raised a palm. "No. Thank you. It was delicious, but I'm stuffed."

Rose nodded. "Truly."

I wasn't sure if she was truly stuffed or my food was truly delicious, but I supposed one went well with the other and moved on. "How's the filming coming along?" I asked, motioning to the paused laptop screen. "Are you getting everything you need? Staying on schedule? Anything I can do to help?"

Rose pursed her lips. "We're okay. A little behind maybe, but that's only because our original schedule was tight and didn't allow for any of the things that have happened since we arrived. Mitzi, the crowds, the bee thing yesterday."

I shivered at the mention of yesterday's "bee thing."

"Online activity has picked up," Quinn said, motioning to the screen. "Bloggers and celebrity newscasters are creating a ton of negative publicity about the documentary. They want to know why we're still taping instead of halting production out of respect for Mitzi's death."

"Bad publicity is an oxymoron," Rose said through gritted teeth. It appeared as if it wasn't the first time she'd explained this and also that she thought Quinn was a regular moron. "Publicity raises awareness, and that was our goal here all along," she continued. "The only reason people are still hung up on Mitzi's connection to our documentary is because someone is leaking pictures of her death. If it weren't for the close-ups of her swollen face cropping up in every article on our film, the public would be throwing money at our project in support of Mitzi's last stand. Instead, they're using images of her death beside images of my face and making the whole thing seem scandalous. Stupid conspiracy theorists."

"I've been looking for one of those," I told Rose. "A blogger, theorist, and Mitzi superfan who calls himself

the Canary. I saw him yesterday before the bee inci-
dent, but I haven't been able to find him since. Do
you know him?"

She looked to Quinn. "Is that the guy who wanted
an exclusive from us about Mitzi's last moments?"

Quinn wrinkled his nose in distaste. "That's the
one."

Rose groaned. "That guy's the worst. He's the one
creating most of the negative hype around us. I hate
that guy. Someone should've thrown him in the bee
box instead of Mitzi."

I tried to control my expression, but my eyes
widened anyway. The flippant remark was in severely
poor taste, and I wasn't sure where to go from there. I
got out my phone and decided to switch gears. "One
more question," I said, buying time as I brought
up Mary Grace's new Facebook profile picture, an
engagement photo of her and Vanders. I turned the
screen to face Rose, then Quinn. "Do you recognize
this couple?"

"Sure," Rose said. "They welcomed us to Charm.
Delivered a basket of local products to our rental and
offered to help however they could."

I quirked a brow. "They didn't try to get you to
fill out some kind of permits for filming or shoo you
away?"

Rose frowned at me. "No, they were very nice."

Quinn made a disgusted little noise, and I turned
to him. "What?"

He shrugged. "They were very nice," he used

finger quotes around the last two words, "because they wanted something from us."

"No, they didn't." Rose bristled. "They were utterly supportive. They even gave us vouchers for meals at local restaurants and offered us the use of their personal golf cart to haul around our equipment."

"And they pitched themselves as a possible reality show," Quinn pointed out. "That was all they really wanted. To schmooze you into making them stars, as if you have that kind of power."

I gaped, unsure if I wanted to laugh or gag. "They pitched themselves as a reality show?"

Quinn's mouth twisted, fighting a smile. "They wanted to call it *The Charmed Life*," he said. "Real-life coverage of the gritty, sexy world of island politics. Told from the perspective of a husband-wife team running a small coastal town."

"Ridiculous," I said for a million reasons, most prominently because they weren't married yet and they certainly weren't running our town. Vanders was standing in as mayor until the election. Mary Grace was making desperate attempts to control her career because her home life was out of control. I knew. I'd visited her house once.

"I agree," Rose said. "I've been in town long enough to know that if there's another documentary worth making here, it would be on your family, not hers."

I blinked. "What?"

"Talking to Clara and Fran is fascinating," Rose continued. "Your family history is remarkable. Tracing your lineage back to the Salem witch trials is practically unheard-of today. And for those women to leave their home and travel all the way here, alone and unarmed, then to found this town? It's unthinkable. It's a movie waiting to happen. Add in all the related unwritten history and rumors of Swan curses, and it would be a guaranteed success. Don't even get me started on Clara's herbal remedies and world-class gardens, Fran running for office, or the sisters' beekeeping…and your dramatic return last year, this amazing tea house, and the fact you solve local crimes."

"I don't solve crimes," I said, grabbing onto the only thing I could.

"That's not what the locals say," Rose went on, her voice growing more dreamlike and airy with each word. "This town loves you, all of you Swan women. You're like some kind of living island treasure."

A few patrons leaned casually in our direction, clearly straining to catch every word.

"It all sounds more interesting than it is," I promised. "And unwritten history is just really old gossip, to be honest. My aunts love it, but it's more of a hobby than a science."

"Then there's this house," Rose said with clear amazement. "Is it true it became available for the first time in decades right when you made your dramatic return, and the owner asked exactly the amount you were looking to pay? Completely cosmic. And this was your childhood dream house, right? Everyone on the island says the place is haunted, and your aunts say the woman it was built for, Magnolia Bane, was a second cousin of yours somehow." Her bright-eyed gaze went contemplative. "From what I hear, that young woman was no luckier in love than the Swan women. Maybe your family curse isn't limited to Swans."

I tried to protest but only a strangled choking sound came out. I had to stop my aunts from repeating that story about the house being haunted. The whole idea was so crazy, I never knew what to say, and my silence was too often mistaken for agreement.

The wind chimes sounded and my gaze snapped up to meet Wyatt's. He removed his hat and nodded at me on his way to the counter.

I closed my mouth with a little effort and politely walked away. Rose was on her own with dissecting my family's alleged curses. I'd wasted too much time on that myself.

Wyatt slid onto a stool at the counter and said something to Denise that had her smiling widely, then tipping her head back in laughter.

She wiped tears from the corners of her eyes as I arrived at her side. "Sorry," she said, attempting to right herself when another round of giggles struck.

"What did I miss?" I asked.

"Nothing," she assured. "It's so silly. Wyatt and I got to talking the other morning when you left us, and it's so goofy. Never mind."

I looked from her to him. His eyes twinkled with mischief. These two had inside jokes now? How long had I left them alone?

Denise laughed out loud again. "That's what cheese said," she whispered, walking away to check on the customers.

The café's landline rang and I grabbed it, grateful for the distraction. "Thanks for calling Sun, Sand, and Tea," I trilled. "Where the food is fantastic and the tea is even better," I added, smiling against the receiver.

"Everly Swan?" a deep and familiar voice asked.

I spun my back to the café and stepped closer to the wall, then lowered my voice. "Canary?"

"Yes. Listen. I know what happened to Mitzi Calgon," he said, sounding a bit out of breath. "I only need one more piece of evidence to prove it, then I want you to take it all to your detective friend."

"Why don't you do that?" I asked, skeptical and well aware my luck wasn't this good.

"Can't. I'm being followed. I have to act when I can."

I considered the possibility he wasn't a killer on the lam, but rather an amateur investigator who'd done a better job than me chasing clues. Now he was on the run from a killer trying to shut him up. The scenario seemed plausible enough, and if it was true, I could finally mark a suspect off my lengthy list. "How will you get the information to me?" I asked. He sure wasn't coming to my place after dark under the pretense of "hiding from the killer."

"Meet me at the lighthouse on the bay tonight. Ten o'clock."

I swallowed a lump of fear and excitement. "Okay."

Grady wouldn't be happy I'd made the plans, but I had a feeling he'd be thrilled to come along.

"Come alone," the Canary said, "and don't be late. I need to leave the island as soon as you have the information."

"Okay," I repeated. "I'll be there. All alone."

Silence stretched across the line until I suspected he'd hung up on me.

"Everly?" His softer, more desperate voice gripped my heart. Maybe he really was afraid and on the run. I'd been there too, and it was awful.

"Yes?"

"Can I trust you?" he asked, the words barely more than a whisper.

"Absolutely."

CHAPTER

EIGHTEEN

I could barely concentrate the rest of the day. Either I'd agreed to meet with a man who knew the name of Mitzi's killer, or I'd agreed to meet with Mitzi's killer. The options were nerve-wracking. I jumped each time someone new entered the café, anytime the phone rang, and once when my blessed fitness bracelet demanded I BE MORE ACTIVE! If only stress and anxiety burned calories, I'd have to binge on chocolate malts and cheeseburgers just to stay alive.

Fortunately, I wouldn't be alone tonight. I'd called Grady after filling Wyatt and Denise in on the situation, and Grady had agreed to come along.

I locked up at seven sharp, then went to change into something appropriate for a secret rendezvous with a potential killer or possible informant on the run. I decided on black yoga pants and a long-sleeved black T-shirt. The nights were still cool, and the wind off the bay would be strong tonight, according to local weather reports. I paired the outfit with comfy white sneakers and pulled my wild, wavy hair away from my face with a large elastic headband, then stopped to check myself out in the mirror. I looked like a plus-sized Tomb Raider. I zipped a light, hooded sweatshirt over the T-shirt and marched in place, wishing I liked cardio as much as I liked cheese.

I checked my window for signs of Grady's truck, then met him on the porch when he arrived. He'd worn blue jeans and a heather gray T-shirt with cowboy boots. I couldn't be sure, but it seemed he wore the boots more often since he'd discovered my nearly debilitating weakness for cowboys.

"Hey," he said in greeting, his gaze raking over my face. "You doing okay?"

"Better now," I said sincerely, and he smiled.

I locked up, followed him to his truck, and waited while he opened my door. Riding in Grady's truck was one of my favorite things. The cab was always warm and it smelled of his cologne, soap, and shampoo. There was sand on the floorboards and country music on the radio. The space was familiar and comfortable when I needed both, and today there were bubblegum wrappers and plastic horses in the cupholders—signs Denver had been there earlier. I especially loved that. The only thing more attractive on earth than Grady in a cowboy hat arresting bad guys was Grady holding Denver's hand.

The driver's door opened and Grady climbed smoothly behind the wheel. "Ready?"

I nodded, and he slipped the truck into gear.

We rode silently through Charm's empty streets. Our town was a different place at this hour. Closed shops. Empty sidewalks. All put on hold for sunrise. Charmers were a morning people. A "greet the day with a smile" people. The sort who walked the beach or boardwalk before breakfast and accomplished more by lunch than most could before dinner.

I stretched an arm through the open window, flexing and curling my fingers around the brisk ocean air. Normally, I enjoyed moments like these. Starry skies and moonless nights. The gentle crash of endless waves. Tonight, however, it all seemed a little eerie. Foreboding even, as we made our way to the lighthouse.

Grady stole a peek at me as we rolled around the corner onto Bay Street from Middletown Road. "I'm glad you called me instead of meeting this guy on your own."

"And I'm glad you agreed to come along," I said diplomatically. Especially since I couldn't be sure the Canary wasn't trying to lure me there and kill me.

Grady gave a quiet chuckle. "You needed me tonight, Swan. Where else would I be?"

He turned down the gravel lane toward the lighthouse, then bounced slowly off the beaten path and parked in a grove of trees not meant for traffic "Before you go out there, I need to do something," he said, unbuckling his seat belt and leaning in my direction until I couldn't breathe. He extended an arm, then opened the glove box.

I heaved a sigh of relief and frustration. No big show of affection, then. Just whatever he kept in the glove box.

Grady straightened quickly, twisting to face me on the bench seat. "I want you to wear this," he said, lifting a pair of strange-looking objects in my direction. "The microphone will let me hear everything that's being said, and the earpiece will allow me to respond to you privately." He leaned forward again, gaze locked with mine. "May I?"

I nodded, then held my breath as he brushed my hair back and slipped the small earpiece into my ear. The rough pads of his fingers grazed the sensitive lobe. The scent of him warmed and enticed me. A memory of our perfect Christmas kiss came back with such force I was sure I could still feel it on my lips. I shivered an exhale, and his eyebrows rose.

Next, he raised the small microphone to my jacket collar and waited for me to nod my acceptance.

"Go ahead," I said breathlessly.

He fixed his attention on my jacket, then pinched the device securely into place, nearly invisible on the breast of my coat. His Adam's apple sank and rose as he backed away.

He tucked an earpiece into his own ear. "Say something."

"You smell nice," I said, my first thought falling out of my mouth without proper vetting. "Sorry." Heat rushed into my cheeks, and Grady smiled.

"You too," he said, his voice coming in a strange

stereo, amplified through my earpiece from the microphone pressed to his collar.

"Once I hear this guy's confession, I'm moving in,"
he said.

"Okay," I nodded, accepting the words as gospel.

"If I think for a second that you're in danger, I'm
moving in sooner, so be expecting that. And if he hurts
you in any way…" Grady's jaw locked and his chest
expanded. "He'll need a medic before the mug shot."

Heat flooded my chest at the sound of his words.

In that moment, I saw a flicker of the soldier
beneath my cowboy. I'd noticed it before and when I
asked, Grady said he had to work sometimes to keep
that side of him buried. He said he was proud of the
things he'd helped accomplish for our country, but he
hadn't always liked doing them or liked himself afterward. I'd thanked him for his service and left it at that.
I hadn't known that guy, but I knew I liked this one
very much. The small-town detective who bought me
lemonade at street fairs and padded barefoot through
the surf with his son on his shoulders. Drove me to
meet cuckoo bloggers for information at midnight.
And loved my family's lemon cake.

"I trust you," I whispered.

Ferocity and pride flashed in his eyes. "Good.
You won't see me, but I'll have you in my sights at all
times. If you get nervous or need me, tug your earlobe
and I'll be there."

I reached for the door, anxiety bunching and gripping my muscles.

"Are you sure I can't talk you out of this?" he whispered as I scanned the deep shadows around the lighthouse base. "I can figure this out without his input and without putting you in danger."

"I know," I said, "but I don't think he's dangerous, and I know he's scared." Hopefully, I was right.

"Telling you someone's after him could have been his way of disarming you and getting you to agree to this," Grady said. "Women meeting men they barely know in secluded locations at midnight doesn't typically end well."

"I'm not alone," I said. "Besides, he loved Mitzi, in a superfan way," I added. "Monitoring her every move was definitely creepy, but I don't think he meant it that way. I think he worshipped her, and he's probably grieving her loss as if she had been an actual part of his life instead of some celebrity fantasy."

Grady pressed the heels of his hands against his eyelids in frustration. "You realize plenty of stalkers who turn violent or murderous claim to have loved their victims, right?" He dropped his hands and turned weary eyes on me. "Unhinged people kill the ones they think they love all the time."

I chewed my lip, weighing cold feet against the desire to know what the Canary knew. He'd pegged the killer in record time, and I wanted whoever that was to be punished. "You'll keep me safe," I said, finding my last breath of bravery before opening the door and climbing down from the truck.

The interior light hadn't come on. Grady kept it

disabled for instances like this one. Nothing gave away a hidden truck's location like a dome light flashing on in the darkness.

I shut my door softly, and the sounds of Grady's door opening and closing followed, but when I turned to say, "Wish me luck," he'd already dissolved into the night.

I lifted my chin and marched toward the lighthouse.

A set of possible scenarios rolled like silent movie footage in my mind. This rendezvous was a trap every time, and the Canary grabbed me. I fought uselessly against his hold and cried silently against a large hand clamped across my mouth. My confidence waned and my pace slowed until I would've lost in a race against molasses. A burdening thought itched at the back of my mind. When I'd seen the Canary yesterday morning, he'd run from me publicly. So, why did he want to meet with me privately tonight?

"You okay?" Grady asked, his voice suddenly present in my ear.

I touched the earpiece on instinct, having momentarily forgotten it was there. "Yes."

"Why'd you stop moving?" he asked.

I looked down at my anchored feet and willed them forward. "Sorry."

"It's not too late to turn back," Grady said. "We can make this an ambush, and I can haul him to the station instead." A bright note of hope in his voice said he'd love nothing more.

Corny as it was, I didn't want to go back on my

word. I said I'd meet him. I told him he could trust me. I wanted it to be true. If he tried anything funny, then Grady could do whatever he wanted, but until then, I wanted to hold up my end of the bargain. "No. I'm okay," I said. "I don't want him to get spooked and run, and I want to know what he knows. He's made his living collecting information on anything Mitzi-related, and he's good at it. Plus, if he's really in danger, he needs protection and you can give him that. I want to offer him your help after we finish talking."

Grady didn't argue, so I kept moving.

I shuffled closer on unwilling feet, crossing a seemingly endless expanse of grass to the foot of the light-house. Shadows hung thick and ominous for several feet around the base. "Canary?" I whispered, straining my eyes for signs of movement or a human shape in the darkness, then turned and moved around the massive cylinder, my senses on high alert.

"What are you doing?" Grady rasped in my ear. "You're leaving my line of sight. Come back."

"I'm circling the base," I said. "What am I supposed to do?" A cartoon image of me on one side of the lighthouse and the Canary on the other, both checking our watches, then walking away, each thinking the other had stood him or her up, popped into mind. "He could be around the side."

Grady grumbled incoherently in my ear, the swishing sounds of wind overcoming his muttered curses.

"Canary?" I tried again, calling softly so I wouldn't startle him if I crept up behind him in the darkness.

"Everly," Grady scolded. "Where are you?"

Dread passed over me as I reached the furthest point from where I'd started, and gooseflesh rode down my spine. "Something's not right," I whispered, as much to myself as to Grady. I just didn't know what. I broke into an ugly run, hurrying back to the beginning of my circular path, desperate to be in Grady's view quickly as possible.

"What happened?" Grady's alarm pierced my eardrum.

"Nothing," I said, rubbing chills from my arms and slowing as the steps to the lighthouse door came back into view. "I just freaked out." Apparently the Canary had too, because I'd made it full circle, and he wasn't at the lighthouse. "He didn't come," I whined. "What if he spotted you, knew I lied about coming alone, and left. What if I blew it?"

"What if you'd come alone, and he'd planned to kill you?" Grady countered.

I grimaced, preferring not to let that thought take root. I went to sit on the short flight of steps and wallow when the lighthouse door caught my eye. "It might be the shadows, but I think this door is ajar." I hadn't noticed when I'd first approached from the other side. "Am I supposed to go in?"

"No." Grady's voice was firm. "Wait there."

I stared at the door—shut but not latched, an obvious invitation—yet I couldn't lift my arm to open it. Fear had frozen my limbs in place.

Why wasn't I brave? Or tough like Denise?

"Hold your position," Grady said. "I'm on my way."

A scraping sound turned me back toward the lighthouse. "Did you hear that?"

"No. What?" he asked, his breaths coming rhythmically now, running, I supposed.

I tipped my head up, as the sound registered again. The icy sense of doom skittered down my back once more.

I moved in the direction of the sound, back into the grass and toward the lighthouse's single brick-trimmed window one hundred feet up.

Something large plummeted out, and I screamed as a heartbreaking thud pounded the ground in front of me.

CHAPTER

NINETEEN

I sat in the grass, several yards from the commotion, transfixed by the crew examining the Canary's body. Grady had confirmed the fallen man's identity when he called for backup. I had taken a closer look despite myself—and Grady's instructions not to. Curiosity was a powerful affliction of mine, and I often paid the price for satisfying it. Now, for example, I'd have the ghastly image of yet another dead body seared into my brain. Forever.

Grady had gone into the lighthouse for several minutes, then stayed with me and the Canary's body until emergency personnel arrived. Then I'd been escorted back a few yards and told to stay put. Obeying had been simple because my wiggly rubber-band legs had no longer wanted to support me. I'd taken a seat in the grass, watching and listening while Grady headed into the nearby trees to search for who-knew-what.

I couldn't help wondering how the night might've ended if I'd been braver. What if I'd opened the door and gone inside? Would I have gotten there soon enough to save the Canary? Could I have stopped him?

A figure moved in my periphery, and I turned to see Ryan's confident stride eating up the distance between us. He winked down at me when he arrived, brandishing a lidded disposable cup in each hand. "Is this seat taken?" he asked before lowering himself onto the grass beside me.

I almost asked how he'd known to come here at this hour. Then I remembered who I was talking to. "Thanks," I said, accepting an offered cup. I inhaled the sweet scent of herbal mint tea.

"It's for your nerves," he said as I downed a therapeutic gulp. "It's not poisoned."

I lowered the cup and glared. "Nice of you to point that out after I drank it."

He shrugged and grinned. "Just trying to lighten the mood."

I grimaced at the body being poked and prodded by men and women from the crime scene department and coroner's office. Emergency lighting from nearby vehicles washed over the already gruesome scene, making it impossibly more ominous. My stomach tightened, and I lowered the tea to the grass, choosing to pull my knees to my chest and hug them instead.

"So what happened? Where's your bodyguard?" Ryan asked, popping the lid off his tea. He sipped carefully as steam rose into the night, sweetening the chilly air.

I quickly recapped the basics, then added, "Grady's searching the perimeter." I pointed over my head to the patchy woods behind us.

Ryan frowned. "Searching for what?"

"I don't know." I released my knees and crossed my legs in front of me like a child at story time, unable to get comfortable in the hard, grassy field. I lifted my tea and curved my palms around the warm cup, pulling it in close. My shoulders rounded and I curled my body over the heady steam. I rarely had the first clue about why Grady or anyone else did anything. Like jump from a lighthouse, for example.

"Does Grady think someone else was here tonight?" Ryan asked.

"He shouldn't," I said. "The Canary came alone."

"How do you know?"

I took another sip of soothing tea, then worked to swallow it. A lump of unbidden emotion clogged my throat. "Because people don't usually bring a plus-one to their suicides."

Ryan's brows tented. "He invited you."

"He had a note in his pocket for me," I said. "He told me on the phone he had information for me, and he did."

Ryan lifted his gaze to the window high above the body and the crowd of emergency personnel. "What did the note say?"

A small sob burst through my lips before I could stop it. I released the cup with one hand to cover my mouth before I drew attention our way.

Ryan set a gentle hand on my shoulder and squeezed reassuringly. "I'm sorry if that was insensitive. Take your time. You've had quite the night." He gave my shoulder a little pat before returning the hand to his lap. "We'll figure this out."

I peeked at him from the corner of my eye. His brow was furrowed as he watched the throng of emergency personnel. "Suicide, huh?"

I dipped my chin once in confirmation.

"So he was definitely alone."

"Looks like," I said.

"But your boyfriend's still in the woods? Maybe he just had to pee."

I laughed unexpectedly at the crude joke. "Maybe."

"I'm not peeing in the woods," Grady's voice barked through the earpiece I'd forgotten I was wearing.

"What?" Ryan asked, scanning my startled face.

I released a ragged breath and lifted a trembling hand to the side of my head. "Earpiece," I said, breathlessly. "I forgot about it, and Grady's been eavesdropping," I added.

"How long have you been listening to us?" I asked Grady. "And why didn't you tell me this thing was still on?"

Ryan's lips curved in delight when I frowned. I suppose the reporter in him couldn't help finding interest in any manner of drama.

"You were alone and upset when I left you," Grady said. "I wanted to be there, but I had to work and I couldn't drag you with me when you could barely stand on your own. I left the microphone on in case you needed me."

Ryan scooted closer until our hips touched, then leaned his head against my ear, clearly attempting to eavesdrop in reverse. "What's he saying?'

I wiggled my shoulders to force him back an inch, then refocused my attention on Grady. "I don't need you right now," I told him as politely as possible while feeling somewhat violated. "I'm doing fine and we can talk whenever you finish what you're doing. Tell me how to shut these things off so I don't distract you."

Ryan stared at my sweatshirt. "Where's the mic?" he asked.

I pointed to the button-sized device, and he lowered his mouth to my collarbone. "I need you," he said, turning his eyes up to mine with devout sincerity.

A passing crime scene woman gawked.

I pushed Ryan back. "Don't put your mouth there. It looks obscene, and people are staring."

"What?" Grady growled.

"Nothing." I planted a palm to Ryan's forehead and shoved when he didn't move on his own. "Grady can hear you just fine without doing that."

"Doing what?" Grady repeated.

Ryan straightened and pursed his lips. "Well? What did he say? Is he coming back? I want to talk to him."

I heaved a sigh and yearned to throw the earpiece and microphone into the ocean. "He'll be back when he finishes what he's doing." Meanwhile, I removed the microphone and earpiece, stuffing them into my pocket. "I hope your night's going better than mine."

He frowned. "I've been with Amelia and her dad. His Mitzi fan club turned on him when they learned he lied on his initial police statement. Without an alibi for the time of her death, he might as well be guilty as far as they're concerned. Now they're boycotting the bookstore. Mr. Butters is holed up at his place, avoiding everyone. Amelia's running the shop alone and she's unsettled by the protesters' constant presence. I helped stock shelves today and ran off a mob with black remembrance bands and signs suggesting that money spent at Charming Reads is money spent supporting a killer."

I rubbed my forehead, where a deep ache was beginning. "I had no idea that was happening." I was a terrible friend. "Why didn't she tell me?"

Ryan chuckled darkly. "In case you haven't noticed, you've got plenty of your own things going on," he said. "Besides, we had it under control."

"Thank you," I said, "for being there for her."

"Glad to do it." Ryan put his cup in the grass and searched me with curious eyes. "So, what did the note say?"

"It was a signed confession," I said, still not quite believing it. "He lured me here under false pretenses. I just don't know why."

"Maybe he'd planned to blame someone else, then had a change of heart," Ryan said. "The lie would've bought him time to flee the island after pinning police focus on someone else."

"Okay," I conceded. "Then, what changed his mind?"

"Guilt?"

I set my tea beside Ryan's in the grass. My stomach was knotted too tight to have another sip.

"What sort of language was used in the note?" Ryan asked. "Was it direct or emotional?"

"Emotional. It was a gushing apology for accidentally killing Mitzi," I said.

Ryan looked horrified, probably a lot like I'd looked when I imagined how the Canary must've felt. "He was her biggest fan."

"I know." I thought of what Grady had said. Sometimes obsessions turned deadly.

"Where was the note?" Ryan asked.

"Back pocket. Grady found the note when he was looking for a form of identification," I said. "The Canary's real name was Skeeter Ulvanich." Yet another reminder that behind the high-trafficked website, Skeet was just a regular guy. Anyone could run a popular blog with the right motivation and content. Even my new website had a growing fan base, and the *Town Charmer* was a hit with locals and tourists. Did an average person, like Skeet or me, run that site too?

"Did he say why he did it?" Ryan asked. "If it was an accident, what had he thought would happen?"

"He was trying to create a scandal he could report on," I said. "Mitzi news had been slow lately, aside from her divorce proceedings, and according to the note, he'd hoped a little harmless drama would be good for business."

Ryan dragged a hand through his hair, watching intently as the Canary's body was zipped into a black bag. "Rough."

"I don't know how I'd live with myself, knowing I'd killed someone," I said. "Especially not someone as important to me as Mitzi was to him. I can't imagine what that must've felt like. The guilt alone had to have been soul crushing."

"So, it's over?" Ryan asked. "Killer's caught. The end?"

"I guess so." I tested the words on my tongue. The night's events seemed to indicate as much.

So why was there a typhoon of uncertainty circling in my core?

❦

I woke with a crick in my neck and drool on my cheek. I hadn't fallen asleep until nearly dawn, then I'd woken repeatedly to nightmares of Magnolia Bane throwing herself from my roof. My unconscious mind had clearly mixed up the images of the Canary's fall with the story of another fall I'd been told about countless times. In the nightmare, Magnolia didn't land in the gardens or on the beach, as I assumed she would have. Instead, she landed in the sea.

And when she landed, she was *me*. I felt the cold, demanding pull of the tide as it dragged me into its depths. Felt the snare of waves pulling my hair and tugging my clothes. Tasted the salty smack and strangle of bitter seawater as I gulped maddeningly for air. The rough floor of broken shells lanced into my bare feet each time they begged for purchase. I tumbled endlessly through the darkness without oxygen, light, or hope. I'd woken multiple times on a gasp—heart thundering, throat burning, and mouth parched—only to drift back into a fitful sleep and witness Magnolia jump again.

I raised onto my elbows and drained the contents of the water glass on my nightstand before settling back on my pillow. Maggie the cat hopped onto my bed and lapped the side of my head with her tiny bristle tongue. Breakfast time for the kitty. I gave her a pat, then forced my weary limbs to move.

Sunlight beamed through my open curtains, temporarily blinding me as I rocked upright and swung my legs over the bed's edge. I'd missed the sunrise for the first time in ages, and I hated that. My whole routine would be off-kilter now.

I rushed through a shower, attempting to make up for lost time, then headed to the café for coffee. I checked my website while the pot brewed. My videos were still getting excellent reviews, and the positive buzz around my recent failure of a livestream was increasing. Ryan had been right. My followers loved seeing the completely unpolished, full-throttle failure of me missing my mouth with a salad-to-go.

I needed to choose recipes for the poll and go live

again soon, but when? I could barely get through the minimum requirements of my day without being side-tracked by some new horror lately.

I checked the weather and tide schedule on the *Town Charmer* blog, then took my time updating myself on local gossip. Thankfully, I wasn't at the center of it and neither was Mr. Butters. The most recent hoopla had to do with the food trucks on Main Street.

Apparently, Chairman Vanders and Mary Grace were leading a movement to relocate food trucks and other unsanctioned vehicles, such as campers and news vans, out of town until they applied for and received the proper permits. Based on the hundreds of comments, our town was divided on the matter. Half the commenters believed rules were necessary to avoid chaos; thus the news crews and food vendors should have to go through the same channels as local citizens if they wanted to park a giant vehicle on Main Street. Campers needed to move to designated camp sites. Period. The other half of the commenters believed special circumstances made receiving necessary permits unreasonable, and the trucks and crews should be allowed to stay.

Mostly, people on both sides saw Mary Grace's loud public interest in pushing procedures for what it really was, a publicity stunt. She wanted to show the town council and great citizens of Charm that she was willing to stand by our protocols, come what may. If elected mayor, she'd continue the hard work she was doing now, keeping the streets clear of food trucks and news crews anytime a national news story broke.

I scrolled on, thankful Charmers weren't being fooled by Mary Grace's sudden appearance in the spotlight. Leave it to her to turn an American silver screen icon's murder into a publicity opportunity.

I froze at first sight of the next headline. MITZI CALGON MEMORIAL.

According to the post, Rose and the Bee Loved documentary crew had teamed up with Mary Grace and Chairman Vanders to host a memorial tonight behind the nature center. There would be a candle-light walk along the bay at dusk with music from the *Blackbeard's Wife* trilogy performed by a local band. Donations would go to helping Mitzi's final earthly cause, saving the American honeybee.

I set my laptop aside and rubbed my forehead. I needed more caffeine to process that mess. I filled a mug with coffee, then grabbed a book I'd borrowed from my family archives. I had my own problems to solve, like which family recipe would become my next baking tutorial. I needed a delicious but easy-to-demo recipe that I could put a personal and modern twist on. And I would find it while enjoying a morning visit with Lou.

I slid the deck door wide, and sounds of the sea crashed over me. Breaking waves, calling gulls, and the distant sound of children's laughter. The world smelled of heat and brine and sunblock, mixed with a bevy of floral fragrances from my gardens. Warm southern sun kissed my nose and cheeks as I lowered myself into a bright red Adirondack chair and kicked my feet up onto the railing.

Maggie sauntered into view and licked her paws, then washed her cheeks.

"Where did you come from?" I asked. I'd left her upstairs with her food and water bowls, then closed the door on my way down.

She paused to flash luminous green eyes at me, as if she had a secret I would never know. Then, she turned to watch a fling of sandpipers racing waves on the beach below.

I sipped my coffee and ran a palm over the replica of an old family cookbook that Clara had copied by hand. The original volume was covered in threadbare red cloth, faded and frayed along the edges. The copy on my lap was new and bound in brown leather. She'd scripted the words *Swan Family Recipes for Joy and Comfort* inside. The year 1826 sat neatly below the words. I traced the number with my fingertip, imagining my ancestor bent over the original pages. A bottle of ink and a pen on her right, a candle or lantern on her left. I wondered if she'd guessed her recipes would outlast everyone she knew. What would she think of me sitting here, reading her words nearly two hundred years later?

I turned the page slowly, admiring Clara's attention to detail.

The original had included a multitude of hand-writings in a variety of inks that crawled over every inch of empty space along the pages' edges and in margins. Clara had included each of those as well. Notes for improving the recipes or improvising ingredients. Hearts and stars as notations for favorites. I was surprised to find that most of the recipes doubled as home remedies. Breads with bee pollen and ginger were suggested for strength and stamina. Peppermint teas for stomach upsets. Bilberry preserves for improved eyesight. Stewed apples for digestion. I smiled.

With all the natural ingredients and notes along the margins, it was easy to see how an outsider might've mistaken the book for a grimoire, or witch's spell book. Especially in times when superstition and fear had ruled the land. Add that to the fact my family had come by way of Salem, and some of the locals' ideas about us made a lot more sense. Thank goodness the misunderstanding hadn't happened *before* my ancestors left Salem.

A low growl rumbled in Maggie's throat, drawing my attention. I watched as her tail swished predatorily and her attention became wholly focused on the sandpipers. Her hair puffed out, as if charged with electricity, but she didn't move.

I turned the next page and smiled at the curlicue letters across the top.

Lemon Cake to Bolster a Hero's Heart.

This was the lemon cake I made for Grady. The recipe hadn't changed much over the centuries, and it worked as well today as I imagined it ever could have. One delectable slice was enough to move Grady from white-knuckled and stiff-jawed to loose-limbed and smiling. The broad, honest smiles that caused his blessed dimple to sink in. I'd copied the recipe years ago from a book created in the nineteen sixties. I'd had no idea the Swan lemon cake had been around so much longer, but I'd cherish it all the more now that I did.

Maggie yowled and I jumped in response to something down below. She tore from the deck in one wild move, claws scoring the wooden deck as she ran. She leaped headlong into the tall grasses of the hillside, disappearing only for a moment before reappearing on the sand below. The sandpipers took flight in an instant, and Maggie sat, watching them sail away. Maybe she was disappointed she'd missed her snack. Maybe proud to have terrified so many little birds at once.

As I leaned forward, watching her soak up the sun, I replayed her leap from the deck in my mind. She'd propelled herself the way I'd always pictured Magnolia Bane had launched from the rooftop widow's walk before crashing facedown against the earth.

So why had the Canary landed so near the lighthouse's side and flat on his back? Was he so depressed that he hadn't bothered to truly jump? Knowing the height would do the trick regardless of effort on his part? Or could he have fallen? Perhaps had second thoughts, lost his footing, and spilled over the ledge?

Or maybe, I thought, the eerie feeling I'd had last night returning, *maybe he'd been pushed.*

CHAPTER
TWENTY

I let Denise in an hour later, surprised to see her so early.

"Denver stayed with the senator last night," she said brightly, tossing her bag under the counter and wrapping an apron around her narrow middle. "She took him to school this morning so I could get a run in before heading over. I even had a long, hot shower and ate my breakfast while seated and not in the car. It was glorious."

I swallowed an internal scolding. Denise had gotten a run in, and I'd practically just woken up.

As if on cue, my infuriating fitness band beeped. BE MORE ACTIVE!

I clamped a hand over it and averted my eyes from Denise's in shame. I'd managed fewer than two hundred steps of the ten thousand that health experts recommended and that my bracelet expected of me. I'd been walking intentionally for a year and rarely went that far in a day. It was depressing, so I'd reset my

daily goal to seven thousand. But I didn't reach that
as often as I should, either. I blamed the tiny island
and all the shops I passed on my walks. Mostly the ice
cream parlor.

Denise freed a broom from the utility closet and
swept it over the floor, her long, blond ponytail swing-
ing jauntily. "I heard about last night," she said nonchalantly, stooping to fill her dustpan. "I'm sorry that
happened, and that you had to see it. It must've been
terrible."

"It was," I said, my thoughts tossed immediately
back to the awful moment. My mouth dried, and I
worked to swallow the sudden punch of emotion. "I
should've gone inside to see if he was waiting for me."

Denise stood, her blue eyes heavy with concern.
"Don't do that. Don't play the what-if game. You can't.
It'll ruin you." Something in the set of her lips said she
was speaking from experience.

I gave a tense nod, knowing there was nothing I
could do to change what had happened and not feeling any better at all about that truth.

"He'd made up his mind," she said, emptying the
dustpan into the trash and returning the broom. "He'd
written a note."

"Maybe," I said, unable to fully silence the notion
that had niggled in me all night and come into form
over coffee. *What if the Canary had been pushed?* I
grabbed my phone and texted the question to Ryan.
He'd been there. After the fact, but still. He knew
everything I knew about what had happened, and he'd

seen nearly everything I'd seen. What did he think of it all by the light of day?

My phone buzzed a moment later with Ryan's response.

Interesting. Are you home?

Yes! Café! I responded briskly, my nerves sparking to life.

On my way.

Fifteen minutes later, Ryan and I were seated at a tall bistro table near the windows with glasses of iced tea and a basket of warm strawberry-and-cream-cheese muffins between us. Ryan, a New York City investigative reporter, normally pale-skinned and impeccably dressed, had a way of embracing the beach life. I suppose blending in was part of his job, and he did it well, if not a little touristy. Today he had sunglasses propped on his head and wore a white V-neck T-shirt and mint-green shorts with a smattering of white sea turtles embroidered on them. His cheeks were rosy from sun, and a dash of freckles had appeared across the bridge of his nose.

I considered remarking on the look but assumed he'd take it as a compliment and never fit his inflated head back through the door.

He bit into a muffin and made a low moan. His eyelids fluttered a moment before he regained himself. "What makes you think the Canary's death wasn't what it seems?" Ryan asked, tracking Denise with his eyes as she wiped down the counter and tabletops in preparation for the café to open.

"I don't know," I admitted. "My gut at first." I chewed my lip. I had nothing substantial to support my theory and hunches weren't enough to open a murder investigation.

"At first," he repeated, "but what now?"

I whispered, hunkering lower over my tea. "I think he fell from the window. He landed close enough to touch the lighthouse with an outstretched hand." I pressed cold fingers to my temple, wishing I could erase the image from my mind. "He definitely didn't jump. And why invite me to talk if his plan was to die? Why pretend he was in danger from the killer if *he* was the killer? Why confess to me at all? Or if he felt he had to do both, why plan them for the same time?"

Ryan leaned forward to match my posture. "My thoughts exactly. And why would he write a note after making plans to speak to you in person? Unless he suspected you wouldn't show, or he wanted you to have something to prove his guilt. Maybe he was looking out for you. Instead of just sending you off with a tale, he provided documentation."

"Very thoughtful of him," I said with roughly fifty percent sarcasm. "I don't buy it."

Ryan lifted his tea jar to me in cheers. "Agreed."

"So the killer's still in play."

He nodded. "I think so. How do you want to proceed?"

I sat back, eyebrows high. "You're letting me decide?" My eyes narrowed. "You always try to call the shots. What are you up to?"

Ryan smirked and the cocky, boyish look, coupled with newly visible freckles, reminded me he was handsome. Usually, he was talking and his looks were easy to forget. "You're right," he said firmly. "I do make the better plans. I'll head back to the rental where Odette and her father are staying. Maybe I can pay their lunch delivery boy fifty bucks to let me carry the food to their door this time. Strike up a conversation that way. Meanwhile, you see what you can get from the documentary's production crew. You've already established a relationship with them that I don't have, and your aunts provide you a reasonable point of access. The film crew stood to gain a lot from a scandal like this. Not cash like Odette and Mr. Pierce, but a spotlight this big, showcasing their work, could potentially change their lives. That kind of opportunity is priceless."

I frowned. There was the Ryan I knew. Overconfident and bossy. "Fine." I straightened, regaining control. "Meet me here after I close, and we'll go over what we know. Seven thirty."

"Can't." Ryan sat back, arms crossed smugly.

"Why not?"

"I've got dinner plans with Amelia," he said, probably knowing I'd never ask him to cancel on her.

So much for retaking control.

He stood and outstretched a hand. "We'll meet up and trade information at Mitzi's memorial. Amelia and I planned to go after dessert. We'll be there by nine thirty."

"Weird way to end a date," I said.

"Oh, that's not how I plan to end the date." He gave his eyebrows an obnoxious wiggle and pushed his hand forward, still waiting to seal the agreement and part ways.

I suppressed a gag and stared briefly at his hand. The gesture seemed strangely formal considering the history between us, but I worried that the alternative was to hug him. So I accepted the shake.

I let Denise know I'd be back after a quick visit to my aunts' house, for a hopefully informative chat with Rose. Then I followed Ryan as far as the boardwalk, where we parted ways.

"Good luck," he said.

"Back at you," I told him.

I checked the time on my phone, then turned on my heels and headed for Blessed Bee. My aunts should've opened their shop twenty minutes ago. With a little luck, I'd find Rose there again.

I eased into long, brisk strides as I thought of Denise and her morning run. The steady rhythm of my purposeful gait settled into my bones, and I daringly increased the pace. Endorphins kicked in and sweat broke across my brow as the stiff muscles I'd started with became pliable and warm. Feeling wistful and ambitious, under the influence of serotonin and stupidity, I launched into a jog. My heart rate spiked and my breaths were instantly labored.

I kept the pace until a stitch in my side nearly toppled me onto the boardwalk. I pressed a palm to my ribs and fell into a clumsy stride, whimpering and weaving a drunken path along the historic planks. I pinched the buttons on my fitness bracelet, hoping to see a sudden mass of accumulated steps. Apparently, I'd barely gone seven hundred steps all day, and the heart rate monitor suggested I call a paramedic. I imagined feeding the device to an alligator.

My stinging throat was dry from gasping, and a charley horse was forming in my calf as I landed on the grassy edge of Ocean Drive. A smattering of pedestrians moved lithely along the sidewalks, the crowds of days prior mostly gone. I squinted against the sun as I made my way to the crosswalk, slightly saddened by how quickly Mitzi's superfans had cleared out and moved on—and missing the food trucks Mary Grace had chased away. I would've sold my shoes for a shave ice.

An oddly familiar cry reached my ears and all thoughts of delicious frozen treats melted.

I raised a hand to my brow and squinted against the sun as I searched for the source of the faint but desperate sound. A moment later, the cry came again, and my senses went on high alert. "Denver?" I forced my wobbly legs into action, darting awkwardly across the road's center and raising a palm to oncoming traffic.

I stopped on the covered sidewalk outside a row of shops I rarely visited and turned in a small circle. "Denver?" I called, smiling politely at passersby who looked slightly concerned.

"Everly!" The unmistakable sound of my name on Denver's small tongue shattered over me like broken glass, and I jolted into a run. I followed the renewed cries into the alley behind the shops, where employee entrances and dumpsters lined a somewhat warped brick road.

Ten yards away, a broad-shouldered man in a black golf shirt and matching casual slacks opened the door to a large black SUV and motioned Denver inside.

The hairs along my arms and neck stood at attention. Fear sliced through my core, cold and sharp, as I realized what was happening. "Stop!" I screamed.

The pair turned to look at me with matching wide-eyed expressions.

"Let him go," I demanded, searching the man for signs he might be armed.

He released Denver's shoulder.

I closed half the distance in slow, measured steps before dropping into a squat and opening my arms. "Come here, Denver."

Denver took one step, and the man's arm bobbed into his path like the gate at a parking garage. He locked cold, blue eyes on me. "No you don't. Get in the car, son."

"That's not your son," I snapped, my hands curling into fists as they fell to my sides.

Denver's ruddy cheeks were streaked with tears, his expression twisted with frustration.

I pulled my cell phone from my pocket, snapped photos of the man and the SUV, then sent the pictures to Grady. When I looked up to tell the man what I'd done, he was stuffing Denver into the SUV.

"Stop!" I screamed, debating my ability to close the distance between us before he could climb inside and drive away. Panic stabbed through my chest as I realized I might not get there in time.

I passed the cell phone into my left hand and curled the fingers of my right around a golf-ball-sized rock from the sidewalk's edge. In one snap movement, I stood and chucked the rock at the man.

The stone collided with his back in a hearty thump, causing him to arch and cuss.

I stooped and grabbed another. "Let him go," I demanded, upright and stalking forward, my voice deep and cold. My gaze locked on the man's head, where my next stone would land if needed. "Now."

The man put a foot inside the vehicle, and I released the second rock with practiced skill.

He ducked a half heartbeat before the stone crashed into the window with a deafening thud and fell to the ground.

I palmed another stone before he returned his eyes to mine. "Don't. Move," I told him, embracing the simultaneous fire and ice roaring through my veins. "I can throw a lot harder and I never miss."

Denver took advantage of the distraction, slid out of the man's reach, and ran for me. He wrapped his arms tightly around my thigh upon arrival, and I circled him with one arm, keeping my next rock poised to throw. "One step in this direction, and I will knock you out with this rock. I've taken pictures of your face and license plate," I said. "I'm sure Denver's father, our local detective, would love to track down the man who tried to abduct his son."

The man's posture relaxed in defeat.

The sound of high heels on concrete pricked at my ears. We weren't alone anymore, which I hoped made Denver and me safe. "What in blazes are you doing?" The senator's seething voice turned me partially around.

The expression on her face made me rethink my personal safety.

I maintained my hold on Denver but lowered the rock.

In a move I'd seen Grady perform countless times, I angled my body to keep the man in my line of sight as I addressed the senator. "I heard Denver crying," I told her. "Then I caught that man trying to abduct him."

Recognition and shock flashed in her eyes.

I looked from her to the man. Could this have had anything to do with her agreement to back her party's next presidential candidate and the controversial bill? If so, would her continued presence here keep Denver in danger? What would his young life be like if the bill passed? I bit my tongue against the urge to tell her to leave town immediately.

She marched forward with resolute determination and grabbed my elbow on her way past.

"What are you doing?" I asked, trying to break free of her grip and dragging Denver along with me.

"Get in the SUV," she snapped.

The man moved aside and opened the passenger door up front.

I dug my heels in and lifted Denver onto one hip, prepared to run with him if necessary. "What's going on?" I demanded. "Do you know this man?"

The silver fox rubbed a palm over his twitching mouth, failing to hide an arrogant smile.

Senator Denver's gaze narrowed. "Yes. I do, and so does Denver. This is my husband. Denver's grandfather, and you've been screaming at him on the street as if he's a common criminal."

"She hit him with a rock," Denver tattled. "And she hit the car!" he added proudly. "Hard!"

Yet the window hadn't broken, I realized belatedly. *Because this was one of the senator's insanely secure vehicles.*

I loosened my grip on Denver, confused and unsure. "This is your grandpa?"

He shrugged and buried his face against my shoulder.

"Why were you crying?" I asked. "I was so scared when I heard you cry."

The senator huffed. "Get in the vehicle, Miss Swan, or I might make someone else cry next."

I shot her a heated look, then settled Denver inside. I slid in beside him and wrapped an arm around his shoulders. The senator climbed in after me and shut the door. Her husband rode shotgun beside a driver I hadn't noticed before—a man who hadn't bothered to get out and help during the commotion. I assumed he'd been given explicit instructions to stay behind the wheel.

We glided away from the curb, and Denver's grandpa turned to look at me over the seat between us. "He knows me," he said. "He just doesn't remember me. He was fine until we split up from Olivia. I brought him outside while she finished at the cash register. I thought he'd enjoy the sunshine, but he started to cry and I didn't want him to draw any attention, so I tried to put him in the SUV. He likes Dominic." He motioned to the man behind the steering wheel.

"Hi," I said, catching the driver's eye in the rear-view mirror.

He touched the brim of his hat with two fingers in response.

"Ha!" The senator snarled at the back of her husband's head. "You didn't want to draw attention? A ticker tape parade would have caused less commotion than the two of you." She swung her livid expression in my direction.

Denver wound his arms around me. "I'm sorry."

I planted a kiss on the top of his head. "You don't have to be sorry. This isn't your fault," I whispered, stroking his hair with my free hand. "It was a misunderstanding on my part."

He rolled wide gray eyes up to me and grinned. "You hit Grandpa with a rock."

"I thought he was stealing you," I said. "I would've hit him with a car if I'd had one."

Denver laughed and snuggled more tightly against my side.

"I've been gone," his grandpa said, sounding a little guilty. "The boy hasn't seen me since he was three, and I wanted to make up for lost time," he said. "Grady allowed him to stay with Olivia last night, so I've been trying to bond. We were on our way to drop him off at school this morning, but I wasn't ready to say goodbye again. So we went to breakfast, then did a little shopping." He watched Denver with rapt curiosity. "He isn't warming to me, and I don't know why."

"You could talk to him as if he's sitting right here and understands English," I suggested. "Or try to be patient. You've just gotten back, and Denver's been through a lot of change since you left. He moved to a new home in a new town and started a new school, all in the past twelve months alone. It would be a lot for anyone. Not to mention his…loss."

"Uprooting him was his dad's decision, not mine," the man shot back. "And he's not the only one who suffered a great loss. Amy was my only daughter."

"And Denver's only mother," I said softly. "And Denver is six. He's perfectly within his rights to like you or *not*." An overwhelming sense of pride and love overcame me, and I realized I would protect Grady's son with my life, against all threats, from strangers or family.

And I didn't give two hotcakes what Grady's former in-laws or anyone else thought about it.

My phone buzzed and Grady's face appeared on the screen.

"Daddy's calling," Denver said.

Denver's grandpa twisted to speak to his wife over the seat while I swiped the screen to accept the call. "This is the woman you've all been talking about?"

"She grows on you," she said as I pressed the speaker button.

"Hello?"

"What's going on?" Grady asked, his voice thickly laced with tension.

"False alarm," I said. "Just a little misunderstanding."

"What kind of false alarm?" he demanded. "Why do you have photos of my father-in-law?"

Everyone's eyes were on me. I cleared my throat before trying to speak. "I thought he was kidnapping Denver."

Grady's father-in-law shot me a grouchy look. "You might've asked who I was," he said, indignantly. "What kind of person hears a child cry and immediately assumes a kidnapping? It's quite a large jump, don't you think?"

"You were stuffing a screaming kid into a vehicle," I snapped. "That's not a jump. It's the definition of kidnapping!"

"Everly!" Grady's voice roared through the speaker, breaking my name into syllables and successfully stilling the passengers around me. "My place. Now."

CHAPTER

TWENTY-ONE

The senator instructed the driver to take us to her place, then she instructed me to advise Grady of the same. She claimed that Northrop Manor had better security and her preferred coffee on hand, which were both true, but I suspected the change of destination had more to do with her need for control than anything else. A subtle reminder that she was the boss of Grady. And everyone. And everything. And after all, this was all about her. Wasn't it?

The driver slowed at the closed wrought iron gates outside Northrop Manor, and I frowned. I realized for the first time how much it irked me that the senator had butted in and bought the place out from under an organization that planned to make the property a living museum.

The massive automated gates opened slowly, and the SUV rolled smoothly through. I did my best to stay on alert in case I needed to defend myself or Denver again, but he'd begun to play with my fingers, making them talk and sing, sometimes fighting one another with sound effects. So, by the time the vehicle stopped outside the enormous stone manor, my focus had turned wholly to the adorable, carefree boy at my side, and my attitude was as light as my heart.

The door beside Denver opened suddenly, and Grady stared inside. His gaze caught on his son, who was molded to my side and playing with my hands. "You okay, buddy?" he asked before pulling Denver into his arms.

"Daddy!"

Grady's heated expression softened as his son's small arms wrapped eagerly around his neck.

I scooted toward the open door, unsure if I was in trouble. Grady shifted Denver onto one side, then took my hand, helping me down.

"I'm sorry," I whispered. "I heard Denver crying. I knew he should've been in school, and I didn't recognize your father-in-law. I was scared and confused." I chewed my lip and winced when I got too carried away.

"It's okay," he said, holding onto me a moment longer than necessary before letting me go. "Thank you."

I furrowed my brow, taken aback by the thick sincerity in his words when I'd been bracing for another argument. "You're not angry?"

"You protected my son," he said.

Denver's head lifted from Grady's shoulder at that. "Miss Everly hit Grandpa with a rock."

Grady's mouth opened. His gaze jumped to his in-laws, already moving toward the house. "What?"

"She said, give me that boy," Denver began in a mock menacing tone, "or next time I'll hit you harder!"

The burn in my cheeks increased furiously. "That's a paraphrase," I said.

Grady set Denver on the ground. "Why don't you go inside and ask Grandma for a snack?"

Denver gave a quick salute and ran for the house.

"I am so sorry," I repeated. "I didn't know."

Grady watched until Denver was safely inside, the massive wooden door shut behind him, then he focused his blank cop expression on me. "I need to talk with Olivia and Martin before I take you home."

I nodded, sensing the caution in his tone. I wasn't sure exactly what was happening, but if Grady was worried, then I was shaking in my sneakers.

He set his hand on the small of my back and guided me into the house.

I clasped my hands in front of me to stop them from shaking and clenched my jaw to stop my teeth from chattering, my body's graceless ways of dealing with the aftershocks of excess adrenaline. The sounds of percolating coffee echoed through the cavernous home, pinging off the high-arched foyer ceiling and ponging from the pristine marble floor. Tendrils of enchanting steam pulled us toward the kitchen. I admired the majestic staircase, beautiful painted landscapes on canvases, and priceless antique chandeliers as we moved. The home's interior craftsmanship was breathtaking, but the parlors and sitting areas I spied through yawning doorways came up barren every time. Aside from a few strategically placed pieces of art and the occasional side table with vase, Northrop Manor was empty.

We stopped at a granite-topped island, across from Martin and Olivia. They were tipped slightly forward, toe to toe and whispering. Their matching scowls said neither was happy, and I suspected I was the cause.

Denver sat on the floor with a plump tuxedo cat and an apple. He'd hooked headphones over his ears and was staring at a handheld device with swimming cartoon goldfish. He laughed as the cat pawed at the screen.

"Well?" Grady said, directing my attention back to the adults in the room. He'd removed his hand from my back in favor of planting it on his narrow hip. "What are you doing here, Martin?" His voice remained impressively civil despite a distinctly dangerous look in his eye.

Denver's grandpa bristled and straightened. "I came to see my wife is safe."

"I told you she was," Grady said. "I told you not to come."

Martin bristled. "I needed time to see where she's staying, explore the town, interview her security staff."

"No. You didn't," Grady said. "I told you I would watch over her, and you promised to trust me."

I eyeballed the two men. They were nothing

alike in appearance, though both were tall and at
the moment, unhappy. To me, Grady always looked
as if he'd just come in from a long day of working
outdoors. He preferred jeans, T-shirts, and boots to
any sort of uniform or suit. He was tan and sculpted
with an ever-present two-day stubble and carefree
wind-styled hair. Martin was lean and sophisticated
in appearance, wearing high-end clothing and dress
shoes. His cheeks were smooth, his skin fair, and his
haircut likely cost more than my wardrobe. It blew
the old adage about women marrying men like their
fathers right out of the water.

Martin's expression sharpened and his stance
turned rigid. "Tell me you wouldn't have done the
same for Amy."

Grady's jaw set. "Don't bring Amy into this. This
isn't about her, and it's not about me. It's about you.
Coming here was stupid and selfish. You have protocols for a reason. You need to get out of here and
follow them." He shot a pointed look at Denver on
the floor. "If anything happens to him because of you,
I will never stop blaming you. Neither would Amy."

Blood drained momentarily from Martin's face,
then his complexion slowly turned red. "How dare
you."

Grady ignored the accusation. "What were you
doing with my son today?"

"Trying to get to know him," Martin snapped.
"He's my grandson and he didn't even recognize me."

"Whose fault is that?" Grady asked. "Not his. He's

had enough loss. I only allow people in Denver's life who aren't going anywhere."

The older couple turned their eyes on me.

I blushed again, taking acute interest in the mosaic tile floor.

"Then you show up, knowing you can't stay," Grady continued. "You say you want to bond with him, but you know you don't have time. For about a dozen reasons, Martin, go home."

I'd been trying to keep up with the conversation until Grady implied I wasn't going anywhere. I wasn't, but did he mean it the way everyone else in the room had taken it? Myself included? Had Grady allowed Denver to grow attached to me because he wanted me to be around?

The senator released a heavy sigh, then motioned us to a table fit for twelve in the next room. "Let's sit. Coffee will be served soon."

Grady seated his palm against the small of my back again, and I curled my toes inside my shoes to deal with the corresponding electric current running through me.

I gawked at the impressive wooden columns, wainscoting, and muraled ceiling above another priceless chandelier. How was every room I entered impossibly more fabulous than the last? "Your home is beautiful," I said, taking a seat beside Grady.

"Thank you," the senator said, inclining her head magnanimously.

Martin watched Grady and me closely, his gaze

making a circuit from one of our faces to the other. "What's your relationship to this woman?" he asked Grady.

"She's my friend and Denise's. And she's important to Denver."

My heart thudded happily.

"She's a tea shop owner," Martin stated. His lips curled distastefully, as if my occupation was akin to *puppy puncher*. "What can the two of you possibly have in common?"

I opened my mouth to protest but I wasn't sure how, and I was more than a little interested in hearing Grady's answer. I folded my hands in my lap and waited.

"Everly was the first friend I made here," Grady said. "We met the day I arrived, and I accused her of murder."

The senator rolled her eyes, as if she might've heard this story before.

Martin frowned. "What?"

Grady's lips twitched, fighting a smile. "I thought she killed an old man. She set me straight. Proved me wrong—and never once blamed me for it. She was the first person here I told about Amy. She was the first to meet Denver, and she has been the one and only person in this town who consistently looks at me as if I'm not about to explode. Even when I am."

I pressed my lips together, fighting a smile of my own.

"She and I have been through a lot together in the

past year, and it's made us close," Grady said. "We have a lot in common. Most of which you wouldn't understand."

"And she's the reason you refuse to return to the Marshals Service?" Martin asked with barely tamped hostility.

"I won't return to the marshals because I'm happy here," Grady said. "Denver is thriving, and I won't put work or anything else before him again."

Martin's anger slowly faded, as if Grady's words had somehow poked a hole in his balloon of rage. "I'm getting out too," he said.

The senator swiveled to face him. "What do you mean you're getting out?"

"I'm retiring," Martin said. "When you told me about the threats made against you, I was devastated. I got into this business to protect people, and I want to spend my days protecting you, not some foreign dignitary. I want to be here for you. I want to be your first man."

Grady glanced at me with one raised eyebrow.

I lifted my shoulders silently. Talk about a sudden change of topic.

"You'll always be my first man," she said. Without warning, the senator threw her arms around Martin's shoulders and kissed him.

Grady and I waited awkwardly for them to wrap it up. They didn't. When the kiss deepened, Grady stood. "Ready?" he asked.

"Yep."

We stopped to visit Denver on our way out. Grady snuggled him and petted the cat. I promised I wouldn't hit anyone with a rock on my way home, and Denver laughed. We left him curled on a window seat a few minutes later, cat purring contentedly at his feet, a book splayed across his lap.

I breathed easier back in the sunshine as Grady ushered me to his truck and helped me inside. The familiar scents and feel of sun-warmed seats turned my tense body to goo, and I melted into the material.

Grady started the engine on a long exhale. "Sorry you had to hear that. Family business is messy for us."

"Family business is messy for everyone," I said. "Do you think Martin will listen? Go back and do whatever he should've done before coming here?"

"I don't know," he said, sounding utterly exhausted. In lieu of giving me an answer, he asked, "How big of a hurry are you in to relieve Denise?"

I dropped an arm across the open window and let the wind rush through my fingers as we turned away from Northrop Manor and headed back into town. "I'm not," I said. Honestly, there was nothing I wanted more at the moment than some answers and time with Grady.

We motored along the bay for several minutes without speaking. I assumed he was searching for words and I didn't want to rush him. When he passed my home and parked in the public beach access lot instead, my curiosity piqued once more.

"You okay?" I asked. "We don't have to talk about Martin if you don't want to. I was just…"

"Curious?" he asked, sliding his eyes briefly in my direction.

"Yeah."

Grady settled the truck's engine. He drummed his thumbs against the steering wheel and stared at the horizon. The long, sandy beach stretched out before us, swallowed slowly by an aquamarine sea, eventually met with a cloudless blue sky.

I inhaled the warm ocean breeze and let my eyelids drift shut.

"Martin's assignment is officially over," he said, effectively springing my eyes open. "He needs to be debriefed, but he's done. It's fitting that he's decided to retire now." Grady dropped his hands to his lap and worked his jaw. "He wasn't supposed to just show up like this. Anyone who followed him from his assignment could have followed him here."

"Do you think that's possible?" I asked, suddenly terrified. I wasn't sure what kinds of people the CIA tracked or hunted, but I imagined they weren't the good kinds.

Grady dragged a hand along his jaw. "It's unlikely. Martin's good, and he's been at it a long while. It just burns me that he'd be so irrational."

I hated to play devil's advocate, but I couldn't stop myself. "In his position, wouldn't you?"

Grady stretched his neck and gripped at the muscles bunched along his shoulders. "I can't believe

I didn't even know he was in town," he said finally, ignoring my question. "I've been so caught up in the Mitzi Calgon case, then Skeeter Ulvanich took a swan dive last night." He stopped short, and I could practically hear him internally berating himself for not being ten top detectives at once.

"You mean the Canary?" It was so strange to think of the man any other way.

"I'm not calling him that," Grady said, shifting on his seat to face me. "What's important is that I've got a solid lead that will probably wrap everything up quickly, and this will all be over soon."

I frowned. "I don't think the Canary committed suicide," I said, needing to get it off my chest.

"Agreed." Grady started the truck's engine and backed out of the parking lot. This time he pointed the truck toward my home. "You hit Martin with a rock." He laughed loud and long, as if he'd just heard a great joke. The sound was boisterous and bright.

I wanted him to elaborate on the fact he'd agreed the Canary hadn't jumped, but I recognized the move. This was Grady's polite way of telling me he had no intention of sharing any more details from his murder investigations with me right now. So I went along with the conversation's new direction and appreciated the warm smile he gave me when he stopped at a stop sign.

"You were going to take on a six-foot, trained CIA operative to save my son," Grady said. His tone sent a fresh round of shivers down my spine.

"I didn't know he was CIA," I admitted. "I thought he might be one of the people threatening the senator and hoping to use her grandson as some kind of threat or leverage."

Grady shook his head in small, deliberate moves. "I owe you everything for your intent alone."

My cheeks heated and I bit into my bottom lip, failing to control a growing smile. "That's what friends are for, right?"

He reached for my hand on the seat between us and squeezed it before easing back into traffic. "You're tougher than you realize, Swan. You never back down when it counts, and you have a big, loyal, fearless heart."

I beamed up at him, temporarily unable to speak.

"I'd love to thank you properly when this is all over."

"Oh." I whispered the word, feeling dizzy with pleasure. "Okay." My stomach knotted and flipped. I wasn't sure what he'd meant by *properly*, but I hoped it involved a stroll on the beach. Preferably with lots more hand-holding.

CHAPTER

TWENTY-TWO

Grady shifted into Park outside my house. "You're staying here now?" he asked. "No more rock-throwing adventures before work today?"

I pursed my lips, interpreting his concern through the jest. He obviously thought I was a trouble magnet. Today I threatened to brain his father-in-law. Last night I had a secret meeting with a man who'd allegedly killed himself. In front of us. Before that, I'd been locked in my family's archives.

Maybe I was a trouble magnet.

"Everly?" he prodded, bringing me back to the moment.

"I don't know," I admitted. "I was on my way to see my aunts when I ran into your in-laws. I'd still like to see my aunts." And talk to Rose about how her week was going. Maybe even get her to say something that becomes a thread I can pull to unravel the mystery of who killed Mitzi Calgon.

"You're torn because you told Denver you'd send

Denise back for him?" Grady guessed. "And you feel obligated to go inside and send Denise sooner rather than later."

I touched the tip of my nose. "Ryan's trying to talk with Odette and Mitzi's husband today. I'm supposed to talk to Rose. I figured she'd be with my aunts, and I could accomplish two goals with one visit."

Grady dropped his head back momentarily. "Ryan," he groaned. "You teamed up with that guy again? Are you trying to kill me?"

"We haven't teamed up," I said. "Ryan and I are... collaborating. And I'm not trying to kill you. He and I are planning to compare notes at Mitzi's memorial. That's all. Do you think it's strange that he hasn't been able to have a single conversation with Odette or Mr. Pierce?"

"No," Grady answered. "I think it's to be expected, especially under these circumstances and with people like them. Mr. Pierce and his daughter have been living with Mitzi Calgon for years. They've been stalked and hounded by paparazzi every day of their lives. They could probably spot a reporter like him from a mile away, and no one wants to talk to a reporter."

"Have you talked to them?" I asked.

He pulled a beaded chain from beneath his shirt. A Charm P.D. shield hung from the chain. "I'm a detective. People like to talk to us. We tend to be helpful."

I considered that a moment. "Criminals don't like to talk to you."

"Not usually, no."

"Did Odette and Mr. Pierce enjoy talking to you?" I asked. Did that mean they were innocent? "Because Mitzi's divorce proceedings have been pretty ugly so far, and Mr. Pierce had a lot to gain without her."

Grady fixed me with the blank cop stare. "This sounds like a theory, but it can't be because I've asked you nicely not to make theories about this case."

"No theories," I said, hoping to sound aloof. "Just a busy mind." I tapped a fingertip to my temple. "I can hardly help wondering why Mr. Pierce and Odette are still hanging around, if not to cover their tracks in the murder."

Grady turned narrowed eyes on me. "That is a theory and you know it."

I feigned offense with an open mouth and wide, innocent eyes.

"Pierce and his daughter are waiting for Mitzi's body to be released from the coroner so they can take her home. They're staying inside to grieve and avoid obnoxious fans and people like Ryan, who try to parlay human loss into a story."

"Have you considered the possibility they're also sticking around to keep tabs on the investigation's progress?" I asked. "That information is essential in covering tracks."

Grady rubbed the heels of his hands against his temples.

"I'm just saying there's a lot of money in it for Mr. Pierce and money is a powerful motivator, that's all. It doesn't make sense for Mitzi's nearly ex-husband to fund the Bee Loved project or for his daughter to stay on as Mitzi's assistant when the women obviously don't get along." I crossed my arms and awaited his rebuttal.

Grady reached across me and opened the glove box. He freed a roll of antacids and put two in his mouth. "Mr. Pierce didn't want the divorce. Mitzi filed. Not him. He's not fighting her on little things to get more from her. He was trying to buy time to win her back. The same reason he made a generous donation to Bee Loved when he heard Mitzi was getting involved in their project. As for Odette, she wanted her dad to be happy, so she stayed on with Mitzi as a bridge between her father and stepmother. She'd hoped to facilitate a reconciliation."

I chewed on that a minute, then tucked the information away for later and moved on before Grady stopped answering my questions. "What made you think the Canary was pushed?" I asked while he crunched aggressively on the pills. "Was it because he landed so close to the lighthouse?"

"No." Grady returned the remaining antacids to the glove box and shut the compartment, then gave me a warning look. He wouldn't elaborate on that.

"What do you think of Rose?" I asked, clearly pressing my luck with Grady's patience. Anything he added to what I already knew was sure to help guide my discussion with Rose when I saw her.

"I think you shouldn't give her or anyone else any reason to believe you're still looking into this," he said. "Including me."

I took note of his tone and narrowed eyes, then lifted my palms in surrender. "You're right."

He didn't look like he believed me, so I changed the subject again.

"I might've found the original Swan family recipe for lemon cake in one of the old books I took from my aunts' archives," I said. "I thought I was using the original version already, but there's an even older one in this book. It's doubly crazy because the recipe itself has barely changed over the centuries."

"Centuries?" Grady tented his brows. "How old is it?"

"The book was started in 1826, and lemon cake is one of the first recipes." I smiled as awe spread over his face. "Thanks to high-tech advances like food processors and refrigeration, the baking is easier and the cakes last longer. But aside from that, not much has changed."

"Say lemon cake again, and I might start to drool," Grady said.

"Oh!" I smiled, recalling another bit of information I loved about the find. "The recipe was called Lemon Cake to Bolster a Hero's Heart. Isn't that romantic? I'll bet the Swan woman who invented it had a lover who was a soldier." I pictured the yellowed pages of the original book, cluttered with inky scribbles. "The book is fantastic. There are dozens of handwritten notes on most of the pages—comments and advice from my ancestors over the years. It's no wonder people have whispered for generations about my family being magical. The book looks like a prop from *Hocus Pocus*."

Grady smiled. "Well, that cake certainly enchants me."

"I'll have to make more soon," I said, admiring the way he looked instantly younger when he wasn't brooding or complaining.

As if he heard my thoughts, his smile widened and his dimple made an appearance. "Tell you what," he said, slipping the truck into gear. "You want to visit your aunts before you start work, and I can't get what happened with Martin and Denver off my mind, so why don't I drop you off at your aunts' place on my way back to Northrop Manor? I'll get my son, and Denise can stay at Sun, Sand, and Tea as long as she'd planned. She has no idea you were considering sending her home early, so it won't make any difference to her."

I made a show of tugging my still-buckled seat belt, then faced forward, ready to go.

We found a sign in the window at Blessed Bee announcing that the store would open late today, so we headed to my aunts' home instead. I prayed silently that the sign wasn't a weird decoy and that my aunts were truly safe. Grady stopped in their driveway ten minutes later. Aunt Fran, Aunt Clara, and the film crew were visible in the side yard. "Call me if you want a ride home," Grady said as I slid down from the cab.

I waved as he drove away, loving the knowledge

that he was the one going back for Denver instead of Denise. Spending some unexpected time with Grady would give Denver a thrill and Grady a much-needed break.

Quinn was the first to notice my approach. He waved a hand overhead in greeting, then met me halfway across the lawn. Aunt Clara stood in the gardens with a basket of flowers hooked over one arm while Aunt Fran made sweeping gestures and described the pollination process to Rose's camera. A stranger held a boom mic over my aunts' heads, and Burt Pendle positioned a massive light reflector just outside the shot. "You always get a police escort?" Quinn teased.

"No. The detective and I had some things to go over, so he offered me a ride." I felt my brow pucker as I recalled the reason I'd gotten into Grady's truck. "My day had a complicated start."

"Did something happen?" Quinn asked.

"Just a misunderstanding. I'm fine," I assured him, working up a smile.

Quinn pulled his lips to the side, considering. "If you say so." He turned to watch my aunts banter about honey. "They're good. People will love them. Are you here to watch the filming?"

"Absolutely. How's it going so far?" I asked.

"We're finally getting some solid material for the documentary, so I call that a win. Your aunts are unbelievably knowledgeable on everything related to honeybees, especially their impact on the environment and vice versa. I've even learned a few things about strategic gardening for maximum bee benefits. Pretty significant since bee science is kind of my thing."

I felt a jolt of pride punch through me. "They are the foremost bee authorities, it seems."

"Cut!" Rose called, stepping back from the camera on her tripod. Her long, dark hair had been wound into a messy knot on top of her head. She wore faded jeans with flip-flops and a yellow Bee Loved T-shirt. The expression on her face was inscrutable. "All right. Come on." She motioned Quinn and me over.

I hurried toward my aunts. "Hey," I said, greeting them with air kisses before turning to face Rose from their sides. "How's it going?"

Rose's eyes were intense as she moved in on us and stopped uncomfortably close. "Detective Hays brought you here," she said, her voice low, her interest obviously high.

I bobbed my head. "He and I were talking, and I wanted to see how the filming was coming along, so he offered to give me a lift."

"Were you talking about the man at the lighthouse last night?" she asked.

My mouth parted, but surprise stilled my tongue.

"It was all over the morning news," she said. "The details were super hush-hush, but I heard you were there." Her eyelids drooped and her lips curved into a tiny cat-that-ate-the-canary smile. "Is it true?"

Unease rippled over me. I'd told Grady I planned to talk to Rose. I'd even asked him what he thought of Rose, and what had he said? *I think you shouldn't give her or anyone else any reason to believe you're still looking into this.* Maybe those words were more telling than I'd thought. I nodded my head in short jerky movements. "It was awful. I still can't believe it really happened."

Her eyes brightened with my confirmation. "I also hear he left a suicide note. Can you confirm that as well?"

I froze. Officers and emergency personnel were given explicit instructions to keep the note out of the press. She couldn't attribute that little detail to the morning news. Could she? Had it been leaked? By whom? I ran through a mental inventory of all the faces on-site last night. None struck me as less than dedicated and professional. "Where'd you hear that?" I asked.

Rose's conspiratorial smile widened to borderline madness. "I spoke to at least three dozen people before breakfast today. Everyone's talking about it. A second death this week is wild on its own. When the second death was that of a man who'd made a life out of stalking Mitzi? Then left a suicide note? That's huge. There aren't a lot of die-hard fans left on the island, but the ones who are here are completely abuzz. Some say he couldn't live without her. They think he'd tied his life so closely to hers that he didn't know how to go on once she died. Maybe it's the producer in me, but if I were writing this story, I'd say the Canary could've killed himself over an abundance of guilt and shame. Because maybe he killed Mitzi."

I took a baby step back on instinct. How had she drawn that conclusion without knowing what the suicide note had said? Why hadn't she assumed the same thing the others had? Was Rose the one who'd pushed him and spread the news about his suicide note? Was this her way of making sure everyone was talking about the Canary's guilt and covering her own?

Aunt Clara slid her arm around mine and squeezed. "Oh, dear."

"What if the Canary's death wasn't really a suicide?" I heard myself ask.

My aunts gasped. "What do you mean?" Aunt Clara asked.

"She means he could have been pushed," Aunt Fran said, brows knitting into a frown. "Why would you say that?"

Rose's crazy eyes twinkled. "Plot twist," she whispered, clearly thrilled.

Aunt Fran stared at me. "Is that what you think? He was pushed?"

"I don't know," I said. "The timing is really weird. The fans could be right about him not knowing what to do with his life now, but Rose's idea is pretty good too. I wonder what the note said." I swept my attention back to Rose. Did she know what the note had said?

Her expression fell. "No one I spoke to this morning knew for sure. I don't suppose you saw it?"

I pressed my lips together and shook my head.

Aunt Clara gripped my arm more tightly. "You're

saying it's possible that whoever killed Mitzi killed this man too? As a cover-up for her murder?"

"It's possible," I said. "Or he could've been her killer and killed himself in an act of guilt and desperation." But I didn't think so.

Aunt Fran looked thoughtful. "I prefer the idea that the blogger was the killer."

"Who wouldn't?" I said. "It's a tidy wrap-up. The guilty one is gone, and everyone can relax."

The pair with the boom mic and light reflectors gave up their pretense of not eavesdropping and moved closer.

Quinn puckered his brow. "I don't understand."

Aunt Clara looked to Aunt Fran, as if she could somehow help gather her thoughts. "If Mitzi's killer knew the Canary made a living stalking her," Aunt Clara began, "then killing the Canary and planting a suicide note based on his guilt would be a devilish way of deflecting attention from the real killer and maybe putting the whole case to rest with that poor Canary going down as the bad guy."

Aunt Fran shook her head scornfully. "Devious."

"Or brilliant," Mr. Pendle said, hoisting the boom mic over one shoulder. "It's a matter of perspective," he added when the group shot him ugly looks.

Rose hooked me with her gaze. "What do you think, Everly? Was the suicide a ruse? A misdirect? A cover-up?"

"Who knows?" I said nonchalantly.

But after this conversation, I was sure of it.

CHAPTER

TWENTY-THREE

I raised my eyebrows at Denise, who stood slack-jawed before me. I poured iced chai tea and held it in her direction. "Take your time," I said. "It's a lot of information."

She accepted the glass with a nod. "Wow."

"Yeah," I agreed. "It's been a busy week."

I'd made up my mind on the walk home from my aunts' house. It was time to fill Denise in on what I'd been up to all week. She and I were friends now, and she worked with me. Both of those facts could potentially put her in harm's way. Plus, she lived with Grady and Denver. She'd been hired by the senator. She should know Martin was in town, that he'd spent the day with Denver instead of taking him to school, and that I'd really put my foot in it by thinking he was a child abductor. So, I'd laid it all out for her, including my various theories on who might've killed Mitzi and why.

Denise sipped the tea, pausing on occasion to

shake her head. "You've been leaving here all week to look into Mitzi's murder? Even after receiving threats to stop?"

"None of the threats have specifically said I should stop. The threats were more implied," I said. "The first just said Don't Bee Stupid, and the next said I should Bee Smarter or I'd Bee Sorry." I shrugged. "That one came with actual bees."

Her mouth popped open in astonishment. "How can you be so calm about this?"

"I don't mean to be," I said. "I've been threatened a lot in the last year. Either I'm learning to take it in stride or it's some sort of psychological defense mechanism." I considered the options a moment. "I'm leaning toward the latter."

"No doubt," she agreed. Denise scanned the café slowly, presumably checking tea levels and patrons' expressions for signs of need. "You had a chance to talk with Rose today?" she asked, when her gaze fell back on me.

"Yeah. She was really interested in gossip about the Canary's death," I said. "In fact, she'd looked a little crazed as she filled me in on everything she'd heard. I couldn't tell if it was the shock factor alone," I added carefully. *Or something else.*

"You think she could be behind this?" Denise asked.

"It's possible," I said noncommittally.

Did Denise have mind-bending capabilities to go along with her supreme fighting skills, or was I really that easy to read? Maybe neither, I realized. Maybe she knew more than I did but wasn't letting on. She lived with Grady, after all, and he'd said he was close to wrapping this up. Maybe Denise had seen or heard something that had helped nudge her in the direction I was going.

I turned the question back on her. "Do you think Rose is behind this?"

Denise wrinkled her nose. "I don't know anything about her except what you've told me. But as a budding producer, she probably has a lot to gain from all the added publicity this week."

"That's what I thought," I said. "And Rose spent the first few days after Mitzi's death interviewing fans instead of working on the documentary. I wasn't sure what to make of it at the time, but now I can't help wondering if she's making two documentaries: the one she came to make and one about Mitzi Calgon's murder."

"So, Rose stands to get a huge career boost, but Odette and her dad just inherited coffers of Mitzi's cash and possibly rights to royalties on her stake in the *Blackbeard's Wife* empire."

"That's what I'm thinking," I said. "Grady doesn't seem to think Odette or Mr. Pierce had anything to do with it, though." Unless he was trying to mislead me to keep me away from his main suspects.

Denise took another long pull on her tea, and the iced cubes clanked against the nearly empty jar. "Have you talked to Odette?"

"No, but Ryan's been following her and her dad all week," I said. "I'm hoping to touch base with him at Mitzi's memorial and hear what he's learned."

"Smart," she said. "That's a great place to rendezvous and trade information on this. I wonder if all your suspects will be there?" She smiled. "This is kind of fun. Making hypotheses and testing them. I haven't used this kind of deductive reasoning since college."

"Well, I have to warn you. Grady calls those hypotheses *theories*," I said, "and he doesn't approve."

Her smile widened. "You keep him on his toes. It's good for him." She set her empty jar aside and leaned her narrow frame against the counter, one palm braced beside each hip. "Speaking of that. I can't believe the senator's husband is here. And that no one told me."

"Believe it," I said.

Denise exhaled, her kind blue eyes looking more tired than I'd ever noticed. "Look, it's not my place to say this, but you've been super honest with me today, and I know you care about Grady."

I waited, unsure how to respond.

"The senator's constant judgment makes him crazy. It was part of why he moved here, someplace no one ever dreamed she'd follow. Since she's been back, he's been uptight and ill at ease. I hate seeing him that way, and Denver notices too."

My stomach pitted. I hated thinking of Grady being bullied by his former mother-in-law without her daughter there to shield him. "He probably wants to make her as happy as he can to honor Amy."

Denise nodded. "Yeah, but the senator's got different priorities than Grady, and it creates massive conflict. She was actually nicer to him when he buried himself in his work after losing Amy. Never mind that he didn't eat, sleep, deal with his grief, or parent his son while he went down that dark rabbit hole. Senator Denver was still happier then. At least she could understand the path Grady was on. That was when she hired me to hold things together. All was well and good until Grady came home one night in a fevered rage with himself. Something had happened at work, someone had hurt their child, killed them, I'm not sure, but it tipped Grady over the edge. He told me he was done. He tendered his resignation, found his current house online, and put in a bid. The senator never quite got over his decision to abandon his career, regardless of the reason."

"That's sad," I said. "For all of them."

"Yeah, but we are who we are, I guess."

"Agreed," I said, forcing a tight smile.

A bubble of laughter broke from her lips and startled me. "You hit the senator's husband with a rock," she said.

I pursed my lips.

"He must've been so mad." Denise laughed again. "I really wish I could have seen that."

"You really don't," I said, fighting a wave of humiliation. "I argued with him about it in the SUV, which might've been even worse. Grandma taught me better than to argue with my elders, but I'd lost my temper." Too many things were happening at once, and none of them made sense. "I made an honest mistake, and throwing rocks was the only defense I had." A fresh and delightful idea entered my mind, and I pinned her with a hopeful gaze. "Unlike you."

"Me?" Her cheeks darkened with understanding. "I didn't mean to attack Ryan. It was instinct and I feel horrible."

"Ryan's fine." I waved a hand dismissively. "He's a good guy, and I'm guessing he appreciates the fact you can protect yourself."

She didn't look so sure.

"I'd love to learn how you did that to him," I said. "It was kind of amazing, and I don't know the first thing about getting away from an assailant after stepping on his foot and screaming for help."

Denise's pretty face twisted in horror. "Stepping on his foot?"

"Yeah. I'm basically defenseless. Maybe you could help me."

"Help you?" She frowned. "How?"

"Teach me to protect myself," I suggested. "Like the moves you learned in your mandatory self-defense class freshman year."

Denise's blush deepened. "I should probably tell you more about that."

"Oh, yeah?" I asked as I made my way to the register, where a local couple waited to cash out. "I could pay you for the lessons."

When I returned to Denise, she'd eaten half the lipstick off her bottom lip. "Can you keep a secret?"

I smiled. "Absolutely."

"When I was in high school, I had a date with an extremely popular boy, and the whole thing went very wrong."

She proceeded to tell me how the boy had forced himself on her and no one had believed her afterward because he was popular, and she was not. They found it hard to believe he'd have any interest in her. It was the last time Denise gave her trust easily, and she found a local boxing gym to work out her issues until graduation. She would never again be a victim. "I was teaching the freshman self-defense class my senior year at Georgetown when I met the senator," she said. "I'd applied to the FBI during an on-campus recruitment event. I guess she got my name from there somehow. She said she was looking for someone who fit my profile for a special, personal assignment."

"And that was how you wound up as an au pair for Denver," I surmised.

"It's been a wild ride," she said with a humorless laugh. "My life hasn't turned out at all like I thought it would. I've done the best I could picking up the pieces, and I'm okay with the trajectory I'm on now. My job with the Hays family, for example, has made me infinitely happy, emotionally satisfied, and financially fit. The senator is a very fair employer." She flashed a mischievous grin. "Plus, I'm making a difference in the lives of two men I've grown to love, and Grady is making a difference to countless others. One day Denver will too."

The pride in her voice swelled my chest. I loved that she truly cared for Grady and Denver. Still, something she'd said rattled around in my head. "You must be really bored working here during Denver's school hours," I said. "If the senator pays well, there must be a ton of things you'd rather do."

"Sometimes," she said, "but you need help here, and I like you."

The words, *too easy* came to mind. "And?" I prodded.

"It's been a great way for me to meet other islanders and make connections to the community outside local kindergarten moms."

That statement had sounded more canned than the last. I fixed her with a narrow stare. "Did the senator put you up to this? Are you here to spy on me?"

Shock widened her expression. "No! Of course not. I'm not a spy!"

I crossed my arms. "You're not telling me something, so out with it. If we're going to be friends, *real friends*, there has to be trust."

She watched me for a long beat—evaluating, it seemed. "Promise you won't get mad."

"I've gotten mad every time someone has started a confession to me with that sentence, so no," I said. "Now, spill."

Denise scanned the café again, more quickly this

time. "I'm here because Grady was worried about you." She flipped her palms up to keep me from interrupting her.

I snapped my mouth shut and waited. My fingers itched to dial Grady and give him a piece of my mind, but I decided to hear Denise's entire story so I could tell him off properly. "Why was he worried?"

"Once he learned about the senator's threats, he reasoned that his connection to you could put you in harm's way. You could become leverage to be used against him. Also, you have a habit of being abducted and threatened with death." She added the last part as casually as if she'd said I also had a habit of brushing my teeth. "He knows I can protect you, if needed. Sometimes Grady and I spar together, and my marksmanship is well above average."

I blanched. "Marksmanship. Did you think you'd have to shoot someone? Are you carrying a gun right now?"

"Not on my person," she said.

My gaze slid below the counter to her periwinkle Kate Spade satchel. "Are you kidding me?"

"Don't be mad," she said. "The kinds of people who threaten a senator are the real deal, and Grady's logic was right. There are two people on this planet that he'd surrender to set free in an abduction situation and you're one of them. I'm with Denver when he isn't at school, so it made sense for me to come here while he was there."

I opened my mouth to complain and an ugly

throaty sound spilled out. Questions and rebuttals piled on my tongue until individual words were impossible, so I paced silently behind the counter.

"You're angry," she said. "Everyone wants transparency until they get it."

I turned back and shook a finger at her, then paced another few laps. "You're going to teach me to defend myself," I said finally. "I'm not mad you're here for reasons that weren't disclosed earlier because they're nice and thoughtful reasons that could have saved my life. But I'm not happy that I've been in potential danger for the last five months and you never mentioned it."

She winced. Good. At least she knew that was a junky thing to do to me.

The proverbial light bulb flickered. "That's why I keep running into you. That's why you swing by my house on your runs and pretend to look for your missing sunglasses. You're my protective detail. Not just when Denver's at school!" I clamped a hand over my mouth when guests began to take notice of my whisper-rant.

"I knew you'd be mad."

I gave a long, dark chuckle. "Yes. I am mad. I feel strangely violated by the stalking and weirdly betrayed by the fact you and Grady executed a plan about me behind my back." That wasn't exactly right. "In front of my face." My blood pressure shot up again. "I also feel completely dense for not figuring it out sooner. My aunts think I have some sixth sense about people, but you two had me duped."

"I'll teach you," she said, stepping into my path

and opening her stance. "You should be able to defend yourself. Everyone should. I'll help."

A measure of frustration slipped away. "Really? When?"

"Before work, a couple days a week. We can use the old ballroom here."

A traitorous smile spread over my face. "I'm still mad."

She nodded. "You can take it out on me during practice."

I threw my arms around her. "Thank you. You have no idea how much this means to me."

She stiffened slightly before hugging me back. "You forgive me?"

"I'm not great at grudges," I said. "Most people have good intentions, even if they go about things wrong." I'd be having a serious conversation with Grady about all of this at my first opportunity, however, and I wasn't sure how easily I'd let him off the hook. Denise and I were just getting to know one another. She had a better excuse for not opening up to me thoroughly. Plus, she was in Grady's employ. He and I were friends who talked about things, or at least we were supposed to. I didn't like that he'd intentionally kept this from me.

"Have you asked Grady?" Denise asked, derailing my thoughts.

"About what?" She'd just revealed their secret to me, and I hadn't used a phone. How could I have asked him anything?

"What he thinks about you getting some self-defense training," she said. "Have you ever talked about it? Has he suggested it before?"

I frowned. If I looked like the kind of woman who'd ask permission for self-defense classes, I needed to get a new look. "No."

"I'm surprised he never offered to teach you himself," she said. "He knows a lot more than I do. I think he'll be happy you're interested."

"I'm not too sure," I said. "I think Grady would prefer I make tea and stay out of harm's way. Period."

She smiled. "I think he likes you just the way you are."

"As a trouble magnet?" I asked.

"Alive," she said. "And since you're pulling in enough threats on your own, we'd better start those lessons soon."

The seashell wind chimes jingled, and Denise slid seamlessly into waitress mode. "Welcome to Sun, Sand, and Tea," she called, grabbing napkins and place settings before the new guests could make an appearance.

Odette and Malcolm Pierce strutted into the café and headed for a table near the rear wall of windows.

"That's Mitzi's husband with her stepdaughter and personal assistant," I whispered before she went to take their drink orders.

She turned her back on them to mouth the words, "No way."

I nodded. "Way."

"I thought Ryan was watching them," she said softly.

Before I could answer, the wind chimes jingled again and Ryan sauntered in. His hair was uncharacteristically mussed and damp, his shirt slightly askew. He took a seat at the counter and smiled. "Hello, ladies."

Denise looked cheerfully at him. "Hey, Ryan. Give me a quick minute, and I'll be right back." She went to greet Odette and Mr. Pierce while I gave Ryan a more careful review.

"What happened to you?" I asked, leaning my forearms on the counter across from Ryan.

He rolled his eyes in Odette and Mr. Pierce's direction. "Guess who didn't order lunch for delivery today?"

I smiled. "You don't say." I offered him a bottle of cold water from my fridge, and he chugged it.

He set the half-empty bottle aside and mopped a napkin across his forehead. The contrast between the white napkin and his flushed skin was drastic. "I had to follow them here on foot, and it's hot outside. I'm burnt for sure." He straightened an arm in front of him for examination.

I took another look at the pair chatting with Denise. They looked fine. "How did they get here?"

"Golf cart," he said, lifting the bottle of water to his lips once more. "I just ran a mile and a half, and I'm not really a cardio guy."

The image of Ryan jogging around the island,

ducking behind trees and mailboxes while trying to tail a golf cart and stay hidden, popped into mind and I smiled. Widely. "Can I get you some food to power-up before the jog home?"

Denise swept past me to pour a pair of iced teas, then returned to Odette and Mr. Pierce.

Ryan lifted a finger and pointed it discreetly in Denise's direction.

"Anything you like," she told them. "On the house. We're real sorry about your loss. If there's anything we can do to make this time a little easier for you, just give a holler."

"She's good," Ryan said. "What's she up to?"

"Probably angling for information. I told her everything," I said. "About the threats I've received and my floundering investigation. I figured I'd want to know what was going on if I were her."

Ryan tilted his head slightly. "You would because you're an abnormally curious person. Most people are happy *not* knowing everything that goes on around them."

"I'm not abnormal."

"But are you sure *she* wanted all that drama dropped on her?" he asked.

A sliver of guilt wiggled in my chest. I'd assumed Denise would want to know. I'd thought it best that she not be kept in the dark, and I'd wanted to include her because my decisions could affect her.

I cringed in belated realization. All those thoughts and intentions were about me.

Denise bounded back to my side and grinned. She cocked a hip and raised her brows. "Okay, what did I miss over here? Oh! Tea." She took Ryan's empty water bottle away. "What can I get you?"

Ryan reviewed the large chalkboard on the wall behind me. "Iced ginger peach tea, please. I'm making my way through the list."

"How about some food?" I asked, repeating my question from earlier.

He hooked a thumb over one shoulder, silently indicating Odette and Mr. Pierce. "Did they order food?"

Denise delivered his tea with a napkin. "Yep. Shrimp tacos for him. House salad, no cheese, low-fat raspberry vinaigrette on the side for her."

Ryan rubbed his palms together in excitement. "In that case, I'd like the baked zucchini strips with basil pesto dip and the stuffed mushrooms."

"You got it," I said.

Denise snapped into action, tossing Odette's salad and prepping Mr. Pierce's tacos.

I dipped pre-cut zucchini strips from the fridge into a whipped egg, then doused them with bread-crumbs and lined them on a baking sheet. I added a foursome of stuffed mushrooms and slid the order into my convection oven before giving the timer a twist.

I prepped his plate and filled a small cup with the basil pesto dip while Denise finished the tacos and ferried them to Odette and Mr. Pierce's table.

Ryan and I watched intently as Denise chatted with the elusive pair before returning to the counter.

"Well?" Ryan asked. "What'd they say?"

She frowned. "The teas are delicious. I already knew that. How do you guys get people to tell you things?"

"Usually unintentionally," I admitted. "My interview skills are abysmal."

Denise gave a woeful smile. "You're just trying to make me feel better."

"She isn't, actually," Ryan said. "She's really very terrible."

I laughed despite myself. "Shut up."

Denise crumpled a napkin and tossed it at him.

"We can't all be investigative reporters," I said, still fighting the smile. It wasn't fair that he could be borderline rude and still seem charming. "He's been trying to talk to them for days," I tattled to Denise. "Don't feel bad."

Several minutes later, the oven dinged, and I removed the tray.

Denise helped me plate the piping hot zucchini and mushrooms, then I set the cup of basil pesto dip beside the plate.

Ryan looked from her face to mine. "That was perfectly choreographed," he said, motioning from us to the plate before him. "How many times a day do you do that?"

"None," I said, but he was right. Denise and I made a great team.

She tapped petal-pink nails on the counter, her gaze distant, lost in thought. "That blogger should've compiled a detailed packet of evidence against the true killer, then made arrangements with a trusted ally to send it to the local police and media if anything happened to him."

Ryan plunged a zucchini strip into his dip cup before stuffing it into his mouth. "I think I saw that episode. *Law and Order*, right?"

Denise ignored the jibe. She pulled her phone from her apron pocket and began tapping the screen. "The blogger world is in upheaval over the Canary's death. There are at least a dozen conspiracy theories going around right now. Some of these are ridiculous." She shook her head at the screen. "Someone says his death was faked to get more hits on his blog. Someone says Mitzi's husband killed him to stop the Canary from sharing more details about her death. Someone says Mitzi's husband killed him because he blamed the Canary's continual coverage of Mitzi's life for leading a killer to her on the island. Someone says the Canary killed himself because he couldn't live without Mitzi in the world."

Ryan popped a mushroom cap into his mouth and chewed. "We aren't short on information or theories this time around. Too bad I don't know what's worth looking into and what's a waste of time. Chasing every lead has me exhausted, frustrated, and spinning my wheels."

"Excuse me." I stepped away to ring up two couples

up at the register and seat a family of four. When I returned to check on my friends at the counter, Ryan's plate was empty and Denise was chewing her thumbnail. "Anything new?" I asked.

"No, but this is a rush," Denise said, looking up from her phone screen with enthusiasm. "So much more exciting than my usual daily duties. I really needed this. I'm going to keep helping."

I shot a proud smile at Ryan. I hadn't dumped my drama on Denise and bummed her out. She was happy to be involved. "Make sure you tell Grady I forbid it."

Her lips pulled into a deep pout.

"What do you think we should look into first?" I asked, turning my attention to her phone screen.

She moved in close to my side and scrolled through a few of the more interesting blog posts with me.

The gentle tinkle of my seashell wind chimes drew our attention a few minutes later.

Odette and Mr. Pierce's table was empty, a small stack of cash tucked under one plate.

Ryan dusted breadcrumbs from his palms, then slid off his seat. "That's my cue." He dropped a twenty on the counter and went after the pair he'd been trailing for days.

I hoped for his sake Grady was right about them.

CHAPTER
TWENTY-FOUR

I spent the afternoon creating a spreadsheet to organize my thoughts about who killed Mitzi. The Canary had been at the top of my suspect list until he'd confessed to the crime postmortem. Now, I realized, my top suspects were either Odette, her father, the two of them working in tandem, or Rose. Grady had discounted Odette and her father, but both Odette and Rose had means and motive, and Mr. Pierce could have gained access through the nature center's open back door, giving him means as well. And he definitely had motive. I made note of that on my spreadsheet. I recalled Odette's strange reaction to the news of Mitzi's murder and Rose's extreme interest in gossip on the Canary's death, and both women seemed plausible as killers. Then someone else's face came to mind.

Mr. Pendle had been at Charming Reads when I met the Canary. He'd witnessed him giving me the folder of information on Mitzi, and he'd quickly become a volunteer on the Bee Loved documentary. Why would a fifty-something attorney do grunt work for free and without an obvious driving motivation?

How much did I really know about Pendle? I'd met him through Mr. Butters. He'd given me his business card, and I hadn't thought much about him after that. But he'd been there the day someone locked me in the archives, and he was there this morning, listening as we'd discussed the possibility the Canary was murdered. He'd called the potential twist "brilliant, depending on perspective." Was he just a strange guy? Merely an obsessed fan? *Or was he something worse?*

I went onto the deck to clear the tables and my head a few minutes before closing time.

Lou greeted me with a throaty caw and an enthusiastic ruffle of his feathers. He spread his wings, showing off an impressive seagull bod and stout little legs, then bobbed and weaved in the ocean breeze as if he were already in flight.

"Looking good, Lou," I said, wiping big wet circles over the tabletops and chairs with a blue polka-dotted rag. "Any chance you overheard who killed Mitzi during one of your flights around the island?"

He cocked his head and fixed one beady black eye on me, then blinked.

"No? Well, do you know who's been threatening me or who pushed the Canary off the lighthouse? 'Cause I could really use some help on this right now."

Lou put down his wings and sidestepped along the railing in my direction.

I froze mid-table-wipe. Lou wasn't normally a close talker. He was wild and skittish, only appearing friendly as long as I respected his space and kept a healthy distance. Then again, I'd fed him shrimp, fish, and scallops through the freezing winter, and I was pretty sure he'd saved my life. Maybe that kind of bonding entitled us to sit a little closer from time to time.

He turned to face me, then opened his beak. When no sound came out, he performed the motion again.

I held my breath in anticipation while ridiculous notions circled my frantic mind. What if my aunts were right? What if Lou really was the reincarnation of the wealthy businessman who'd commissioned the house and was now destined to haunt it? What if he was about to tell me what I needed to know?

"Caw!"

I yipped and stumbled back, then burst into laughter. What was wrong with me?

"Everly?"

I spun to find an amused-looking Wyatt in the doorway behind me, one hand braced on either side of the open deck door.

"Whatcha doing?" he drawled, white teeth gleaming in a spectacular smile.

I straightened my expression and my posture, then went back to wiping tables. "Nothing."

"You sure?" he asked, moving onto the deck with me. "Because it looked like you were talking to that seagull and expecting an answer."

"Caw!" Lou screamed, and I jumped again.

Wyatt laughed.

I motioned him back inside, then slid the door shut behind me.

"Caw! Caw! Caw!" Lou hopped to the deck floor and screamed at us through the window. "Caw! Caw! Caw!"

"Maybe he wants to place an order," Wyatt suggested.

I gave Lou a long, contemplative look, then remembered that my aunts were full-on bananas—it was part of their charm. But I was sane, and seagulls weren't reincarnated businessmen.

I leaned a hip against the counter and smiled, feeling utterly foolish. "How about you? Are you here because you're hungry, or did you come to check up on me again?"

Wyatt patted his washboard abs. "I'm always hungry, especially if you're cooking."

"Smart man," I said, easing around to the business side of my counter. "What'll it be?" I glanced at my watch. "It's after seven, and I'm officially closed, so you can consider this a visit between friends and disregard what's on the menu board. You name it. I'll make it."

"That's awfully accommodating," he said. "What's on your mind?"

"What do you mean?" I asked, pulling a skillet from the rack and setting it on the stove. Wyatt only ordered one thing when I gave him carte blanche. Grilled cheese. Plain white bread. American cheese.

"You could've made me pick from the stuff you have mostly prepared already, but you didn't. You're willing to make anything I want from scratch at closing time. That tells me you're looking for a distraction. I'm here and willing to listen, so you might as well talk it out."

I sighed. "Sometimes I forget how well you know me." It was easy to remember the bad times that had led to our breakup, probably because losing someone as important as Wyatt had hurt like crazy. Focusing on why it was good that he was gone made it easier. Remembering he was a good guy who treated me well and loved animals, the beach, and my town but wanted something different out of life made it harder to recall why we couldn't work it out.

A mischievous smile curved the side of his mouth. "I used to know you very well."

I grabbed a fresh-baked loaf of bread and a knife. I shook the long, serrated tool at him. "Whatever image just went through your mind, forget it immediately." I sliced the loaf carefully and buttered two slices.

"All right," Wyatt said. "I'll take a grilled cheese, please."

And it seemed I knew him too. I heated a pan, then fished a slice of American cheese from the refrigerator. "How's life for an island cowboy these days?"

"Not bad. Seems I'm doing better than the local tea shop owner," he said. "I hear you're having quite the week."

I assembled the sandwich and set it in the skillet,

then told myself not to kill the messenger. Wyatt hadn't been the one gossiping. He'd been the one who heard something that sent him my way. "So you *are* here to check on me."

"Do you mind?" He clasped his big hands on the counter. "It's good to be cared for, isn't it?"

"I can't exactly complain." I flipped the sandwich and tried to imagine who would have talked to Wyatt about my harrowing week. My inner circle wasn't very big. I couldn't believe Ryan was the leak and getting information from Grady was like getting cash from Scrooge McDuck. It was possible my aunts had confided in Wyatt. They loved him. And I couldn't help wondering if Denise had said more than she should. There had definitely been a spark between her and Wyatt the last time I'd seen them together.

I plated the finished sandwich and turned off my stovetop. "Who talked?" I asked bluntly. "Or am I the lead story on our gossip blog again?"

Wyatt tore the sandwich in half with his fingers, creating a stringy yellow bridge between the golden slices. "Nope. Nothing like that. I ran into the guy from the documentary at work today and we got to talking."

"Quinn?" I asked.

Wyatt shoved the corner of one half of the sandwich in his mouth. "The one with the schoolboy haircut and hipster clothes," he said around a mouthful of toasted bread and cheese.

"That's Quinn," I said. "And he wears normal

clothes. I'm not sure how he can stand the long-sleeved shirts in this heat, but to each his own." I was a little relieved to know it had been Quinn who'd spilled my stories instead of Ryan or Denise. They knew I wouldn't have appreciated it. Quinn probably hadn't given my feelings a second thought. News was just news to him. "What did he say?" I grabbed a tea jar and filled it with ice, then set the cubes afloat in a flood of old-fashioned sweet tea.

"I guess I started it," he said, accepting the sweet tea with a smile. "I introduced myself and asked how the documentary was going. He remembered me from the luncheon. He saw me taking your aunts home, so he asked if I'd heard about what happened to you at their house. Freaked him out."

I rolled my eyes. "Yeah, I'm sure my being locked in the archives and threatened with bees must've been terrifying for him."

Wyatt laughed. "To hear him tell it, yes. That guy's all about the science and the bees. This whole week has been a little too much for him, but he thinks your aunts are brilliant. I don't think he's too impressed with the lady doing the filming."

"I get the same feeling," I said, "and I don't disagree. I actually think she might be trying to create a special on Mitzi's death while making the Bee Loved documentary on the side. Aunt Clara and Aunt Fran said they barely did any filming until the last two days. Before then, all Rose wanted to do was interview the Mitzi Calgon fans."

"You don't like Rose either," Wyatt said, stuffing the last of the sandwich between his lips.

"I don't like that she's my main suspect right now and spends a huge chunk of her time with my aunts every day."

Wyatt frowned. "I assume you've told your detective about this. What does he say?"

I bit my tongue against the truth. Grady wasn't mine, and he didn't like it when I shared theories. "Mostly, he thinks I should stay out of his investigation," I said.

Wyatt laughed. "He always says that."

"Well, he doesn't say much else on the matter, so I'm left making guesses."

"Anything I can do to help?" Wyatt asked.

"Not unless you know anything about a middle-aged attorney and visiting Mitzi-fan named Burt Pendle. Short. Bald. White beard," I said.

Wyatt shook his head. "Nope."

"It's okay. I'll figure it out."

"You always do." Wyatt finished his tea, and I refilled him without asking. He cocked an eyebrow. "Something else on your mind?"

I leaned my forearms on the counter and focused on his sincere, handsome face. "Are you really thinking about giving up the rodeo?"

He sighed. "Why? You worried about me, E?"

"Little bit," I said. "I've never known you without it. It's part of who you are, or at least it was." My heart pinched as I voiced the concerns I'd been toiling with since he first mentioned quitting. "I don't want you to give up on your dream."

"People get new dreams," he said, a lazy half-smile tilting his lips. "I like that you worry about me, but my life is good here."

"But will it be enough?"

He nodded, slow and steady. "It is enough."

I felt my smile return. "You're sure?"

"Sure as I can be. Sure I haven't been itching to get back in the saddle. I haven't been re-watching my old tapes, looking for ways to improve my technique. Heck, I eat here more times a week than I work out, and it feels good."

I bit my tongue against a comment on his physique, which looked good.

"Feels like freedom," Wyatt said. "You know what I do these days?"

"You laugh more," I said, enjoying the gleam in his eye.

"I do, and I watch sunrises and sunsets. I track the wild mustangs and teach folks about them. I hang out with my buddies from work. I got my lifeguard certification last week. For the first time in my life, my world's about more than bulls and blood. I haven't been to the emergency room in a year. I might actually pay off all my hospital bills if I keep this up."

I laughed, and he lifted his tea in cheers and took a long drink.

"I'm happy, Everly."

"Then you'll stay in Charm?" I asked, realizing I'd

been a little worried he might leave. "You're not going to get bored and run off?"

"Nah." He locked his fingers behind his head, elbows pointing out. "I'm thinking of buying a house."

I took a minute to let that sink in. He was planting real roots, and he was doing it in Charm. "I can absolutely get behind that. Where are you looking?"

"Up the beach." He tipped his chin and dropped his hands to his lap. "Four-by-four country."

"Four-by-four-country," I repeated, feeling the perfection of his choice in my marrow. Locals lovingly referred to the narrowest strip of our island, at the northernmost tip, as "four-by-four country." It was the least modernized and most secluded. The roads were bad to nonexistent, and folks needed a four-wheel drive vehicle to access it. Homes were short and stout, built on pillars in the surf because the sea at high tide didn't leave much dry. Four-by-four country was also quite possibly the most peaceful, natural, beautiful land on earth, definitely in all of North Carolina. The maritime forest curved along the tip and ran down the eastern side. The bulk of Charm's wild mustangs lived there. Wyatt and I used to picnic there. It was fitting that it would be his home. "That sounds perfect."

He winked, then stretched onto his feet and pulled me into a hug. "You asked what I'll do instead of rodeo. I'm thinking of starting a weekend school for little cowboys. Maybe kindergarten through middle school or whatever age boys discover girls and start thinking it's not cool to attend a school for little cowboys."

He laughed, and I joined him. "All right," I said. "I love it."

"I'd teach basic care of horses. Feeding. Grooming. Stall cleaning. Offer beginner riding lessons. Maybe teach some roping. Go hiking. Talk to them about respecting their folks, neighbors, friends, animals, and nature." He shrugged. "That's if the nature center accepts my program proposal. If so, we'll put out some flyers, see if any local kids bite."

I pressed my cheek to his solid chest and squeezed. "That sounds amazing."

There was pride and satisfaction in Wyatt's eyes when I stepped back to take a closer look at the man before me. He seemed lit with hope and enthusiasm, and I loved it. "Will I see you at the memorial tonight?" I asked.

"Yeah. Me and some of the nature center employees volunteered to help. Management asked us to hang out, just be present in case anyone has questions or gets rowdy. That sort of thing."

I walked him out, then went through my evening routine in the café. I left a few minutes later, hoping to catch my aunts at home and walk with them. I had questions for Rose and possibly Mr. Pendle, if they were together. If not, I'd ask my aunts for feedback and opinions on my theories. Aunt Clara and Aunt Fran were never short on either.

I cut across town, internally gagging at the upcropping of Mary Grace for Mayor signs. I considered pulling them down or drawing mustaches on her image, but I decided to be the bigger woman. I also wondered briefly if I'd been too quick to dismiss her as a suspect. Would Mary Grace really kill to make Aunt Fran look bad at election time? She was certainly using the Mitzi commotion to her full advantage, saving the town from unlawfully parked food trucks and news vans. Anything to keep herself in the spotlight.

"Everly!" Mr. Waters waved from his post outside Molly's Market, where he swept the sidewalk.

"Hi, Mr. Waters," I called, crossing the street to greet him.

He stilled his broom and cupped his hands over the handle's top. "Beautiful day."

I took in the soft evening light, the sun dipping lower in the sky with each passing hour and the majestic amber and apricot hues coating our world. "It really is."

"Are you attending the memorial on the bay?" he asked. "A real shame what happened to that poor lady."

"I am," I said. "I'm trying to catch my aunts so we can walk together."

Rose and Quinn appeared at the mouth of the alley, drenched in the waning sunlight and clearly at odds over something. She flung her hands wide, then let them flop to her sides before walking away. Her conservative black suit and heels were a drastic departure from the usual jeans and T-shirt—an ensemble presumably chosen for her appearance at Mitzi's memorial, the unexpected joint effort between Bee Loved and Mary Grace Chatsworth.

Quinn shook his head at her retreating form.

"Evening, Quinn," Mr. Waters called.

Quinn blanched when he saw us watching him. A moment later a smile formed and he headed our way. "What are the two of you up to?"

"Sweeping." Mr. Waters smiled, facetiously stating the obvious. "How are your arms and back?"

Quinn blushed. "Better. Thanks." He turned his eyes on me. "You're not sweeping?"

"No." I chuckled. "I'm going to catch my aunts before the memorial. You?"

"I'm headed back to my rental." He looked at his blue-striped button-down and chinos. "I have to change."

I nodded, trying not to wonder how my outfit stacked up. The black walking shorts and gray silk blouse had felt fancy until I'd seen Rose's suit. "Which way are you headed?" I asked.

Quinn pointed, and I swooped a hand through the air, indicating he should join me. "See you later, Mr. Waters."

Quinn and I moved through town in the awkward silence I was beginning to associate with him. When the buildings and traffic faded into the background, I turned to him, multiple questions jockeying for position in my mind.

"Can I ask you something?" I said.

"Sure," he said. "What's up?"

"I've been looking into what happened to the Canary," I said gently. "You were the last person I

know that he talked to, and I'm still trying to understand why he ran from me on the boardwalk that
day only to call later and request that we meet up."
I looked both ways before stepping off the curb into
the crosswalk. With some luck, Quinn wouldn't shut
me down or be upset when I told him what I thought
about Rose. They'd gone to college together and they
were partners now, but I needed him to be willing to
share information and hear me out. "I have a theory
about who killed the Canary and Mitzi," I said, finally
finding my nerve.

"Me too," Quinn said softly, raising a hand to
my neck. "Sorry," he whispered as the sting of metal
buried deep into my skin.

CHAPTER

TWENTY-FIVE

My knees went weak, and Quinn hooked an arm around mine to steady me. His long sleeve rode up a few inches to reveal a set of deep red scratches. "How about we take a walk on the beach?" he suggested as I struggled to keep up, both physically and mentally. "Tide's coming in, and I found an easily accessible, but quite private, little cave not far from here."

"Your arm," I said, clearing my throat several times before I could form the words. "Cat scratches."

He peered at me with a sour expression. "Your psychotic cat should be euthanized. She chased me relentlessly through the marsh and down alleys. She tore up my arm and my back when I finally refused to run anymore. I dropped the file twice and half of it was ruined by marsh muck. If I had time, I'd find that cat before I go home and throw her in the ocean."

My hackles raised. "That's why you're always dressed like this. To cover your wounds."

"It's not as if I can go around in shorts and sandals with long sleeves, now can I?"

"I hope they hurt," I said, feeling spiteful for Maggie's sake. "Why'd you care what was in the file?" I snapped. "It had nothing to do with you."

"I didn't know that," he said. "Skeet collected information about the documentary because it related to Mitzi. I needed to know if he had information about me because I was involved in the documentary. I couldn't risk the cops tracking her death back to me through the sedative I used. It's produced at a lab in my office building. Probably at a hundred other sites across the country too, but the fact I had access to this one could have been my undoing. I needed to know."

"There wasn't anything like that in the file," I said, my mouth growing pastier by the second.

"I know now," he snapped. "And I didn't hurt you to get that file. I covered your head gently with a clean pillowcase and ran away. I never meant to hurt anyone," he said with a crushing squeeze of my arm. "Everything has gotten completely out of control, thanks to you."

"Me?" I blinked to clear my vision as Quinn looked both ways before steering me across the street, toward the beach. "You pushed the Canary out of the lighthouse window," I accused, my addled mind fitting pieces together one by one. "You wrote the fake suicide note to wrap things up and save your hide. He ran from me when he was with you because you'd threatened him. You probably forbade him to talk to me."

"He ran from me when you saw us because I'd just threatened his life and you became a witness. He took the opportunity to escape."

My tingling jaw dropped. "You've been behind all of this. You sent that creepy poem and those island stalker photos. I'll bet you even sent the letters to Mitzi back in California." My ears rang and my speech began to slur. "You befriended the Canary so you could use him. You wanted him to use his blog and influence to lead people down the paths you created. You wanted him dead because he could point the finger at you for all of that!" A bit of drool slid over my bottom lip, and my eyelids drooped.

"Smart girl," he said. "But so, so dumb."

As Quinn checked for nonexistent traffic, I willed my numbing hands to free my phone from my back pocket, opposite him. We'd moved too far away from the action to be noticed at this hour, and the setting sun was quickly replacing light with shadow.

I stole fleeting blurry glances at my phone each time Quinn's head jerked in the opposite direction, drawn by distant sounds or his own paranoia. My scrambled mind struggled to remember how to dial for help, and my buzzing hand was losing strength. With hope and a prayer, I aimed my heavy, uncoordinated thumb at the little icon Ryan had put on my home screen and gave it a thump. My arm fell limp at my side a half heartbeat later, and I begged my fingers not to let go.

"What are you doing?" he asked, tugging me

forward as he scanned the area for witnesses to his crime. "Hurry up."

"You drugged me," I said, the words falling from my prickly tongue in slow, thick slurs. "What did you think would happen? Why did you do that?"

"Quiet," he snapped, his voice low and controlled. "You're going to draw attention."

"Are you working with Rose?" I asked. "Did she put you up to this?" Each word came loud and messy. Had I imagined the wrong homicidal duo all along? I'd suspected Odette and her father when the real killers were Quinn and Rose? "What did you do to me? Are you going to kill me too?"

Quinn tightened his grip on my arm until I squeaked in pain. "I said shut up. I gave you the same sedative I gave Skeet and Mitzi. They didn't feel a thing and neither will you in a few minutes. Now, keep moving before I have to carry you." He paused when our feet left solid ground and sunk deep into mounds of dry sand at the beach's edge. The ominous crash and roll of waves was suddenly clear and unhindered. "I doubt I can carry you in this," he said, scrutinizing my body. "Or at all." He jerked me back into motion. "Just keep moving."

My muddled mind was stupidly hurt by his words. Clearly spoken by someone who'd never struggled with his weight. Did he think I wanted to be this size? That I wanted to get winded running up my stairs? A tear slid over my cheek, and I hated myself for caring about my dress size when I was obviously being taken to my death. It was all just too much.

"Get up!" Quinn yelled.

I puzzled over the order. Up where? I opened my eyes, not realizing they'd closed, and the warm caress of sand on my skin finally registered. My legs had buckled, and I was lying on the beach. A perfect twilight sky stretched overhead, streaking shades of violet and periwinkle across the heavens.

Quinn cursed.

I strained to see him past my feet, where he'd taken position and begun to pull.

My lifeless arms went over my head behind me as he dragged me from the dry sand to the heavy-packed and painful stuff near the water's edge. My phone was gone, and so was my lifeline, if I'd ever really had one.

"You just couldn't let this go," Quinn complained as he grunted and pulled. "Neither of those people meant anything to you, and you still had to take up a personal crusade over a gossip blogger and a washed-up movie star. Ridiculous. I didn't even mean to kill her. Should I spend the rest of my life in jail for an accident? A mistake? Everyone makes mistakes. I'm not a doctor. I took syringes from the lab across the hall so I could drug Mitzi and embarrass her. I just wanted her to leave Rose's precious project. How was I supposed to know the old lady was allergic to bees? What kind of lunatic attaches herself to a *save the bees* project when their stings will literally kill her?"

Quinn stopped to catch his breath at the edge of the water, and the cool tide licked my face and hair.

Panic welled in me. I couldn't swim in my condition,

but maybe I could float if I could stay awake. The sea and I were kindred spirits. She wouldn't kill me if I could just keep my eyes open and not float so far away that a wave knocked me under. Maybe I could even float into someone's view down the beach. Surely there were couples still walking along the surf at this hour. The entire island wasn't attending the memorial.

When the water retreated, it pulled a large portion of sand from beneath me, and the next rush of tide crashed against my ear, flooding my face and choking me.

"Come on," Quinn said. "You can't drown there. Someone will find you before I get off this wretched island." He repositioned his grip under my arms and dragged me into a shallow earthen cave, worn into the side of a small hill. The space was nothing special and it smelled of dirt and mud. The hill protruded above us and curved out a few feet on each side, just enough to conceal me as I drowned.

Quinn propped me against the back of the cave and stripped the tie from around his neck.

He tied my wrists together with the silken accessory, then released me with a grunt.

The jagged mud-and-stone wall held me upright, legs sticking out before me, bound hands lying uselessly on my lap.

"Hopefully, the drugs will knock you out completely before the water reaches your face," he said. "The others were unconscious by now, but they both weighed less. Just give it a few minutes."

Another hot tear ran down my cheek. Then another. "You don't have to do this," I cried, the words barely more than rasps and whispers.

"I'm going to do better when I get home," Quinn said. "I'll double down on the good I can do with science and research. I won't get drawn into Rose's nonsense again. I don't need to be a part of her artsy schemes to raise money for my work. I'll use my theories and findings to wow minds and raise interest on my own."

He rubbed a palm against the back of his neck and turned to watch the water. "All I wanted was to stop Mitzi Calgon from supporting this documentary so we'd have to start over looking for funding. Rose only got the money because your aunts gave her Mitzi. Without her, this would have been my project. I'd raised enough to cover the cost of a short scientific film, but Rose landed big money and took the reins. Now she calls the shots and I'm little more than a silent partner. The film she's making won't help anyone but her. She's made a mockery of your aunts, who are brilliant." He shook his head as water rushed into the cave, washing over his feet to cover my legs and bottom. He lifted his soaking shoes as the tide pulled sand from beneath them. "I've got to go."

"Please don't," I begged.

But he was gone.

My mind lightened and floated as the world outside my tomb grew dark. I dreamed I was a kid again, between smacks of cold water. Running on the beach, flying kites, building castles with my grandma. She was young and so were Aunt Clara and Aunt Fran. They wrapped me in their arms and told me stories of ancestors who'd beaten all odds. Swan women were cursed in love, but we were safe on our island. We belonged here. We were enchanted here.

My head rolled against the earthen wall and water lapped my chin, popping my eyes open again.

I sucked in a sharp breath, my will suddenly restored. Adrenaline surged in my veins and fought against the drugs. The water was deep, and my arms floated in front of me like disembodied zombie limbs. *Help!* I thought. *Help!* But the word didn't come.

I opened my mouth to try again, and water ran inside. The briny sting burned my eyes and nose. I choked and gagged as another wave crashed over me, covering my face for an eternity before retreating briefly, then coming again.

"Help!" The word erupted from my burning throat and echoed in my ears, absorbed instantly by water in the filling cave.

"Everly!" My name came back to me on the wind, distant and weak. A whisper that had traveled too far. A hallucination. Or maybe an ancestor coming to collect me from the grave.

Except, I didn't want to be collected. Or in a grave.

I wanted to live.

I opened my mouth again as the next wave retreated, freeing my nose and mouth. I tipped my head back, keeping my air passages temporarily clear.

And I screamed. The next wave rode over me, enveloping my face before I could prepare.

I gagged and choked, swallowing gulps and lungfuls of the ocean, no longer able to find air.

The tide had won. The water covered me.

And I would die like I had in my dreams of Magnolia Bane. Lost to the sea.

CHAPTER

TWENTY-SIX

Something gripped my arms and pulled me into the sea. I was floating. Flying. *Dying,* I thought, the heartbeat that had echoed in my ears growing soft and thin.

I was dying.

My back collided with something hard and rough, stealing the lovely ethereal sensations from my limbs, and replacing them with a steady rocking pressure against my chest.

Then, I heard the angry voice.

"Come on, Everly!" the voice demanded. "Breathe! *Dammit!* Breathe!"

Something was wrong. Someone was angry, and I felt…*bad.*

My chest constricted and ached. The burn spread across my torso, cracking my peace like an eggshell. Spilling the lovely warmth from my bones and replacing it with icy chills. I opened my mouth and gave up the water that had filled me.

"Everly," an angel whispered. "I knew you could do it. You're a fighter. Stay with me, now." His breath sweet on my cheek. His hands familiar in my hair. "Over here!" he called. "Hurry!"

I peeled my stinging, blurry eyes open and found Grady staring back.

His face was as white as the moon above us, his eyes as glossy as the sea. "Stay with me," he said again, and a set of tears fell over his stubbled cheeks. "Don't go, Everly. Hear me?"

I nodded as a pair of people in matching EMT uniforms landed in the sand beside us.

Grady had found me. He'd saved me, and he was right. I was a fighter.

❧

Four weeks later, I fought with my unruly hair, a body-shaper designed in Hades and the zipper on my new dress. Then, I collected myself and my beaded clutch before stepping bravely into the night. I would have preferred to curl up in my old home forever like a conch in her shell, but I had a party to attend.

"I still can't believe you agreed to come to this with me," I said an hour later, sinking my teeth into a strawberry I'd dunked in chocolate. Maybe it was the near-death experience, being saved by Grady's impressive mouth-to-mouth skills, or the fact I was eating tons of delicious foods Mary Grace Chatsworth-Vanders had paid for, but I was in heaven.

The ambience Mary Grace's reception planner had created was lavish and decadent. They'd been right to choose the historic home on the bay for the event. It was like a scene from *The Great Gatsby*, except everything was white and drenched in wedding-themed décor. Hundreds of roses filled dozens of crystal vases, their petals adorning every flat surface from tabletops to windowsills. Collections of flameless pillar candles were arranged in mounds of sand and surrounded by clusters of seashells and sand dollars—a tribute to our island I couldn't help but love. The food had been flown in from a hoity five-star catering service on the mainland, and it was delicious. My taste buds took extensive notes on foods I wanted to try at the café.

Grady stole the rest of the strawberry from my fingertips and stuffed it into his mouth. "It's not as if I could have told you no," he said. "Most of the town is here, and you're wearing that dress."

If he knew about the commercial grade spandex keeping me from busting a zipper or taking a deep breath, he would've been less impressed. "You clean up pretty well yourself, Detective Hays," I said, giving his lapel a little pat.

He stared at my lips a long moment before smiling back at my eyes. "How are you feeling?"

I paused to make an internal assessment. It was my first official outing after my run-in with death, but all things considered, I was doing okay. I'd only closed Sun, Sand, and Tea for a few days before returning to business as usual. The doctors had prescribed rest when they released me from the hospital after a night of observation, but too much peace and quiet had made me antsy. Cooking and baking had always been my drugs of choice, so I'd done that instead. The processes of chopping, measuring, and mixing soothed my mind. The soft tick of a heating oven helped me process the trauma and re-center my thoughts. Owning and operating my café had been just the therapy I needed.

Denise, Amelia, and my aunts had done the things I couldn't, like shopping and errands. It had taken two weeks for me to venture off my porches and decks. I still hadn't gone farther than my garden alone, but I was getting braver by the day. It was strange how quickly my body had recovered from the trauma of the cave and how tightly my mind was holding on.

"Everly?" he pressed, stepping closer, looking acutely unsure.

I forced a tight smile and selected another strawberry. "I'm good."

He narrowed his eyes, evaluating me. "It's a crowded room. New place. Lots of noise."

"I'm okay." I patted his chest. "I'm not alone or in danger. I'm with you."

Grady was convinced I had a touch of PTSD, and I didn't want to think about whether he was right or wrong. I just wanted to press on, and tonight seemed like a good time to begin.

"I don't mind the crowd," I said. "I know almost everyone, and they've all been very sweet and kind. The atmosphere and location are posh and inviting. Food and music are great. Company's not bad." I smiled. "I feel a little like a nineteenth-century debutante entering society. Plus, my appearance tonight should stop the incessant gossip over my well-being. Half the town has seen me looking poised and happy tonight."

Grady smiled. "I've always wanted to dance with a debutante." He relieved me of my plate and lifted my right hand in his. Then he twirled me.

My creamy sheath dress flared at the knee as I spun.

When he pulled me against his chest and secured a strong arm around my back, I nearly swooned. I was pretty sure I could spend eternity like that and never want for anything else.

"Oh, get a room." Ryan's voice reached my ears before I saw his approach. And despite myself, I smiled.

Grady groaned and released me. "Does he live here now or what?" he asked quietly as Ryan and Amelia approached from the nearby dance floor.

Her dress was sky blue and floor length. It accentuated her petite frame with an elegant neckline and sexy side slit to her knee. She'd worked her blond hair into a side chignon and added rhinestone earrings and a necklace. I envied her sense of style and ability to remain upright in four-inch, open-toe heels.

I hugged her immediately. "You look beautiful," I whispered.

"Thanks, you too." She kissed my cheek and released me.

"Va-va-voom," Ryan said, leaning in to kiss my cheek as well. He straightened and extended a hand to Grady. "I don't know, detective, but I think we might be here with the prettiest ladies on the island tonight. The bride must hate that she invited you."

"Oh, she does," I said. "The bride hates me."

"The bride hates everything," Amelia said.

Grady accepted Ryan's handshake. "Welcome back, reporter. You here on another big story?"

"I'm here on a big date," Ryan said, winking at Amelia.

She beamed, and I couldn't help liking Ryan a little more. I had to give the man credit. He made her happy.

Ryan gave me a long look. "How are you?"

"Annoyed."

He barked a laugh, then looked to Grady and tipped his head in my direction. "How's she doing?"

"Not bad," Grady said. "She's tough. Brave. Resilient. And gorgeous in this dress that I'm betting she can't wait to change out of."

Amelia smiled at him. "Agreed."

"Is it that obvious?" I asked, fighting the urge to tug at my plunging neckline.

Grady's eyes sparkled. "No, but I know you'd rather be on the beach. I would too, which is why I brought a change of clothes for later."

An instant smile split my face. "Do you think there'll be time?"

Grady and I had ended most nights this month

with a walk on the beach. I looked forward to our
walks like I'd once looked forward to birthdays and
Christmases. The hot summer nights were perfect for
bare feet in the surf. Sharing a blanket on the sand and
staring at the stars. "I thought you'd have to go home.
You know Mary Grace will drag this out all night."

"I'm not staying here all night," he said. "I have
things to do."

I grinned.

Ryan watched Grady and me, his keen gaze moving
from my face to his.

My cheeks heated furiously as I imagined what was
going through his know-it-all head.

"What happened with Quinn at the arraignment?"
Ryan asked, momentarily confusing me. "Off-record,
of course. I'm just dying to know you got this
son-of-a—"

Amelia cleared her throat.

"Biscuit," Ryan finished.

Grady cast a guarded look at me as he stretched
taller, angling himself protectively against my side. It
was his standard physical response to questions made
about my captor or that day in my presence. At first,
I'd assumed his predictable tension was about me,
about whether or not I was up to hearing the details
again. Lately, I'd been wondering which of us was
struggling with my abduction more. He thought he
should've been there—instead of at the nature center,
awaiting Quinn's arrival.

Quinn had been right to worry. Grady had traced

the sedative in Mitzi and the Canary's systems to a lab in the building where Quinn worked. He'd found evidence of correspondence between Quinn and the Canary before either of them had left California, and he'd gotten our local news reporter to name Quinn as a source in the leaked photos of Mitzi's death. He'd pulled Quinn's prints from a page of the Canary's folder that had been dropped in the marsh, and he'd matched the pillowcase put over my head in the gazebo with one from the beach rental Quinn shared with Rose. She'd immediately granted Grady access to Quinn's room, and the evidence had stacked into an airtight case. There were receipts for three burner phones from Hilton Head, all with numbers matching the call and texts Mitzi and I had received. A search warrant for Quinn's laptop had done the rest. Grady had followed the facts, he'd identified the killer, and he'd been waiting to take him in.

"It's okay," I said. "It's all good news, and I'm glad."

Ryan took a tray of champagne flutes from a passing waiter. "It's all right," he told him, "I'm with Detective Hays, and we need to commandeer this vehicle."

The waiter rolled his eyes and left the tray with Ryan, who placed it on the nearest table and pulled out a chair for Amelia.

I helped myself to a flute, then chugged it before taking a seat beside her.

I was dealing better each day with what had happened to me in that cave, but it didn't mean I was over it. "Go on." I motioned from Grady to Ryan.

The men unbuttoned their jackets, then took their seats, Grady at my side and Ryan at Amelia's.

She curled her hand over mine on the table and gave my fingers a firm squeeze before releasing them.

"Quinn pleaded guilty to involuntary manslaughter for Mitzi Calgon," Grady began. "He stuck to his claim of only wanting to ruin the documentary with a scandal. He initially tried to end Mitzi's involvement with the Bee Loved project by creating the illusion of a stalker in California. He leaked the details anonymously to Skeet, who was supposed to share them with his followers and raise hysteria within the community. In theory, the stalker would send Mitzi back into hiding. But she was never hiding. She was retired, and a few letters didn't worry her. Quinn continued the charade here with calls to her cell phone, weird poems, and photos. It was unfortunate for Mr. Butters that his painting matched the tone and mood of the poems and letters." He cast an apologetic look in Amelia's direction.

She nodded magnanimously. "It's okay. We're just thankful you're good at your job."

His lips turned down in disagreement, but he nodded back in solemn thanks. "When the stalker didn't send her packing, Quinn resorted to his backup plan—sedatives he'd stolen from a lab in his building. Unfortunately, he didn't know anything about medication interactions or dosages, and he gave each of his victims a deadly amount."

Ryan turned wide eyes on me.

"Her too," Grady said, his voice low and seething. "Despite Quinn's assertion that he wanted to foil the film without committing murder, stealing the sedatives shows premeditation. It will be hard for his attorney to prove the plan wasn't murder all along. I've brought charges against him for stealing and administering the drugs too. Quinn forged the suicide note he left in Skeet Ulvanich's pocket, so first-degree murder charges apply there. He followed Skeet to the lighthouse, then injected him with the drugs and guided him to the top of the steps. He opened the window, balanced him on the ledge, and pushed. Add the kidnapping and attempted murder of Everly..." His voice caught on my name, and he cleared his throat. "Quinn will go away for a long while. I'm making certain of that."

Ryan swirled the bubbly in his glass, considering the statement. "Utilizing some of your most powerful connections, I see."

"I've wrapped this case airtight on my own," Grady said. "He's never walking free."

"Good," Ryan said. "That's everything I'd hoped to hear."

I smiled at Ryan, feeling the sting of emotion in my eyes. "Your dumb livestream app saved my life, you know. I've never properly thanked you for that."

Ryan's jaw tightened. "I know," he said. "I was watching."

I looked to Amelia. We hadn't talked about the specifics of that day, but I knew that the footage of my abduction was streamed to all my followers as it happened. Most of them lived too far away to help or truly understand what was going on, but according to Grady, there had been a search team of Charmers on the beach within minutes.

"We went the wrong way," Amelia said. "I was sure we should start looking near your house."

Ryan gripped her hand on the table, then lifted it to his cheek.

Mr. Waters, apparently also one of my livestream followers, had called Grady and pointed him in the right direction. He'd known I was with Quinn and that we'd headed toward my aunts' home when we left him on the sidewalk. Grady had gone onto the beach and moved in that direction, keeping watch on the unchanging sand and surf image being transmitted by my phone.

"Grady got there in time," I said. "That's what matters. I'm okay, and Quinn can't hurt anyone else."

Anguish washed over Grady's tight expression, and I could practically see the memories replaying in his mind.

He'd found my phone, but the little cave was already underwater. It had looked like any other hill from the beach where he stood. Still, Grady said something had called to him.

Afterward, he'd leaned over the silver rail of my hospital bed and pressed a fist to his chest. He said he'd felt an undeniable need there. A compulsion that had pushed him into the surf despite any logic or evident reason, and that was how he'd discovered the opening. That same sensation had compelled him to swim inside, and he nearly hadn't. He'd almost let logic overcome his instincts, and he beat himself up for it regularly.

The music changed and guests clapped, sharply reminding me of where we were. The DJ played "Do the Funky Chicken" and locals, including Amelia's dad and my Aunt Clara, took to the dance floor in elated droves.

Amelia whistled long and loud as her dad flapped his bent arms like a chicken. "What did Rose decide to do about the documentary?" she asked, pulling her attention off the silliness on the dance floor.

I smiled and sat straighter. This was the fun part of the story. Rose had been so horrified to learn that Quinn had done all those awful things under her nose, she refocused on the documentary she'd come to make, vowing to make it her best work ever. She'd even stayed an extra week to collect serious footage with my aunts and gather enough details to produce a first-class film. "She finished editing last week and is sending my aunts an early review copy very soon. She's even pulled some strings to secure a November 1st release date. Aunt Fran's hoping it will create some pre-election buzz."

"Perfect!" Amelia turned her attention on Grady, curiosity changing her expression slightly. "Is your mother-in-law still running for mayor? I don't think I've seen her entourage around."

"It seems so," he said flatly. "And it sounds as if her husband will be retiring to Charm as well. Not that Olivia's retiring. She's looking forward to making small-town politics the Act Two of her political career."

"Bummer," I said, honestly. "I'd kind of hoped she'd go back to DC with Martin and Northrop Manor could become the living museum Charm had originally planned. My aunts already have ideas for some of the costumes and exhibits. Aunt Clara wants to volunteer as a weekend candlemaker and Aunt Fran is pulling favors from a local war reenactment group to help with the grand opening weekend. Plus, our family archives have detailed firsthand accounts of the evolution of Charm that can be used to ensure authenticity, at least from one family's perspective."

Grady shifted beside me, and the corner of his mouth kicked into a lazy half-smile. "I could get behind that. Olivia and Martin belong in the city. We belong here. Look," he said, his gaze tracking Aunt Fran to the sundae bar with Denver.

She'd pulled a chair up to the table for him to kneel on so his limited height wouldn't hinder his access. He filled a bowl with ice cream, then dug into the toppings with gusto. When he finally put the tiny tongs down, his chocolate ice cream had vanished beneath a pile of crushed cookies and candy. Aunt Fran added a flood of hot fudge and caramel to the top, then gave him a high five.

Amelia laughed, and I realized she had been

watching them too. "I don't think Denver will ever run short of grandparent figures around here."

As if on cue, Amelia's father and Aunt Clara moved in on the sundae action, shaking whipped cream cans and spraying them into their mouths.

Grady smiled.

The music slowed and a spotlight trailed Mary Grace and her new husband to the highly polished parquet dance floor. Her white beaded gown was stunning, a lovely contrast to his black suit as he took her into his arms. The image of a billowing American flag appeared on the large white wall behind them.

"Oh boy," Amelia groaned. "Nothing's too subtle for these two."

I caught sight of Aunt Fran's unhinged jaw and laughed. It was going to be an interesting November this year.

Grady stood and buttoned his jacket, then reached for me. "How about a dance?"

Amelia and Ryan followed us to the dance floor, along with a number of other couples.

"Well, what do you think of that?" Ryan asked as Wyatt and Denise came into view, swaying close and smiling.

I wasn't sure who the question had been intended for, but I answered anyway, in case Grady was worried about Denise. "Wyatt's a good guy. He deserves to be happy, and I don't think he would hurt her."

Ryan snorted. "I don't think he *could* hurt her."

I laughed. "No doubt."

"I hear he's leaving the rodeo," Amelia said, "is that true?"

I watched as he and Denise spun and laughed. I saw an ease and comfort there I'd never seen in Wyatt before, and I recalled her words. "I think so," I said. "It seems Wyatt fooled around and accidentally put down some roots. He found a life he cares more about than bulls and glory."

"This place does that to a man," Grady said, spinning me away from Ryan and Amelia. He watched me intently as we moved in sync to the sweet song. "I asked Denise about Olivia's intentions when she hired her," he said. "The bit about her meeting all my needs. Do you remember?"

My cheeks flamed hot. Of course I remembered. I'd had a crush on Grady since the moment I'd set eyes on him, and the senator had made a point of telling me she'd hired Denise to handle *everything*. Denise lived with Grady. She was five years younger, gorgeous, and fit. I'd eaten my weight in Häagen-Daz after that nightmarish revelation. "What did she say?"

His smile widened. "She called me a pervert and said she was hired as personal protection, in addition to child care and general household administration. Nothing like you'd assumed."

I buried my face against his shirt and laughed. "Did you tell her I was the one who'd told you that?"

"Yes." His chest rose and fell in silent bursts of laughter. "She thought it was funny after she got past the shock."

I dragged my gaze to his and rested my chin against his chest. "She must think I'm an idiot."

"She thinks you might've been jealous," he said, looking light and youthful as he spun me around the dance floor.

"You're not so bad," I said. "And I like how you move. I also appreciate that you keep saving my life."

His expression darkened and his body slowed to an easy sway. "Speaking of that," he said. "I hear you're in the market for some self-defense lessons."

"I am," I said. "Denise promised to help me as soon as I'm ready." The brush with death had set me back emotionally by a few weeks, but I was having fewer nightmares and feeling more like myself every day.

"How would you feel about getting the lessons from me?" he asked, his expression guarded and a little vulnerable.

I nodded. "Okay."

"Yeah?" he asked, a hint of disbelief in his tone.

"Sure," I said, feeling a rush of heat hit my cheeks once more. "But I've never done anything like it before, so try not to hurt me."

"Never," he breathed, pulling me close.

I pressed my cheek back to his jacket and watched as my friends and family danced, laughed, and mingled. My heart expanded until it hurt. I'd never expected to find a perfect moment at Mary Grace's wedding reception, but this one was incredibly close.

Grady lowered his lips to my ear. "What are you thinking, Swan?"

"That I'm happy," I said. "That I feel safe and peaceful and proud."

I felt the curve of Grady's smile against my cheek. "Me too," he said. "You want to get out of here before someone ruins it?"

"Absolutely."

Grady lifted a hand in goodbye to Amelia and Ryan as we headed for the door.

"I'm thinking we eat lemon cake on the beach and look at the stars," I said.

Grady held the door and watched me as I passed. "I can do you one better."

"Doubtful," I said, narrowing suspicious eyes on him. "How?"

He led me to his truck and leaned smugly against my door without opening it. "I've got about two hundred letters in there that I busted out of evidence this afternoon."

Instant tears blurred my eyes. "You have my grandma's letters?"

"No," he said. "You do." He opened the door for me to climb inside.

I threw my arms around his neck instead, and I knew our night was only going to get better.

RECIPES FROM SUN, SAND, AND TEA

Ginger Pear Iced Tea

A Swan family favorite that's sure to be yours too!

Yield: 8 servings | Total time: 2 hours 30 minutes

8 cups water
2 ripe pears, cored and cut into slices or chunks
1 ginger root, peeled and sliced
4 dates
1 cinnamon stick
Sugar (optional)

Combine all ingredients in a pot and bring to a boil.

Reduce the heat, partially cover the pot, and simmer up to 2 hours, until the pears are soft.

Remove from the heat, cool, and strain out the solids.

Pour over ice and sweeten with sugar as desired.

Mango Shrimp Spring Rolls

Yield: 8 servings | Total time: 30–40 minutes

8 spring roll wrappers or rice wrappers
16 large cooked shrimp, peeled, deveined, and
    tails removed
½ ripe mango, peeled and cut into strips
Fresh cilantro
Bean sprouts
Mint leaves (optional) or chili powder (optional)

Set up an assembly line with items prepped and
ready to go.
Slice the shrimp into 2 pieces long ways.
Prepare the rice wrappers by placing, individually,
into a bowl or skillet of warm water until moist
(3–4 seconds).
Arrange 2 shrimp (4 slices) on the prepared wrapper. Top with the mango and remaining ingredients to taste.
Garnish with mint or chili powder (or neither).
Fold the wrapper's ends in first, then roll as tightly
as possible into a tube or cylinder.
Tip: Serve with soy or a light peanut sauce for dipping.

Swan Family Rum Cake

Everly's homemade rum cakes are going faster than she can make them, but you don't have to wait for yours! Try her from-the-box version that's easy as can be! It's ready in about an hour and will have your family and friends begging for more!

Yield: 8 servings | Total time: 1 hour 15 minutes

1 (15.25-ounce) box yellow cake mix
1 (3.5-ounce) box instant vanilla pudding
4 eggs
1/2 cup vegetable oil
1/2 cup water
1/2 cup spiced rum
1/2 cup chopped walnuts or pecans (optional)
For Glaze:
1 cup sugar
1/2 cup butter
1/2 cup rum
1/2 cup water

Preheat the oven to 325°F.
Grease and flour a Bundt pan.

Prepare the cake as instructed on the box.

Stir in the rum.

Place the nuts in the bottom of the pan.

Pour the mix into the pan.

Bake 1 hour, until golden brown and pulling away from the pan along the edges.

Glaze:

Melt all ingredients in a saucepan over medium heat, and simmer 2 minutes, stirring constantly.

Pour over the warm cake, still in the pan.

Cool completely, then turn out on a cake plate, cut, and enjoy!

ACKNOWLEDGMENTS

Thank you, sweet reader, for joining Everly and the gang on another island adventure. You make my dream possible! I owe you all a debt of gratitude and delicious iced tea! Thank you Anna Michels for your incredible guidance and feedback. You challenge me and make my stories stronger. Beyond that, you allow me to be part of the amazing Sourcebooks team, and that is priceless! Thank you, Jill Marsal, my magnificent agent, advocate and friend. Your support and encouragement are changing my life. Thank you Darlene Lindsey, World's Best Mother-in-Law and dearest friend. None of this could happen without you. None of it. Thank you, Mom and Dad, for making me believe I can do anything and for instilling a lifelong love of the seaside. And finally, thank you family for putting up with a goofy, pajama-clad, daydreaming author-mom like me. My heart and head are so full of love for you that there simply isn't room for basic domestic skills and culinary excellence. I'm glad you understand.

CHAPTER
ONE

Welcome to Sun, Sand, and Tea." I perked up at the precious sound of seashell wind chimes bouncing and tinkling against the front door of my new café. "I'll be right with you."

A pair of ladies in windbreakers and capri pants smoothed their windblown hair and examined the seating options. Sounds of the sea had followed them inside, amplified briefly by the opening door.

I bopped my head to a Temptations song and tapped the large sweet tea jug behind the counter. Until three months ago, owning and operating an iced tea shop on the shore of my hometown had been nothing more than a childish dream. I'd thought being a grown-up meant working a job I hated while wearing uncomfortable clothes, so I'd toed the line for a while, but my looming thirtieth birthday and a broken heart had changed all that.

Now I did what I wanted—in comfy clothes for significantly less money, but at least I could wear flip-flops.

I set a lidless canning jar of Old-Fashioned Sun Tea in front of the man sitting at my counter and beamed. "Let me know if I can fix you anything else, Sam."

He frowned at his phone, too engrossed or distracted to answer. Sam Smart was a local real estate agent. He'd arrived in Charm during the years I'd been away from home, and from what I could tell, he was a type-A, all-stress all-day kind of guy—a little sweet tea was probably just what he needed. I nudged the jar closer until his hand swept out to meet it. "Thanks."

"Everything okay?" I asked.

He flicked his gaze to mine, then back to his phone. "It's Paine." He shook his head and groaned.

"Ah." I grabbed a thin stack of napkins and patted Sam's shoulder on my way to welcome the newcomers. "Good luck with that."

Benedict Paine had been a thorn in my side since the day I'd approached our town council about adding a café to the first floor of my new seaside home. Owning a sweet-tea shop was my dream come true, and honestly, I couldn't afford the house's mortgage payments without the business income. Despite the home's fixer-upper condition, the price tag had been astronomical, making the café a must, and Mr. Paine had fought me the entire way, complaining that adding a business to a residential property would drag down the neighborhood. I could only imagine the kind of headache a man like Paine could cause a real estate agent.

The space that was now my café stretched through

the entire south side of the first floor. Walls had been strategically knocked out, opening the kitchen and formal dining area up to a large space for entertaining. The result was a stunning seaside setup, perfect for my shop.

From the kitchen, a private hallway led to the rest of the first floor and another thousand or so square feet of potential expansion space. A staircase off that hall provided passage to my second-floor living quarters, which were just as big and full of potential. The stairs themselves were amazing, stained a faded red, with delicate carvings along the edges. They were mine alone to enjoy, shut off from the café by a locking door. I could probably thank the home's history as a boarding house for my substantial second-floor kitchen. The cabinets and fixtures were all older than me, but I couldn't complain—the café kitchen was what mattered, and it was fantastic.

Seating at Sun, Sand, and Tea was a hodgepodge of repainted garage sale and thrift shop finds. Twenty seats in total, five at the counter and fifteen scattered across the wide-planked, whitewashed floor, ranging from padded wicker numbers with low tables to tall bistro sets along the perimeter.

The ladies had selected a high table near a wall of windows overlooking my deck.

I refreshed my smile and set a napkin in front of each of them. "Hello. Welcome to Sun, Sand, and Tea."

They dragged their attention slowly away from the rolling waves and driftwood-speckled beach beyond the glass, reluctant to part with the amazing view for even a second.

"Can I get something started for you?"

The taller woman settled tortoiseshell glasses onto the ridge of her sunburned nose and fixed her attention to the café menu, scripted on an enormous blackboard covering the far wall. "Do you really make twenty flavors of iced tea?"

"Yes, ma'am. Plus a daily array of desserts and finger foods." The selection changed without notice, sometimes with the tide, depending on if I ran out of any necessary ingredients.

"Fascinating. I came in for some good old-fashioned sweet tea, but now you've got me wondering about the Country Cranberry Hibiscus. What's in that?" She leaned her elbows on the tabletop and twined her fingers.

"Well, there—there's black tea, hibiscus, and, uh, rose hips, and cranberries." I stammered over the answer to her question the same way I had to similar inquiries on a near-daily basis since opening my café doors. It seemed a fine line between serving my family's secret recipes and sharing them ingredient by ingredient.

The woman glanced out the window again and pressed a palm to her collarbone as a massive gull flapped to a stop on the handrail outside the window. "Dear!"

"Oh, there's Lou," I said.

"Lou?"

"I think he came with the house."

She lowered her hand, but kept one eye on Lou. "I'll try the Cranberry Hibiscus," she said. "What about you, Margo?"

Her friend pursed her lips. "Make mine Summer Citrus Mint, and I'd like to try your crisp cucumber sandwich."

I formed an "okay" sign with my fingers and winked. "Give me just a quick minute, and I'll get that over here for you."

I strode back to the counter, practically vibrating with excitement. After only a month in business, each customer's order was still a thrill for me.

The seashell wind chimes kicked into gear again and I responded on instinct. "Welcome to Sun, Sand, and Tea." I turned on my toes for a look at the newest guest and my stomach dropped. "Oh, hello, Mr. Paine." I shot a warning look at Sam, whose head drooped lower over his tea.

"Miss Swan." Mr. Paine straddled a stool three seats down from Sam and set his straw porkpie hat on the counter. Tufts of white hair stretched east and west from the spaces below his bald spot and above each ear. "Lovely day."

I nodded in acknowledgment. "Can I get you anything?"

"Please," he drawled, giving Sam a thorough once-over. It wasn't clear if he already knew Sam was mad at him, or if he was figuring that out from the silent treatment.

I waited, knowing what the next words out of Mr. Paine's mouth were going to be.

Reluctantly, he pulled his attention back to me. "How about a list of all your ingredients?"

Sam rolled his small brown eyes, but otherwise continued to ignore Mr. Paine's presence.

I grabbed a knife and a loaf of fresh-baked bread and set them on the counter. "You know I can't give that to you, Mr. Paine. Something else, perhaps?" I'd been through this a dozen times with him since Sun, Sand, and Tea's soft opening. Swan women had guarded our tea recipes for a hundred years, and I wasn't about to hand them over just because he said so. "How about a glass of tea instead?"

I cut two thin slices from the loaf, then whacked the crusts off with unnecessary oomph.

Sam took a long pull on his drink, stopping only when there was nothing left but ice, and returned the jar to the counter with a thump. "It's very good," he said, turning to stare at Mr. Paine. "You should try it. I mean, if you'd had it your way, this place wouldn't even be open, right? Seems like the least you can do is find out what you were protesting."

I didn't bother to mention that Mr. Paine had already tried basically every item on the menu as I plied him with free samples to try to get in his good graces.

Mr. Paine frowned, first at Sam, then at me. Wrinkles raced across his pale, sun-spotted face. "It's a health and safety issue," he groused. "People need to know what they're drinking."

"Yes." I arranged cucumber slices on one piece of bread. "I believe you've mentioned that." It had, in fact, been his number one argument since I'd gotten the green light to open. "I'm happy to provide a general list of ingredients for each recipe, but there are certain herbs and spices, as well as brewing methods, that are trade secrets."

"He doesn't care about any of that," Sam said. "He just wants to get his way."

Mr. Paine twisted on his stool to glare at Sam. "Whatever your problem is, Sam Smart, it's not with me, so stow it."

Sam shoved off his stool. "And your problem isn't with her." He grabbed the gray suit jacket from the stool beside him and threaded his arms into the sleeves. "Thanks for the tea, Everly." He tossed a handful of dollar bills onto the counter and a remorseful look in my direction.

I worked to close my slack jaw as the front door slapped shut behind him. Whatever grudge match Sam and Mr. Paine had going, I didn't want a ticket for it. I put the unused cucumber slices away and removed a white ceramic bowl from the fridge.

Mr. Paine watched carefully, teeth clenched.

"Maybe you'd like to try the Peach Tea today," I suggested. "Whatever you want. On the house."

Preferably *to go*.

"How much sugar is in the Peach?" he asked, apparently determined to criticize. "You know I don't like a lot of sugar."

I pointed to a brightly colored section on my menu that highlighted sugar-free options. "How about a tea made with alternative sweeteners, like honey or fruit puree? Maybe the Iced Peach with Ginger?" I turned to the refrigerator and pulled out a large metal bowl, then scooped the cream cheese, mayo, and seasoning mixture onto the second bread slice, turning it face down over the cucumbers. "There's no sugar in that at all."

"Fine." He lifted his fingers in defeat, as usual, pretending to give up but knowing full well he'd be back tomorrow with the same game.

I had quit hoping he'd start paying for his orders two weeks ago. That was never going to happen, and I had decided to chalk the minimal expense up to community relations and let it go. Though if he kept walking off with my shop's canning jars, he'd soon have a full set—and those weren't cheap.

"Great." I released a long breath and poured a jar of naturally sweetened peach tea for him. He was lucky I didn't serve it in a disposable cup.

"What's in it?" he asked.

"Peaches. Tea." I rocked my knife through the sandwich, making four small crustless triangles.

"And?" Mr. Paine lifted the tea to his mouth, closed his eyes, and gulped before returning the half-empty jar to his napkin. He smacked his lips. "Tastes like sugar."

"No," I assured him. "There's no sugar in that." I plated the crisp cucumber sandwiches, then poured the ladies' mint and cranberry teas, grateful that they were too busy ogling Lou out the window to notice the delay. "Fresh peaches, honey, ginger, lemon, and spices. That's it."

I knew what my tea really tasted like to him: *defeat*. He'd tried to stop me from opening Sun, Sand, and Tea because businesses on the beach were "cliché and overdone." According to Mr. Paine, if I opened a café in my home, Charm, North Carolina, would become a tourist trap and ruin everything he lived for.

Fortunately, the property was old enough to have been zoned commercial before Paine's time on the town council. Built at the turn of the nineteenth century, my home had been a private residence at first, then a number of other businesses ranging from a boarding house to a prep school, and if the rumors were true, possibly a brothel. Though, I couldn't imagine anything so salacious ever having existed in Charm. The town was simply too…charming. And according to my great aunts, who'd been fixtures here since the Great Depression, it had always been that way.

The place was empty when I bought it. The previous owner lived out of town, but he'd sent a number of work crews to make renovations over the years. I could only imagine the money that had been slowly swallowed by the efforts. Eventually it went back on the market.

Mr. Paine eyeballed his drink and rocked the jar from side to side. "I don't see why you won't provide the complete list of your ingredients. What's the big secret?"

"I'm not keeping a secret. The recipes are private. I don't want them out in the world." I wet my lips and tried another explanation, one he might better understand. "These recipes are part of my family's lineage. Our history and legacy." I let my native drawl carry the words. Paine of all people should appreciate an effort to keep things as they were, to respect the past.

He harrumphed. "I'm bringing the ingredient list up at our next council meeting. I'm sure Mayor Dunfree and the other members will agree with me that it's irresponsible not to have it posted."

"Great." He never seemed to tire of reminding me how tight he was with the mayor. He'd used their relationship to the fullest while trying to keep my shop from opening, but even the mayor couldn't prevent a legitimate business from being run in a commercially zoned space. I refilled Mr. Paine's jar, which had been emptied rather quickly. "Let me know if there's anything else you'd like to try."

Mr. Paine climbed off his stool and stuffed his goofy hat back on his mostly bald head. "Just the tea," he said with unnecessary flourish.

"See ya." I piled the ladies' teas and sandwich on a tray and waved Paine off. "Try not to choke on an ice cube," I muttered.

ABOUT THE AUTHOR

 Bree Baker is a mystery-loving daydreamer who got into the storytelling business at a very young age, much to the dismay of her parents and teachers. A few decades later, no one seems surprised that she's made a career of it. According to Bree's husband and three saucy children, she's never short on words or imagination and can't seem to use one without the other. Her favorite tales involve the sea, intrigue and honor, humor and heart. Bree Baker is a member of Sisters in Crime, International Thriller Writers, and Romance Writers of America. You can learn more about Bree and her books at breebaker.com.